STREETS OF STONE

STREETS OF STONE

An Anthology of Glasgow Short Stories

EDITED BY

Moira Burgess and Hamish Whyte

1985
The Salamander Press
Edinburgh

The Salamander Press Edinburgh Ltd
34 Shandwick Place, Edinburgh EH2 4RT
113 Westbourne Grove, London W2 4UP

ISBN 0 907540 62 7

Made and printed in Great Britain
Typeset in Edinburgh by Hewer Text Composition Services
Printed and bound by Whitstable Litho Ltd
Whitstable, Kent
Designed by Paul Minns

Contents

❖❖❖❖

All raptures of this mortal breath,
Solemnities of life and death,
  Dwell in thy heart alone:
Of me thou hast become a part —
Some kindred with my human heart
  Lives in thy streets of stone
ALEXANDER SMITH 'Glasgow' (1857)

Introduction

❖❖❖❖

THERE has been a remarkable growth of Glasgow literature—writing about Glasgow and writing by Glasgow authors—in the last twenty-five years. In the fields of poetry and the novel this creative flowering has already been recognised, and the present editors (among others) have begun the process of recording and charting its development.[1] Glasgow short fiction, however, has not perhaps had its due share of attention, even though such writers as Alan Spence and James Kelman have recently produced work of outstanding originality and style. This anthology presents a selection of short stories set in Glasgow.

A case could be made for extending the scope of such a collection farther back in time than has been done, to include such authors as John Galt, Neil Munro and J. J. Bell, and other, more minor, writers. It was felt, however, that a more coherent picture of the Glasgow short story proper, as opposed to the sketch or episode which certainly flourished around the turn of the century, would be obtained by concentrating on the fifty years or so of writing from the nineteen-thirties to the mid nineteen-eighties (although some of the stories are set earlier).

We would possibly disagree with Geddes Thomson[2] when he says that the Glasgow short story 'is, in terms of achievement, of recent vintage: late sixties and seventies'. It has been exciting to find, in half-forgotten literary magazines of the thirties, a story by J. J. Lavin,

---

[1] *Noise and Smoky Breath: an illustrated anthology of Glasgow poems 1900–1983*, edited by Hamish Whyte (Third Eye Centre and Glasgow District Libraries, 1983).

The Glasgow Novel: a bibliography, compiled by Moira Burgess (Scottish Library Association, 1972. 2nd edition forthcoming).

[2] THOMSON, Geddes, 'The Glasgow Short Story', *Chapman* 33, Autumn 1982, vol. 7, no. 3, pp. 5–8.

author of the fine novel *Compass of Youth*, and several stories by George Friel, including the interesting 'Onlookers' which we have chosen. The forties and fifties appear from the viewpoint of the present day as a time of consolidation, when some of these stories were collected in book form or became part of novels.[3] In the sixties, certainly, began the flowering referred to above. The authentic voice of Glasgow speaks as clearly in these modern short stories as in any contemporary novel. (Does the laconic quality of characteristic Glasgow speech perhaps find natural expression in the necessarily concise and well-crafted short story form?) Our selection draws heavily on work of the seventies and eighties, a golden age for the Glasgow short story, and we include, to bring the picture as far up to date as possible, some pieces previously unpublished.

We have probably, as indicated earlier, preferred the literary short story to the sketch, and on similar grounds have not included anything in the 'book of the programme' genre, examples of which made an early appearance in the form of Helen W. Pryde's McFlannel books (1947–51), and nowadays follow almost inevitably on popular TV series.[4]

If we have a benchmark, it has perhaps been the truthful depiction of some aspect of Glasgow life, or (less tangibly) the expression of some essential trait of Glasgow character. The child's-eye view, a recurrent feature in Glasgow short stories, is represented here by Lavin's 'By Any Other Name' and Spence's 'Tinsel', moving on to adolescence in Gaitens's 'Growing Up'. While women writers do not figure largely in Glasgow short fiction of this kind, the stories by Thornton, Ure and Margaret Hamilton sensitively treat different facets of female experience, as, perhaps, do Mulrine's 'A Cold Coming' and Montgomerie's 'Daft Jenny'. We wanted to reflect the recent experimentation with Glasgow speech patterns, and have chosen Alex Hamilton's 'Moonlighting', Kelman's 'The Hon', and the two pieces by Leonard. With these we also move into the field of Glasgow humour, memorably extended by Gray's straight-faced 'The Crank That Made the Revolution'.

While we have included stories recording sectarian differences

---

[3] GAITENS, Edward, *Growing Up, and other stories* (Cape, 1942).
Dance of the Apprentices (Maclellan, 1948).
HENDRY, J. F., *Fernie Brae* (Maclellan, 1947).

[4] cf. BOYD, Edward and KNOX, Bill, *The View from Daniel Pyke* (Arrow Books, 1974) and HOUSE, Jack, *The House on the Hill* (Richard Drew, 1981).

INTRODUCTION

(Spence's 'The Rain Dance'), problems of an immigrant population (Thomson's 'Pride of Lions'), and poverty (Turner's 'The Shoes'), our selection has not been on purely utilitarian lines. We have often chosen a story simply for its quality of reading well and lingering in the mind, like McBain's 'Supper on the Wall' or Gilkison's 'Atthis'.

We may fairly be accused of omitting many stories which should have been included, but in many cases the reason for this has been sheer lack of space. We think that those we have included well deserve an audience. Beyond this, perhaps we should leave the stories to speak for themselves.

GEORGE FRIEL

Onlookers

◇◇◇◇◇

BEFORE the newlyweds moved in, the single apartment looking on to
the main road was occupied by a man and his wife who fought every
night. Regularly, just after midnight, the woman's screeching haran-
gue was heard rising above the deep growling of her husband, and
their only child squalled in unheeded terror. The whole block lay
wakened in darkness, waiting the climax. After the rumble of overturned furniture came the sharp report of hurtled crockery breaking
against the wall, and then the woman's loud wails. The neighbours
lived in expectation of murder, and with heterosexual sympathy the
gossiping wives blamed the woman for provoking the poor man and
not knowing when to hold her tongue. Unfriended and unregretted,
the quarrelsome couple moved after four months, and the tenement
looked forward to peace at midnight again and sleep unbroken by the
noise of battle going on till two and three o'clock in the morning.

The newcomers were different. The neighbours were sure they
would never quarrel outrageously, for Mrs Gannaway and her
husband were clearly suited to each other, agreeably placid in
temperament. And Mr Gannaway had a small tobacconist and news-
agent's shop, on the same side of the street as his house. Because
of his attentiveness, it was always busy, steadily gaining trade from
the muddled stores kept by slovenly old women in the district. So
his wife would never need to quarrel with him about money, as her
predecessor in the single apartment had done with her husband,
a man who had never worked.

The tenement returned to tranquillity then, and although Mrs
Gannaway did not gossip with the neighbours and had no confidant
among them, they had nothing against her. They saw her as a
slow-moving, dreamy young woman, who smiled readily with a vague
friendliness. And from the cut and cloth and number of her
husband's suits, as well as from the changes in costume she had
herself, they considered the newlyweds were quietly prosperous,

free from the worry over money which obsessed everyone else in the tenement.

But slowly the matrons began to see something more than a leisurely content in Mrs Gannaway's slow walk and more than the happiness of an unworried bride in her bright colour. Mrs Higney declared that the young wife was consumptive, and before long all the wives in the block were taking her guess as a statement of fact, a statement made years ago by somebody, long forgotten, who had known it as a certainty. Within the year, Mrs Higney was proved correct. After a doctor had visited her for a month, Mrs Gannaway went to Ruchill Hospital, across on the north bank of the canal, to the sanatorium there for consumptives.

Mr Gannaway stayed on in the single apartment alone, attended more industriously than ever to his shop, and greeted his neighbours with brief politeness. His small business went on improving, and he increased its stock, throwing into contempt the paltry holdings of the old wives who had kept similar shops in the district long before him. Walking the few hundred yards from his shop to his home, he had the air of a man who knows he is doing well because he deserves to. His greetings to the neighbours he passed had in them something of tolerance for the shiftless and condescension to the unsuccessful, and he never mentioned his wife. As a result, the women on his own side of the street were not quite sure if they liked him or not; they were not quite sure if he were callous and secretive, or just naturally a man of few words.

But before she had been much longer than a month away, Mrs Gannaway came back from the sanatorium and slept alone every night on a long couch placed against the window, which was opened wide at top and bottom. And she rested. She rested all day. Peeping discreetly behind their curtains, the housewives on the other side of the street watched her and her husband at the window of the single apartment, and discussed with each other all they saw, alluding to it casually as if they had seen it just by accident.

Then at night, the tenement was again kept awake by a disturbance in the single apartment, less violent than it had suffered from the quarrelling of the couple who had previously lived there, and with none of its screaming terror. But it had a horror all its own, and aroused the neighbours more intermittently. It was the sound of the young wife coughing, and the way it seemed to choke and rack her made them shudder and turn round with the blankets pulled over their ears. Sometimes, when she was at her worst, she had barely time to recover her breath from one attack before she was in the grip of another, coughing harshly all through the night. And once they were sure she was as good as dead. A fit of coughing at three o'clock in the morning faded away in an exhausted rattling in her throat, and in the little brick boxes around and across from her the tenement-dwellers stared unsleepingly into darkness, waiting and wondering. But then they heard another spasm seize her, showing by its vigour that she was still very much alive. Some nights they heard an especially lengthy paroxysm end in a long low moaning, as if she were weeping.

'That's terrible!' muttered Mrs Higney. 'You'd think it was tearing her inside right out, the way it comes. She'll kill herself some night, coughing like that.'

And the woman in the little dairy down the street, which opened at six o'clock in the morning and served the early-rising matrons with rolls and milk, began to ask regularly, as a ritual greeting to her customers, 'Did you hear her last night? I think she's getting worse.'

'There was once I thought she had burst something,' the customer would answer. 'It seemed to be sort of wrenching her apart.'

'That cough alone,' said the dairywoman, 'would be enough to kill anybody. It's something awful.'

But as if to confute their pessimism and reject their robust sympathy, Mrs Gannaway began to get better. She coughed less often at night, and she began to get up oftener and go out for a walk. For nearly three months she seemed to improve, and the neighbours were almost forgetting she had ever been ill. Then, as if just idling for a few days, she returned to her couch alongside the window and lay there unmoving. She began to cough again at night, with fiercely concentrated attacks that left her gasping. But the neighbours had heard worse from her before, and insensitive to it by custom, they heard it drowsily only as a minor spasm and fell unworriedly asleep. And while they slept, Mrs Gannaway coughed despairingly on, coughed as if she were fighting to suppress it, with something apologetic in it all, until the attack won out in its full deathful insistence and left her helplessly panting in exhaustion, her head lolling over the edge of the couch.

Three weeks after she took to her bed again, early in a morning of April when the clear spring sunlight slanted over the tall tenements of the main road and made its tram-railed broadness seem clean and joyous, she died at the window while her husband, risen from his bed

3

in the other corner of the room, sat on a chair beside her, chafing her hands in a panic.

'She's dead,' said the dairywoman to her first customer at six o'clock, so impatient to tell the news that she could not wait to hear the customer's order.

The stout, slippered matron who had come in for a dozen rolls and a pint of milk gaped in disbelief as she had seen film actresses do, and slowly said, 'But I thought she was getting better.'

'You should have heard her last night, just before she died,' said the dairywoman, nodding her head wisely to hint at all her customer had missed. And to every customer who came in that morning she said at once, 'Did you hear Mrs Gannaway was dead?' And every customer gaped a while and then slowly said, 'But I thought she was getting better.'

The funeral took place the following afternoon, and three deep against the kerb on both sides of the street the neighbours stood impatiently waiting for the coffin to be brought down to the hearse.

'There's nearly as big a crowd here as there was the time they buried the man Reid,' said Mrs Higney, looking round approvingly. 'You remember he cut his throat.'

With increasing boldness the matrons on the Gannaways' side of the street discussed Mr Gannaway with whispering hostility, their heads nodding in agreement as they listened to each other.

'If he had only cared to spend some money on her,' said Mrs Higney in low-voiced righteousness. 'God knows he could afford to. It's a wee Klondyke, that shop of his. But damn the ha'penny he ever spent to try and help the poor girl.'

'Imagine keeping her there in a single apartment,' whispered Mrs Farquhar. 'How did he ever expect any woman to get better in that place? Why, she hadn't even room to move!'

'He could easy have got her a better house than that,' said Mrs Stevenson, supportingly. 'A single apartment, on the money he's making in that shop! Just shows you how some folks'll put up with anything to save a shilling or two.'

'Aye, as long as they're all right,' said Mrs Higney. 'And damn the rest! And she came back from the sanatorium, where she might have stayed in comfort, just to do her duty as a wife. Fine way he showed his appreciation, letting her stick in that pokey wee place!'

'Even the other side of the street would have been better,' said Mrs Martin. 'We just get the sun for a couple of hours in the morning. They get it all the rest of the time over there.'

'The other side of the street!' cried Mrs Higney contemptuously. 'He could have got her a place in the country. But he never had a thought for that poor girl. All he could think of was his shop, his shop, all the time.'

'He was always running back there,' said Mrs Farquhar. 'He couldn't stay at home in peace with his wife. Afraid he'd miss a penny or two, maybe. Some husband he was, leaving her alone like that.'

'What kind of a life had she?' demanded Mrs Stevenson. 'Cooped up there in a single-end all day, with nobody to keep her company or give her a helping hand.'

'And he was never up nor down about it,' said Mrs Martin. 'Always the same smug smile when he passed you. Too sweet to be whole-some. And her there, hardly fit to raise a hand. She'd have been better staying in the sanatorium away from him, for all the attention she got when she was trying to do her best for him.'

'You'd never have thought his wife lay dying, to look at him,' said Mrs Farquhar. 'But that poor girl knew it. You could see she knew it.'

Over on the other side of the street, the matrons who, peeping behind their curtains, had watched the Gannaways at the window of the single apartment across from them, stood silently waiting. Then slowly, like the ripples in water caused by a thrown stone, talk moved among them in whispers.

'I'm sorry for that poor man,' said Mrs Houston. 'He must have had a terrible life with her. I've seen him at that window washing dishes.'

'Washing dishes!' cried Mrs Lennie. 'He did all the cooking and cleaning in that house. He even sewed on his own buttons.'

'She sat there all day doing nothing,' said Mrs Buchanan. 'Surely she could have done some wee thing for the man. But not a hand's turn did she ever do. She'd have been better staying in the sana-torium, instead of coming back to be a hindrance.'

'Oh, it wasn't good enough for her,' said Mrs Plottel. 'She was so sure she could do it all at home. Rest, says she. Rest and fresh air, that's all the treatment they give you. So she came back and slept there with those windows wide open. Quite content to let that poor fellow look after her, when there were proper nurses for her in Ruchill. What kind of a life had he?'

'Maybe he's better without her,' said Mrs Lennie. 'She had to go, sooner or later. And she was no wife to him. A wife only in name. He did all the housework. He even served her with her meals, and she slept alone on that couch every night.'

5

GEORGE FRIEL

'And all day too,' said Mrs Houston. 'He had to get his brother to look after the shop for him. He was always running up from it to attend to her. And you never saw him complain. Always put a pleasant face on it. He took it well, that man. There's not many men would have even bothered with a sick wife the way he was.'

'Well, they can't say he wasn't good to her,' said Mrs Buchanan. 'He gave her every attention. He wanted her to leave that single apartment and take a house outside the city. But not she! She said she'd miss the view on to the main road.'

'I know he was never done giving her money,' said Mrs Houston. 'Do you know, a week before she died he gave her five pounds he won on a horse. And what do you think she did? She bought herself a fine new dress. It'll do me in the summer, says she!'

'It just shows you,' said Mrs Buchanan. 'They never believe they're bad, these consumptives . . . Look, there he is now!'

Bearing the front right-hand corner of the pall, Mr Gannaway came through the close. When the coffin was placed in the hearse, he turned with his brother and opened the door of the first carriage. Letting his brother enter first, he pulled out a handkerchief and blew his nose, fumbling as he did so to brush a corner of the linen over his eyes. Then, round-shouldered and head down, he went in beside his brother.

'That poor man!' whispered Mrs Houston. 'It's really better for him as it is, a young man like him, with all his life before him. And yet he feels it just the same. Did you see him wipe his eyes?'

'Did you see that?' whispered Mrs Higney. 'Wiping his eyes so as everybody can see him! Aye, it's easy to cry when it's too late. If he had only thought more about her when she was living, maybe she wouldn't be dead the day. A young woman like her, with all her life before her.'

EDWARD GAITENS

Growing Up

❖◇❖◇❖

THE boy lay awake all night in the light of dreams about the adventure of his first job. He was fourteen years old. It was only a month since he had reluctantly left school, but he forgot now how bitterly he wept when his mother told him he must go to work and contribute to the family income. Because only last night his father had asked him: 'Would ye like tae come wi' me to the shipyards tomorrow, son?' and his mother chimed in: 'Aye, take him wi' ye. Mebbe ye'll get him a start wi' big money.' And the boy nodded eagerly: 'Oh, yes, da!'

His father, who had been a long time unemployed, had suddenly addressed his wife with unusual optimism. 'Ye know, Mary, I've a feelin' I'll get a start tomorrow for sure! They're layin' a big ship down at Clydebank. They say it'll mean a year's work for hundreds o' men.' The wife looked sceptical, but the boy believed his father would find work and that he, himself, would get his first job in the shipyards, away out where the Clyde neared the sea!

His father had washed and shaved to avoid a rush in the morning, for they had to be up at half-past four, take a hurried snack and cup of tea and catch the five o'clock tramcar. The boy washed also, exulting as he laved arms, neck and face, and went through the lobby to the concealed bed in the front room, his glow of anticipation burning away desire for sleep.

A job in the shipyards! He had often listened intensely to his father and brothers talk of those worlds of fabulous energy and mighty achievements where thousands of men and boys toiled night and day and the clang of hammers never ceased. He would see battleships launched and immense ocean liners. He would help to build one and earn big money! He was dazzled with pride.

Night and the wonder of quiet was ending; he heard the homeward footsteps of nightshift workers and day workers going forth, then the hum of the first workmen's tram from afar, as dawn stared at the window, innocently entering, filling the drab room with beauty of light. Slow-fading silence, the slow growth of clarity and rising tempo of sounds, thrilled and awed him. Soon he would hear, through the wall, from the set-in bed in the kitchen, where his parents slept, his mother saying: 'Eddy, will ye get up, now! It's half-past four!' and his father exclaiming: 'Eh! Wha-a-at? My God! Eh! What's up?' and jumping agitatedly to the floor, as he frequently did. Then, the boy was aware, it would be hardly after four.

'She won't have to wake me!' he boasted to the silence, smiling at the cracked, blistered whitewash of the bed-ceiling. He would be up and dressed before his da! He regarded his two elder brothers who were sleeping with him with condescension. They would be abed for three more hours, then James, the eldest son, would return from nightshift at seven, have breakfast, read a newspaper and retire to the yet warm bed at eight o'clock. But he did not envy them!

Quivering with eagerness he rose, pulled on his flimsy tweed trousers and slung minute braces over his boyish shoulders, disappointed that he hadn't moleskin trousers, a thick, leather, heavy-buckled belt and big hobnailed boots, like his da. He was still enjoying the novelty of his first pair of long trousers. Aye, he was a man in these! And they were more comfortable, too. They didn't chafe him above the knees like the short breeks he had thrown off a week ago! He heard the kitchen window-blind whirr up and the clang of a tin kettle planked on the stove. That was his mother up. Wouldn't she be surprised when she called him and he was all ready! Perhaps he had better say a prayer to the Blessed Virgin? She would get him a job! Quickly he put on stockings and cheap boots with papery uppers, and kneeling at the bed held forward clasped hands to a coloured china effigy of the Madonna, gracing the centre wall. Unaffected by the raucous snoring of John, he muttered two very quick, devout 'Hail Marys', then, half-ashamed, added the improvisation: 'Hail, Queen of Heaven, the Ocean Star, pray for me and get me a job this day!' He rose pleased, happier, firmly believing the 'Holy Mother' would intercede with the powers that dole out work to men, and went into the kitchen.

His father was leaning against the bed pulling on his trousers, his mother, at the gas-stove, was frying thick slices of bread in dripping for their snack, and the kettle whistled a plume of steam into the room. While he stood by to let his father wash first, in the iron sink at the end of the dresser, his mother turned, pouring boiling water in a large enamelled teapot, and said, half-sullenly: 'Ye'd better put yer collar on. Go an' clean it. An' don't spit on it! Wash it properly wi' soap an' flannel. Ye must be respectable!'

He returned to the parlour, his eagerness dimmed by her sullenness, and lifted a celluloid collar and stringy brown cotton tie from a glass dish on the sideboard where he always placed them when undressing. He had wanted to go like other apprentices, like his da, with a knotted muffler or nothing at all round his neck, and he regarded the collar indignantly. That wasn't like a working man! Did she take him for a jessie or a message-boy?

While his father dried himself he washed the collar at the sink, rubbing it vindictively with a piece of red flannel, then washed himself, anxiously hoping his parents wouldn't quarrel. They were often sulky and short with each other, and sometimes he had been wakened at this hour by a brutal altercation, when his father had struck her and rushed out, crashing the door, and she had yelled after him she hoped he'd be killed at his work. He could not understand the real cause of the strain between his parents—their thin love blasted by the worry of recurring unemployment; his mother's suspicion that her husband didn't try hard enough to get work and his offence at her distrust.

Their tea was ready and he ate the hot, fat-soused bread and drank the bitter brew deliciously, his appetite big with excitement and pleasure. They stood to eat, his father glancing continually up at the clock. His mother said: 'Yer pieces and tea and sugar are ready, there!' At the corner of the table lay two lunches wrapped in newspaper, a huge one for the man, a smaller one for the boy, and on top of each a penny Colman's Mustard tin filled with dry tea and sugar. The boy felt manly as he regarded it; he had begged it from his mother, who had made up his tea and sugar the night before in a screw of paper, and, in good mood, she had emptied the newly bought tin into an egg-cup, gratifying his wish to be as possible like his father. They were ready to leave and stuffed their pieces into their jacket pockets, the boy imitating his father's movements.

His father begged the loan of a sixpence and the wife answered complainingly: 'Och, shure I lent ye sixpence yesterday! Could ye no' walk some o' the way?' but she took her purse from under her pillow, where she kept it to prevent him filching coppers while she slept, and gave him the coin unwillingly. Suddenly he exclaimed: 'Isn't that Saint Peter's bell just striking the half-hour? Och, ye've got us up too soon. We could have slept longer!' Unperturbed, she answered: 'Well, ye're better to be early. Ye'll have time tae say an Our Father an' three Hail Marys for a job!' He slung his cap irritably on a chair and knelt in unprayerlike mood at the bed, making the sign of the cross. The boy, palpitating to be off, was almost in tears. 'You say a wee prayer, too,' advised his mother. 'Och, maw, I said two Hail Marys before I came ben!' he grumbled. 'Say another two an' make sure!' she answered obdurately. He knelt beside his father and while their mumbled 'Aves' ascended to holy images on the bed walls, the woman sat to drink a cup of tea. The man cocked an eye frequently at the clock and suddenly crossing himself, rose, donned his cap and said: 'We'd better be gettin' away now!' The boy rose simultaneously and as they went out his mother warned her man to do his best and not be too late home!

The boy was aware of an outreaching sense of freedom when they emerged from the narrow entry. At last they were away! As they boarded a tram he ran before his father to capture a front seat and leant forward gallant and unenclosed as a charioteer, while the packed tram passed all stops. He saw smoke jut from hundreds of chimneys, blinds shoot up, curtains parted and here and there a woman leaning akimbo on a sill four storeys high, contemplating the street. He tried to see into rooms, but speed blurred his vision and he laughed at the phenomenon. Ah, this was better than rising at eight and crawling to school at a quarter to nine. This was rare! And perhaps tomorrow or next day he would be dashing along like this while his former schoolmates were asleep. And when the tram stopped at a crossing where services went all ways, the names CLYDEBANK, YOKER, SCOTSTOUN, ANNIESLAND, DALMUIR, DUMBARTON, glowed with romance, magic as the names of foreign lands to him who only knew back-streets. And here they were in Dockland! The funnels of liners and masts of sailing ships above the warehouse roofs, the flags of many nations afloat in the warm breeze.

Shortly the shipyards' region surrounded him with new wonder. His father decided to call at a firm ten miles out, and as it was still very early they sauntered about the vicinity till starting-time. The boy glued his eyes on great cranes rearing over housetops like figures in a monstrous ballet, and his spirit followed their rhythm while he fired shrill questions at his father, who answered in his detailed, laborious manner. Then at a minute to six they followed the last worker going through the wicket door of the immense gates, and his father craved an attendant commissionaire's permission to enter and interview various foremen. The personage let them pass and immediately the boy was stunned in an ocean of sound, then as soon, struck by a tragic stillness. A procession of begrimed, bareheaded workers, bearing two stretchers, wended towards the ambulance-house at the gate. The boy's father stopped; other men paused a moment, removing their caps, then hurried to their work. The procession passed, the man on the first stretcher gallantly smoking a cigarette, smiled at the boy, but the face of the body on the following stretcher was covered.

The father removed his cap, bowing his head; the boy copied him. 'My, there's been a man killed already! It's terrible. Terrible!' The boy looked up, asking: 'Do they not stop the works when a man's killed, da?' His father answered, 'No, the work goes on, son. The work goes on!' The shipyard ambulance appeared, the bodies were placed within, a nurse closed the door and the vehicle sped through the gates.

The boy forgot the dead man as they went on through the yard amid mammoth sights and sounds. He saw a warship near completion, the mere ribs of ships just begun, liners in repair dock and the pathetic end of a worn vessel in the hands of the breakers. All men seemed midgets here, the riveters' catchboys everywhere in the skeleton ships, like imps, handing red-hot rivets from portable fires to the holder-on, and his small self had never felt so insignificant. Then in pride at being here, he strutted along cloaked in rare distinction. 'Ye can smell the sea here!' said his father, but he only smelled rust, iron and steel, machine-oil and the smoke and heat of furnaces.

All the while seagulls decorated the air, but their cries were unheard in the symphony of Labour. The boy crouched within himself as cranes swung overhead steel plates vast as two floors of his tenement home, and his father showed him a steam-hammer pounding gargantuan objects of molten steel. 'I've seen a hammerman place an egg there and bring the hammer down to rest on it and not break it! They get so skilful!' The boy marvelled, breathless with questioning, while his father hurried to interview foremen in various shops and the holes and corners of ships—great, strapping men who shook their heads distantly or spoke amiably, and canny little gaffers with frowsy moustaches, glasses and peaked caps, who sized up his father shrewdly.

None had jobs to offer, and when the breakfast-time buzzer blew, his father took him to the smiddy's shop, unhitched a tin can from his belt, filled it with water and boiled it on a smiddy fire. Never had he seen so many smiddy fires gathered in one place, nor water boil so swiftly as he worked the bellows handle and his father held the can on a rod. They washed down their food with milkless tea, sitting on a great anvil, while his father discussed with the blacksmith the chances of work in another shipyard.

Crossing by ferry to the opposite shore was the next brilliant event. Now the river was mad with sunshine and against passing and anchored ships the water splintered like golden glass. Amidstream, his father pointed out famous shipyards. 'Yon's Fairfield's away back, and there's Harland & Wolff's. That's John Brown's where we're going next, and yonder's Beardmore's! Yon's the highest crane on the Clyde!' and the boy looked far through smiling space at the goliath moving with relentless deliberation at its task.

And once again they were at shipyard gates, hanging about till the dinner-hour, when his father rushed forward to intercept a little man in a dungaree suit, spectacles and a sailor's cap among the hundreds of men streaming out. While the interview proceeded the boy could not take his eyes from the man's ardent red nose, abnormally small, above his grey moustache. 'Weel, I'm no sure!' said the foreman, 'I'm no sure! I'm pretty full up the now. But see me here tomorrow at six! And is this yer wee laddie? Will ye be wantin' a job for him, too? Weel, bring 'im wi' ye! One o' my platers wants a boy. Ye'll be puttin' him to a trade later on?' and walking in a queer, staccato style, he left them without waiting reply.

'God be praised!' the boy's father exclaimed jubilantly. 'That means a start for me tomorrow! He wouldn't tell me to come if he hadn't a job for me! An' you'll get a job, too, son, wi' fifteen shillin's a week!' The boy couldn't believe it. Fifteen shillings a week! Fifteen shillings a week! Immediately he was rich and in imagination scattering money right and left, buying long-desired things for himself, presents for his mother, father and brothers, making fabulous plans. They walked along with more inspirited step. 'Ye'll have a pay-poke on Saturday the same as me!' said his father, and the boy set his cap a little rakishly, plunged his hands into his pockets manfully and looked at life with tremendous satisfaction!

They could not afford to buy tea in a coffee-shop, and his father took him to a lodging-house where he could boil his can on the hot-plate. They turned down a side street into a narrow lane. From a distance the boy read the black letters on a white-glassed, antique lamp over the narrow door: GOOD BEDS FOR MEN, 4D AND 8D PER NIGHT, and when they reached the place, THE THISTLE HOTEL above the entrance.

They passed into a hot, low-roofed room, with settles and a long, narrow table at which two shirt-sleeved youths played cards with a dog's-eared pack. The place stank vitally of foul life; on a form against the wall a powerful, barefooted negro lay asleep. The boy was amazed at his cavernous mouth, slackly open, exaggerated by full, negroid lips, then his frightened glance fixed on an elderly tramp with one raw, blear eye, the other large and glowing, huddling against a brickwork stove which occupied an entire end of the room, shivering, scratching himself and unwrapping dirty toe-rags from his feet. He stared hypnotised at the brilliant orb as the old man ogled him with a toothless grin.

'You sit there, sonny,' said his father, placing the tin of tea and sugar on the table and going to fill his can at a hot-water tap on the stove. The boy waited timidly, afraid to look about the villainous surroundings, and he started, alarmed, as a thick-set, apish man who leant against the stove reading a newspaper padded across on rope-soled slippers and stood over him. The boy's glance travelled slowly up his loose, greasy trousers and recoiled at the black hair, thick as a dog's, on his enormous arms and breast, showing through his open shirt. The man's little red eyes regarded him with savage contempt, and as the young face turned away he calmly lifted the mustard-tin, turning its oval in his fingers. That moment the boy's father turned and shouted: 'Hi, you! Put that down! That's mine! Put it down!' The brute swung round, deliberately removed the lid, poured the contents on the table and threw the tin at his feet.

The boy was transfixed by that black-and-white spill, a lurid insult, like a spit in his father's face. He jumped back as his father leapt, his left hand seizing the bully's shirt, his right followed by all his weight smashing into his face. He heard a crack and a ripping sound and waited, petrified, certain the big man would beat the life out of his da, that all here would set on him! The two youths started up, the negro shouted, swaying, staring like a sleepwalker, the tramp cackled like a crone: 'Heh, that was a rare smack ye gied 'im! My, that was a guid yin! Right on the chin! Right on the point!' But no one interfered and the big man sprawled back on the table, breathing heavily, then sat up dazed, rubbing his jaw, his torn shirt slopping between his thighs, hair showing down to his paunch. The boy's father pranced, shaping up to him. 'Come on, ye bastard! I'll beat the jelly out o' ye, big as ye are!'

They all turned as the dosshouse proprietor, a stout, carroty-haired man, rushed in tucking a soiled white apron at his waist, shouting furiously: 'What's goin' on here? What the bloody hell! Here, you! Get to hell out of here! Come on, out you go! You don't pay for a bed here! What's yer bloody game, comin' here to use my hot-plate without payin'?' The boy's father faced him defiantly, inclined to fight him also, but he only said: 'All right! Keep yer shirt on, man! We're goin'! Come on, sonny!'

In the lane his father hitched up his belt arrogantly, pleased at besting the dosshouse bully. 'Did ye see that, sonny? One good right, straight from the shoulder, an' down he goes, the get! I bested the cur!' He went through the fight again, shooting out his fists, then swaggered along at tremendous pace, thumbs in his waistcoat armholes. He put an arm round his son's shoulder. 'Eh, we're a couple o' rare fighters! They can't best us!' he chuckled and walked faster, looking slyly down. The boy strove to pace him till his heart pounded and he fell behind. His father slackened with a great laugh. 'My, ye're a rare wee walker, sonny!' and the boy smiled, breathing hard. How proud he was of his da! He was the best da in the world! 'Come on!' cried his father. 'We'll eat our dinners down by the water. Damn the tea!'

They walked by the river along the grassy banks. The boy clutched at his father, crying excitedly: 'I can smell the sea now, da! I can smell it!' He lifted his head and inspired and the adventurous tang filled his little breast. They ate their pieces and his father smoked a clay pipe, then lay down with a big, white-spotted red handkerchief over his head. And the boy sat beside him watching river-life—barges, yachts, pleasure-boats, tramps and great liners from all corners of the world, going along the sun's path of gold, always to the accompaniment of riveters' hammers, clanging on bulkhead and deck. 'Oh, da, look at yon bonny boat! It's like a swan, isn't it, da?' and he pointed at a suave steam yacht, white as snow, anchored midstream, its brass-work and gold paint flashing as it bowed to the smooth flow. His father said: 'Eh! What's that? A swan? Ay, a swan!' and fell asleep, snoring outrageously, and the red handkerchief burbled on his face.

And the boy's happiness rose with the waning day. This warm, light-hearted May day seemed eternal, and he could have sat here for ever, watching life, listening to the echo from shipyards across the water, sending his heart to follow the wild gulls. He was not lonely because his father slept. In this hour all life was his. He was content. He thought how the river widened to the ocean, and only then felt lonely for a bit as a sense of the world's immensity overawed his tiny comprehension. Then a liner from India in tow of pilot tugs crawled past, shutting the white yacht from view for several minutes. A crowd of half-naked lascar sailors leant on the ship's rail, chattering, laughing, singing an Eastern song. One waved a bright scarf to him and he waved with his cap. He had often watched lascars shopping in the slum markets. Why were they always happy and laughing? The liner passed. At once the world was friendly, all his happiness was restored and he smiled again at the white yacht.

His father started awake when the sun was some way down, and exclaimed: 'My God! It's late! Yer maw'll be mad wi' us. We'd better get home!' The boy was in a state of sheer bliss with all he had seen that day. No boy had seen the wonders he had witnessed, and all the long ride home he fought sleep, wishful to miss nothing. When he had gulped down his tea he rushed into the back-court to tell his tenement friends. They were rooting for any objects of interest housewives might have thrown into the communal midden, which was beginning to exude its summer stink. They rallied, a charmed, envious circle, while he narrated, a little Homer of the back-streets. He had seen a dead man and the highest crane on the Clyde! His da had knocked a man 'right oot' over a table!—by now his father's adversary had attained prodigious proportions—and he had got a job in the 'Yards' with 'big money'. Suddenly he broke off importantly with: 'Well, I'll have to be gettin' home now. I've got to be up gey early for my job, ye know!' and swaggered away.

There was unusual tranquillity in his home that evening. His mother was pleased because all her menfolk would be in jobs, and she and her man were almost friendly. The boy tried to read a book, but the print danced and he could think of nothing but his fine job with big money. He would give his mother every penny. Keep nothing for himself. He would be a good son to her. She would see! He stumbled to her where she sat smiling, knitting a sock. 'Ye won't let me sleep in tomorrow, will ye, maw?' he said. She tousled his hair. 'No, son. I'll call ye fine an' early.' His father shook his shoulder ruggedly. 'Ye're a fine standing-up man, sonny! Ye'll soon be as big as yer da!' He staggered through to the parlour bed, drunk with the sweet opiate of healthy fatigue, hearing his mother say: 'Puir wee soul! He's gey tire't!' and his father: 'Ay, he's had a long day for a wee laddie.' Immediately he fell asleep, thinking vividly of the morrow's job, smiling, with the cries of seagulls in his ears.

All night he dreamt of exalted shipmasts and tall cranes bowing, proudly lifting, swinging their loads, while wild birds circled around them in brilliant sunshine. And the gallant Clyde, pursuing its historic journey to the mountains and the sea, flowed through his dreams.

EDWARD GAITENS

The Sailing Ship

❖❖❖❖❖

MRS REGAN yelled at her son: 'Get up, ye lazy pig! Rise up an' look for work an' don't shame me before the neebors!' She stopped sweeping the floor and approached the set-in bed, brandishing the brush over him with insane gestures. The veins bulged in her scrawny neck, her eyes were crazy, she was red from her brow to the top of her breast, like a person in the throes of suffocation. 'Get up, d'ye hear? Get out o' this house an' never come back, ye lazy coward! Ye'll not be lyin' there day-in day-out an' neebors whisperin'.' She came closer, sneering: 'D'ye ken whit they call ye? "Johnny Regan, the dirty Conshy, the wee gentleman that's too good for work!"'

He stared in silent misery at the wall, holding in his rage, conquering the inherited violence in his blood. How he hated her! He would always hate her. Always! When she was long dead and gone, her memory would be nauseous! His hands gripped the undersheet in the vehemence of restraint. She screamed down at him: 'A conshense objaictor! My, ye're a rare son! A conshense objaictor an' socialish! Ma braw Terence is lyin' deid in France, while you're lyin' here safe an' weel!'

Why must she taunt him so horribly; make him itch to inflict the brutality he had witnessed so often since childhood? He had gone to prison, driven by wild idealism, believing his action would end life like this! He turned on the pillow and said quietly: 'Ach, shut up, will ye? Don't make yourself uglier than you are!' He could have plucked out his tongue. He had not meant to say that. But her nagging would enrage a saint! She became speechless and struck him with the broom handle, hard, vicious blows. Any reference to her disfigurement always infuriated her.

One of her aimless blows hit his elbow and he felt sick with sudden pain. He must stop this! He leapt from bed, as he was, in pants and semmit, and seized the broom handle. 'Stop it now, Mother! Stop it, for God's sake! D'ye hear me!' he shouted, pleading, at her crazed face. 'Have you gone mad? You'll hurt yourself!' But he could not wrest the brush from her, and he regarded, with horrified interest, her thin, red arms, amazed at her strength. Then rage gusted through him like a furnace blast. One good blow would settle her! He trembled, blinded by emotion, and let go his hold. She began receding from him as though from a ghost, walking slowly backwards holding the broom straight in front of her, terrified by the burning fixity of his gaze. He followed, slowly, ominously, with clenched fists. As she got round the lop-sided table, she darted from the room, slamming the door after her.

For several minutes he stood trembling and staring as if she was still there; then, aware that his bare feet were wet with the sodden tea-leaves she always threw down to lay the summer dust, he exclaimed: 'Ach, hell!' and stepped uncomfortably to the shallow window-bay, where his socks and trousers lay heaped on a chair. He pulled them and his boots on and sat regarding the street. Inflamed by a base desire to rush into the kitchen after her, he clapped his hands to his eyes. 'No! For Christ's sake! Not that!' His own mother! He ought to pity her and all warped people. A sense of the waste of life deeply affected him. One set of people embarrassed or bored by possessing much more than they needed, while others were continually distressed and dismayed by the lack of common human needs. Five years after the appalling waste of beautiful human energy and lives in war, he saw it still around him in slums, unemployment, preventable ignorance and disease.

Waste!

No one could call him a coward. He would have shouldered a rifle in a revolution. Let them whisper 'Coward' behind his back: none of them had the courage to step up and say it. But returned soldiers had said: 'Ah wish Ah'd had the pluck tae be a Conshy, like you, Johnny. It was four years of hell.' And those same men were unemployed, their lives as aimless and empty as his own. How gladly he would man any gun used to batter these tenements to the ground!

Why did he linger on here anyway? Some queer loyalty was keeping him, some faint hope of a return of the humble prosperity and friendliness and cheer that once had brightened this sad house. If only that recurring sickness did not afflict him. He would have adventured from here long ago. That two years' imprisonment, with underfeeding on bad food, had left him with some mysterious weakness. For days it disabled him; and these nights, crushed with three others in that bed, it was impossible to sleep for the heat and the bugs.

He stood up vigorously and hustled into his waistcoat and jacket, trying, by activity, to divert his thoughts from their dark channel. What was the matter with him? He was only twenty-six and Life, fascinating, beautiful, waited for him to turn his youth to account.

He thought of going into the kitchen for a wash, but he knew she would set her tongue on him, and once more his feelings darkened. He looked at his collar and tie on the back of the chair. Why worry? Why bother putting them on! Why worry about anything? He strode into the lobby and met her waiting there, sullenly contrite. 'D'ye want ony breakfast, son?' she asked. He opened the door and passed out. 'I'm not hungry!' he cast back at her.

Ay, sure she would give him breakfast! he reflected as he turned out of the dark close into the main road. With his father and two brothers out of work like himself, bread and margarine and stewed tea was all the poor soul had to offer him this morning. And she would have nagged him like one of the Furies while he ate it. His heart turned back to her; he should never forget that she wasn't responsible for those mad fits; her nerves were fretted raw by worry and care; he believed she loved him, but he was aware that affection is a delicate thing, driven deep into people and lost behind the tough exterior they develop to face a sordid life.

Ach, if only he had a Woodbine! He raked his pockets for a stub. Across the street he saw a man stoop and pick a fag-end from the gutter, wipe it on his sleeve and stuff it into his clay pipe. His ache for a smoke tempted him to do the same, but with no food in him the idea made him squeamish. Never mind! He might get a few hours' casual work. Then his pockets would jingle!

The sky was sprinkled with gay clouds that sailed and shone as if there were no unemployment and slums in the world. At least he could smile at the sky! Perhaps the sea was like that today, limitless, deep azure, with ships roving about it like those clouds. He saw a cloud shaped like a swimming man with arms stretched in the breast-stroke. It sailed to a good wind, and he watched it awhile, wondering how long it would keep its form, till the wind tore it and bundled it into another shape. He laughed, and his heart stood up in him cheerful and fearless, his shoulders squared and he walked with manlier step.

From every by-street the sounds of the hordes of tenement children, on holiday these times, came to him; laughing and calling, each day they marvellously discovered happiness, like some lovely jewel, in the gutters and back courts of the big city. His soul joined with them as they sported and ran, and he was lightened with belief that war and poverty would sometime vanish away like an evil dream and that wakened Man would stand amazed at his blundering and turn to find happiness as simply and innocently as those ragged children were finding it now.

So exalted, he realised he had walked, without tiring, the four miles from his home to the docks. He entered the wide gates and strolled through crowds of idle dockers, vigorously discussing football, religion or politics in the assertive Scottish manner. Small chance of his getting work here! And even if he did, he would have to quit if the union delegate demanded to see his membership badge and card. But he was not saddened. The dazzled waters of the harbour immediately foiled his disappointment, and he inhaled the breath of travel and the smell of merchandise from the abounding light and heat. Flashing pinions curved in the blaze; he sensed them like a wreath around his head and smiled at the pigeons crooning their passion and quarrelling on the warehouse roofs, or seeking spilled grain and indian corn among the very feet of the men.

He watched a big tramp steamship manoeuvring into the first great basin. It was the only vessel there, and he recalled the prosperous days of the port, when every basin was so crowded with masts and funnels that it was hardly possible to row a dinghy between the herded ships. He sauntered around and, lifting his head to watch a wheeling gull, saw the towering masts and cross-trees of a sailing ship peering over the stern of a steamship. It was ten years since he had beheld a sailing ship and one of such a size as the height of those masts hinted she must be, and he almost ran towards her in delighted excitement.

He stood close and contemplated her with amazement as though she was a phantom which had sailed out of the past of buccaneers and pirates and which might at any moment fade from sight. She was a long, slim three-master, newly painted a pale blue, with the name *France* glittering in solid brass letters on her prow that pointed proudly at the bluff stern of the steamship like an upheld spear. She looked all too slender for her great calling; her spars were crowded white with resting gulls, still as sculptured birds, and as Regan gazed past them at the sky he was taken by desire to get a job on her.

He walked smartly up the gangway. There was apparently no one aboard, and he was elated by his solitary experience as he looked along the clean, bare decks where every hatch was battened down and everything stowed away. If only he might get work on her! That would be a manly break with the mean life of the tenements. Once he had faced the seas with her, he could never return to that life again. There was hardly a part of the ship he could have named, but he placed his hand fondly on her hot rail as though he had sailed with her for many years and knew her intimately. He leant over the side and saw hundreds of monkey-nuts floating, bright in the narrow space between the quay and ship. He had not noticed them when he hurried forward, with all his eyes for her, but now he saw them plentifully scattered about the dock and on the travelling crane, under which they shone like nuggets of gold on the coal-dust lying where a vessel had been coaled.

Monkey-nuts! They must have fallen from the hoisted sacks; they must have been her cargo; she had come from the tropics! His fancy wandered into passionate depths of tropical forests, he heard the chattering scream of monkeys, saw small bodies swing and little eyes flash in the green gloom; and he felt convinced that the tropic heat, soaked deep in her planks, was mounting from her decks through the soles of his feet into his body.

He turned to see an immensely tall, broad man in sea-going uniform stepping from a cabin away forrard. His heart bounded. Here was his chance! He walked towards him, summoning all his spirit to ask for a job, without the vaguest idea what to say, regretting his ignorance and inexperience of sea-life. The sailor, tanned and handsome, with blond hair gleaming under his officer's cap, stopped and looked dumbly at Regan, who felt most painfully at that moment the complete absence of breakfast in his belly. Trembling, he removed his cap and said shakily: 'Good-morning, sir! Do you need any sailors?' while he felt his blood scald his cheeks and seemed to himself the utterest fool alive. The officer stared a moment, then took a long, twisted black cheroot from his mouth and waved it vaguely about, as if taking in the whole harbour. 'All my grew iss 'ere!' he said. It was a Scandinavian voice. 'I haf no yobs! You haf been a sailor? Ya? No?' He replaced his cigar and stared stonily, then removed it and burst out with an uproarious laugh, pointing it at the dizzy masts: 'You could yoomp up there, ya? No, I sink you are yoost too schmall!'

Regan wanted to run off the ship. What a bloody fool he was! Fancy the likes of him expecting to get a berth, with hundreds of seasoned seamen unemployed! He felt mortified by the officer's scorn of his physique. He was the last and slightest of eight strong brothers, but he had never been regarded as a weakling.

'Hi!' The officer was calling him back, and hope flared up in him again. As he approached, the officer took a cheroot from his outside breast pocket and offered it silently, with a vast grin on his face. Regan accepted it and descended to the dock where he stuffed his pockets with monkey-nuts and sat on the big iron wheel of the crane eating them and flicking the shells over the quayside. He shrugged his shoulders. Ach, well! At least, he could admire the beauty of the ship if he couldn't sail with her! He loved the way her slim bows curved, like the flanks of a fawn. *France*: that was a light little name that suited her beautiful poise. He had heard it said that the Clyde would never see a windjammer again; that they had all been requisitioned, dismasted and turned into steamships for war service. And here was a lovely one whose decks he had walked!

When he was sick of monkey-nuts, he begged a match from a passing docker and lit the black cheroot. It was pure tobacco leaf and he thought he had burned his throat out with the first inhalation, while his head swam and he coughed violently. He stubbed the cheroot out against the crane and put it in his pocket as a souvenir.

In this great basin, where there were only three ships, all the light of day appeared to be concentrated, and in the intense path of the sun floating seagulls vanished as if they were burned away, like the phoenix bird consumed by its own fire, and Regan blessed his luck for coming upon this ship in such glad weather.

The steamship was unloading a cargo of Canadian wheat, through an elevator projecting from her hold on to the warehouse roof. He went and leant against the sliding-door of the shed and watched the wheat pour an aureate stream to the ground in a rising, golden hill. Then he saw a big, red-headed man descending the gangway of the wheat boat. It was 'Big' Willie McBride, the stevedore, who lived in his neighbourhood and picked up a living as a street bookmaker, when there was no work at the docks. 'Hi, young Regan, come 'ere!' he called. 'D'ye want a job?' he asked as Regan came over. 'It's light work, shovellin' wheat for a couple o' days, an' worth thirty bob tae ye?'

What luck! Regan smiled eagerly. 'You bet, Mac! Glad to get anything! I'm skinned!'

McBride took him aboard the steamship and sent him down the hold, where he was handed a light, flat-bladed wooden shovel and joined nine other men, five of whom fed the endless belt of the elevator with wheat while four others poured it into huge sacks which were tied, roped together in fours and hoisted above by a steam-winch on deck.

Regan set-to shovelling the grain into the cups on the revolving belt. It was stifling down here; very soon he breathed with great difficulty, and his head was throbbing painfully when the ganger shouted: 'Come on, boays! Up on deck for yer blow!' They climbed up and were replaced by ten others. They could only work in shifts of half an hour, with fifteen-minute spells on deck, as the wheat-dust clogged their throats and nostrils, turning to paste in the moisture of breath.

At every turn on deck, Regan leant on the stern-rail and gazed down on the *France*. One time, in the evening, the other men joined him, curious at his quietness; and Paddy, a six-foot, handsome young Irishman, in dirty flannels and a blue guernsey, said loudly: 'Take a good look at the old hooker, me buckos, for she'll mebbe never come up the Clyde again!' Someone said: 'Ay, it's three years sin' she was last here. D'ye ken her, Paddy?' Paddy replied: 'Dew Oi know her! Shure Oi sailed wid that same win'-jammer three years ago. Her skipper was a darlin' sailor an' a dirthy slave-driver. A big, yella-haired Dane, he was, wid a wallop on him like a steam-hammer. Shure Oi seen 'im knock a dago clean across the deck wid a little flick uv the back uv his han'! She was a hell-ship, I'm tellin' ye, an' her grub wasn't fit for pigs, so Oi left her at Ryo dee Janeeraw an' sailed home to Belfast in a cattle-boat!' Regan, listening to him, knew proudly that he would have sailed with her had he got the chance, no matter how hard might be the life she gave him.

After midnight, when they all sat up on deck again, gratefully breathing the sweet air, Regan blessed the *France* for his luck. Her holystoned decks and every detail of her shone clear in the glow of the moon, as he whispered down: 'Thanks, lovely ship, for getting me this day's work!' Behind him, Paddy, who was tipsy, produced a bottle of whisky and sat swigging and humming by himself. Someone said: 'Give us a song, Paddy!' The Irishman stood up proudly, swaying, and passed the bottle round. 'Shure, Oi'll give ye'se a song!' he shouted. 'Oi'll lift yer hearts to the mouths of ye! Sing up, ye sods! Sing up!' They all laughed and joined him, singing:

> 'Oh, whisky is the life of man,
> Whisky, Johnny!
> Oh, whisky murdered my old man,
> So it's whisky for my Johnny!'

Regan turned and joined them. 'Shut up, everybody!' he cried. 'Let Paddy sing by himself! Give us a solo, Paddy,' he said. 'Do you know

"Shenandoah"?' He realised that the Irishman had a fine voice, but he was spoiling it with the drink. He wanted to hear a song that would honour the sailing ship, a sad old song of the sea. Paddy stared at him in drunken amazement and cried thickly: 'Dew Oi know "Shenandjo"! Will ye'se listen to him? Dew Oi know "Shenandjo"! Shure Oi lisped it at me ole man's knee!' He began singing. The lovely old shanty gripped him, and he sang it seriously, with romantic sweetness:

> 'Oh Shenandoah, I long to see you,
> Away, you rolling river!
> Away! We're bound away,
> Across the wide Missouri!'

Someone produced a mouth-organ and played it softly and well, and it sparkled in the moonlight.

> ''Tis ten long years since last I saw thee,
> Away, you rolling river! . . .'

From the ship across the basin a cook cast a pail of slop-water over the side. It flashed an instant tongue of silver and vanished in the dappled iridescence below, and the cook let the bucket dangle while he listened to the song quavering tenderly about the harbour. Regan was deeply moved. Ay, this was the song for a sailing ship! 'Shenandoah.' It was a poem in a name, and it sang of simple men who had travelled far, who carried pictures of relatives or sweethearts and were always promising to write home and always failing, men who had died abroad and never saw their homes again—the forgotten legions of wanderers in the long history of the sea. Ach, he must escape from the prison of the slums!

> 'Oh, Shenandoah, I love your daughter,
> Away, you rolling river! . . .'

The big form of McBride suddenly loomed before them, and his mighty roar burst amid them like a thunderclap: 'Heh! Whit's this? A bloody tea-party? Get doon below, ye shower o' bastards! Yer spell's up ten meenits ago! Jump to it, ye lousy bunch o' scrimshankers!' They all scuttled down the hold, except Regan and Paddy, who, gleefully swinging his bottle, lurched into the stevedore, and the two big men faced each other. Highlander and Irishman, they were of a size and breadth, and they measured each other's splendid build with admiring, mocking eyes. Paddy offered McBride the bottle and the stevedore thrust it away. 'Tae hell wi' yer whisky, man! Ah've goat tae get the wheat oot o' this ship. Ah'll hiv a dram wi' ye efter that's done, no before!'

In spite of his hatred of the violence in himself, Regan sat watching, thrilled, expecting a fight. Paddy suddenly vented a great laugh and stumbled down the hold, shouting: 'Ach, we're buddies, Mac!' McBride shouted after him: 'Sure, we're buddies, but you buckle intae that wheat, sod ye!' Then he turned. 'Whit's the matter wi' you, Regan?' Regan jumped out of his trance. 'Okay, Mac! I thought there was going to be a scrap!' McBride laughed good-naturedly. 'Ach, Ah wouldnae scrap wi' Paddy. He's okay! Noo beat it doon below!'

All night the wheat hissed down the elevator chute and the steam-winch rattled, hoisting up the sacks. Then the flanges of the bulk-heads showed clear and the many tons of wheat sifted surely down till the floor of the hold was visible. Late in the next afternoon the elevator stopped, the last few hundredweights of wheat were hoisted up in sacks and run down the gangplank in trucks on to the dock, and the whole gang left the wheat-boat to be paid off in the warehouse. 'It's me for the boozer an' a bloody guid wet!' Regan heard some of them say as they went away with their money. For two days' and a night's work he had earned over thirty shillings. He thrust it into his pocket and went and sat on the wheel of the crane. He was very tired, his head ached, and he coughed up wheat-dust from his throat, while he gazed longingly at the sailing ship till dusk descended. He had decided what he would do. He would give his mother half of his earnings, buy himself a second-hand pair of strong boots and tramp to London with his few shillings. But not before he had watched the *France* sailing down the Clyde. When he had bade her farewell he would never return. She would speed to the ocean, he would take to the road, and with every mile that he walked his thoughts would follow her.

After supper he picked up the newspaper which his father had just laid down and his eye fell on the 'List of Sailings'. Only a dozen ships were listed, but with excitement he read that the *France* was sailing next day on the afternoon tide. He threw the paper aside and hunched by the fire, staring at the invisible, voyaging with a sailing ship, till his mother, fretted by his immobility, said: 'Whit are ye starin' at, Johnny? Ye look daft, glarin' like that! Ye should go oot tae the pictures or doon tae the chapel for an hoor. Ye hivnae been tae Mass since ye came hame fae London'—she was always ashamed to mention the word 'prison'. He rose and thrust past her. 'Ach, I'm tired!' he said and went into the parlour, undressed and lay down, wakeful a long while, thinking of the *France*.

At her hour of departure next day he was by her side, waiting while ropes were cast aboard her from the pilot-tug, watching every pause and turn she made in the great basin till her prow pointed away from the city. At last she set out, very slowly, in the wake of the tug, with that tall blond man prominent on her deck, shouting instructions, the man who had given him the cheroot. Regan took that out and looked at it, and the keepsake seemed to bind him to her more as he followed along the dockside till his way was barred. Then he hurried out to the road and jumped on a tram and rode till he came to another free part of the river, and stood on the shore waiting till she came up. This way, riding on trams and buses, he followed her slow progress, while his heart grew sadder with every mile that she sailed beyond Glasgow. The flood was opening wider for her, the shores receding; she was leaving the grand little river, with its long and plucky history of shipmaking, maybe for ever. He recalled the Irishman's words. He would never see her again!

At the end he took a bus out to Dumbarton and stood on the shore nearby the great Rock. He saw the tug leave her and turn towards home with a hoot of farewell from its siren, like the cry of a timid friend deserting a gay adventurer. Then, like a gallant gesture, she unfurled all her sails and made her beauty terrible for his eyes. She was lovelier far than he had seen her yet as she came slowly on like a floating bird unfolding its wings for flight. She had a dream-like loveliness, and as she came opposite where he stood alone, he impulsively tore off his cap and waved it, then threw it on the ground and stood with his head proudly up, ennobled by her grace.

Sunset met her like a song of praise and his heart went after her as she rippled past. Ach, if he could only have served her on her last few voyages, before she was dismasted and broken up! She dipped slowly into the dying sun and the waters fanned out from her bows like flowing blood. Then the sun went swiftly down and her beauty was buried in the darkness. 'Goodbye, lovely ship!' he called after her. 'Goodbye! Goodbye, *France*!'

So ecstatic was his concentration upon that vanishing ship that he felt her decks quiver under his feet, saw her high spars tremble, heard the flap of her sails, as he gazed with uplifted head. He was sailing on, away from unemployment and slums and wretchedness, far from the ignorance and misunderstanding of his parents, to the infinite nobility of the sea! His eyes were moist, his hands in his pockets painfully clenched, his limbs shook like a saint's in the ardour of prayer. And for a long time he stood there bareheaded, unaware that darkness, with small rain and a cold wind, had enveloped his transported body.

ALEX GILKISON

Atthis

✦✦✦✦✦

THEN the rain came down and put an end to it. Which was no great pity. It had been only meant as a stroll. Simply an exercise. Something to suit a Sunday morning. Something with no real purpose or intention. Just a stroll, through empty streets, while nobody was about.

Rain of a sort. A smir. The rain that builds up from deep in the August heat. Rain that evaporates, not unpleasantly, in a shimmer. But not the weather for walking alone. It had only been meant as a stroll. Exercise; till the rain came down.

There are the hot houses. Worth a visit. Often visited. Not necessarily with a purpose. You don't need reasons.

YOU DON'T NEED TO READ
THE LATIN NAMES.

Nobody does, that I've ever seen. You walk around in a circle.

A circle so slow, curving, easy and deceptive that you never quite know when you'll return to the vestibule. The goldfish lie still in the water, thriving on the tropical stillness.

You can hear, without listening, conversations. Far around. Almost along the diagonal. The sound carries so far on the still air. You feel embarrassed when you pass them. Lovers sometimes.

SO BE CAREFUL WHAT
YOU SAY.

You can visit without a purpose. Out of the rain, on any other day.

You could walk down past the hospital. Gothic revival. Black and towering. Skyscraper additions. Mongrel architecture, fitting the requirements of the years. Latin plaques that are read.

HAEMATOLOGY AND NEUROLOGY,
CARDIOLOGY AND UROLOGY.
BLOOD AND BRAINS,
HEART AND GUTS.

Each is given a ward, a floor, or an extension.

Carcinoma.
MORE LIKE A PURGATORY
BLESSED BY RADIOLOGY.
A KIND OF
INCANDESCENT DOVE
THERAPY.

Opening up the tomb: praying for us now.

At the time of our deaths, the mortuary. Still and clean. Draining boards and cotton wool. A pink chest open. Elbows locked. Fists digging into hips. Head reclining. Mouth open, full of air.

Sculptured Life.
A CLEANING-UP JOB.
WAITING IN TRANSIT.

No red ochre. Only white light. What else do you expect? Candles and shrouds? Sweet perfumes? Disinfectant and pickled bottles. Praying for us now.

Outside, passing on buses, women in headscarves chant Latin rhymes.

The public house is always worth a visit. Life in the dark. Closed just now, but never mind. It's not essential. More pubs than shops suggests a requirement well met. Cans at home never seem right.

She would not approve: silently, not criticising. She'll be up by now, washing and dressing. Narrow-breasted Atthis. No, not really! How would I know anyway! Or would want to know. There's a purpose in the correct ignorance. Draped and sculpted. Longing for thy narrow breasts. Sculpted innocence, like in the gallery quattro-cento. Raphael understood, painting without models. For some things there are no models to find. I long for thy narrow breasts. Beatrice, four-syllabled, on the pontevecchio. From Tuscan came my lady's worthy race. All narrow-breasted. This is becoming a pre-occupation. Walking in the rain before breakfast. Geraldine she

27

hight. Utter madness, though I've never felt saner in my life, that I can remember.

Pubs named after Persian poems and medieval Spanish states. Indian and Greek restaurants. Degas's less than half a mile from the Masonic Arms. The Orangemen met outside the Galleries. Where the rose in all her pride, goes the old song. Christ of Saint John of the Cross head down, looking away from the rabble. My grandfather called me Micky. So if the Pope says no, we'll have another go, on the banks of the Kelvin. Tooraloo. Tooraloo. The tune that it played. King William on a white horse wielding Excalibur.

The rain falls heavier, but still not unpleasantly. It forms like precious jewels on her window. She'll look out past the veil when she notices that I'm gone. She'll wonder, how long. She'll notice that the teapot's still warm.

Sunday morning admissions to radiotherapy. Some poor sod asked for physiotherapy, with a sore on his lip as big as a ten-penny piece. You have to laugh. Admissions can be embarrassing. Like the old lady telling how she hadn't married her man, but had taken his name for her son's sake. I know you've got to get it right, son. Why get you into bother. Mortifying the student nurses with her tales of the size of her husband. Mortifying me! She died three nights into a coma. Her son prayed beside her bed. I'd meet him with his cigarettes in the basement when I collected the soiled linen. Hello never seemed the thing to say. One day I opened the fridge and saw her with the cloth off. They'd left her eyes open. I covered her up decently. It sounds a morbid subject, but there is more life in that place than in all your schools' seminars, libraries and publishers. Purposes and Intentions.

She listens to him silently. She never fakes surprise or incredulity. She never yawns or does not understand. She listens without flattering. Narrow-breasted, swan-necked, slender-hipped. The Italian masters modelled Virgins on their mistresses, the Infants on their bastards. Little greasy Christ-children, clutching a handful of nails. The Vespucci wasps mingling with the satyrs. Languid Mars: Venus erect. She'll have bathed fully. White skin soft as the Madonna lily. Slender ankles, letting her feet touch the carpet so as not to cause a stir.

There used to be a croquet lawn next to the green. Without the

flamingos, of course. Croquet under the shade of the Govan cranes.
I'll invite her down for a game of tennis. Assuming the rain's off. It'll
only settle the dust. How will I begin? I was thinking, you've not been
down for a while, it's usually pretty quiet . . .

And the sweet smile. The polite refusal that makes you feel so
courteous. A correct humility. She makes you feel as though you don't
offend her. I half-expected that she'd go to church. God knows why.
What a stir she'd cause! They'd count every statue straight off! Mater
Gloriana. Made strong the fountains and made fresh the springs.
They'll never believe this when I tell them. Will you? Say it's all made
up. Sprung from the veins of fancy on the wings of poesy! A wee lie.
Why should I care! If only she'd come down once more.

Beatrice has four syllables. A rose by any other name. If the rain
stops then I'll ask her. I'll say. I'll start. Just for a walk. I wonder if
she's sleeping? Upon a small white bed you fell into a dream. I sat up
all the night and I watched thee. I would have. Just to watch. How
would you start to describe her? Her hair is soft and brown. Her eyes
are blue-grey. There's no stone to match them.

I long Atthis, for thy slender breasts. That's correct: finally.
Slender-backed. Wearing white. You know, she could wear red, and
not many women can. Grey tenements all around; sandstone
mausoleums inhabiting the living. Cracked façades. Running down
like open sores in the winter.

As he approached the closemouth the rain that had fallen for the last
half-hour faded into a sun-streaked haze. The roads looked like
canvas spread on a green to dry. The smell of greenery cut through
the still afternoon. As he stood at the stairway his head turned to the
highest window.

Well, that was a damn-sight worse! It demands both direction and
purpose. Who has either nowadays? Becket's the best and he's
reduced to conundrums. That's the Irish in him I suppose. All his
visions fragmented with memory. Diaghilev made his into dancers.
Loie Fuller. Isadora. Pavlova. A whole, swirling, sensuous dream.
Joyce had a girl on the beach. Keats had a faery child. Even Webster
had a devil, and Tourneur a skull. Fowles has had two, but finds it
difficult to talk about it. But hang it all, Ezra Pound, there is only one
Atthis,

> Restless, ungathered;
> I long for thy lips.

The clarity in the words. The clarity of the girl. The purity of being. That's what makes her special. Not the looks. Not the breasts. Or the flowing hair, or the legs as long as willows. Not even the eyes. But the simple clarity that remains unspoken. Pure thought. Non-illusory. Purpose in the pure vision.

Narrow-breasted Atthis. If only she would walk on the street, her hand on my arm. Then they would have to believe. I would wear a tie, shave, and part my hair behind. She'd have been nice on the croquet lawn. Impressionist figures on a cracked and fading canvas. A white dress, tattered at the hems.

You're beginning to wonder if she really exists! Listen. I know this street. These railings are close enough to touch. The road is still wet. She'll be there. Waiting. Vision in a dressing-gown. Talking about the weather, about trivial matters. I know you don't believe me any more. Have you lost interest? There is a point to all this. Please read on. There is a conclusion. New paragraph. Check your references. Keep it tidy.

Three flights of stairs to climb. At the turning of the first flight I passed an old lady, descending. When I spoke to her she hurried past. At the turning of the second flight I looked out between the boards that covered the window. Below, in a yard filled with hawthorn blossom, a woman hung washing on a line. She sang an old song in a loud clear voice. At the third turning I met a young girl carrying a doll. Dry tears clung to her cheeks. Almost done. All that's left is the door. Key out quietly in case she sleeps. Quietly now. In through the door. Good morning.

ALASDAIR GRAY

The Crank That Made the Revolution

◇–◇–◇–◇

NOWADAYS Cessnock is a heavily built-upon part of industrial Glasgow, but two hundred and seventy-three years ago you would have seen something very different. You would have seen a swamp with a duck-pond in the middle and a few wretched hovels round the edge. The inmates of these hovels earned a living by knitting caps and mufflers for the inhabitants of Glasgow who, even then, wore almost nothing else. The money got from this back-breaking industry was pitifully inadequate. Old Cessnock was neither beautiful nor healthy. The only folk living there were too old or twisted by rheumatism to move out. Yet this dismal and uninteresting hamlet saw the beginning of that movement which historians call The Industrial Revolution; for here, in seventeen hundred and seven, was born Vague McMenamy, inventor of the crankshaft which made the Revolution possible.

There are no records to suggest that Vague McMenamy had parents. From his earliest days he seems to have lived with his Granny upon a diet of duck-eggs and the proceeds of the old lady's knitting. A German biographer has suggested that McMenamy's first name (Vague) was a nickname. The idea, of course, is laughable. No harder-headed, clearer-sighted individual than McMenamy ever existed, as his crankshaft proves. The learned Herr Professor is plainly ignorant of the fact that Vague is the Gaelic for Alexander. Yet it must be confessed that Vague was an introvert. While other boys were chasing the lassies or stoning each other he would stand for long hours on the edge of the duck-pond wondering how to improve his Granny's ducks.

Now, considered mechanically, a duck is not an efficient machine, for it has been designed to perform three wholly different and contradictory tasks, and consequently it does none of them outstandingly well. It flies, but not as expertly as the swallow, vulture or aeroplane. It swims, but not like a porpoise. It walks about, but not like you or me, for its legs are too short. Imagine a household appliance devised to shampoo carpets, mash potatoes and darn holes in socks whenever it feels like it. A duck is in a similar situation, and this made ducks offensive to McMenamy's dourly practical mind. He thought that since ducks spend most of their days in water they should be made to do it efficiently. With the aid of a friendly carpenter he made a boat-shaped container into which a duck was inserted. There was a hole at one end through which the head stuck out, allowing the animal to breathe, see and even eat; nonetheless it protested against the confinement by struggling to get out and in doing so its wings and legs drove the cranks which conveyed motion to a paddle-wheel on each side. On its maiden voyage the duck zig-zagged around the pond at a speed of thirty knots, which was three times faster than the maximum speed which the boats and ducks of the day had yet attained. McMenamy had converted a havering all-rounder into an efficient specialist. He was not yet thirteen years of age.

He did not stop there. If this crankshaft allowed one duck to drive a vessel three times faster than normal, how much faster would two, three or ten ducks drive it? McMenamy decided to carry the experiment as far as he could take it. He constructed a craft to be driven by every one of his Granny's seventeen ducks. It differed from the first vessel in other ways. The first had been a conventional boat shape propelled by paddles and constructed from wood. The second was cigar-shaped with a screw propeller at the rear, and McMenamy did not order it from the carpenter, but from the blacksmith. It was made of sheet iron. Without the seventeen heads and necks sticking up through holes in the hull one would have mistaken it for a modern submarine. This is a fact worth pondering. A hundred years elapsed before the *Charlotte Dundas*, the world's first paddle steamer, clanked along the Forth and Clyde canal from Bowling. Fifty years after that the first ironclad screw-driven warship fired its first shot in the American Civil War. In two years the imagination of a humble cottage lad had covered ground which the world's foremost engineers took two generations to traverse in the following century. Vague was fifteen years old when he launched his second vessel. Quacking hysterically, it crossed the pond with such velocity that it struck the opposite bank at the moment of departure from the near one. Had it struck soil it would have embedded itself. Unluckily, it hit the root of a tree, rebounded to the centre of the pond, overturned and sank. Every single duck was drowned.

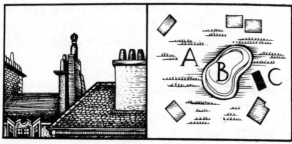

Left: Modern Cessnock shortly after the implementation of the smoke abatement act.
Right: Old Cessnock from General Roy's ordnance survey of 1739.
 Fig. A represents the swamp, B the duckpond, C the McMenamy hovel.

Left: Unimproved duck, after the watercolour by Peter Scott.
Right: McMenamy's Improved Duck.

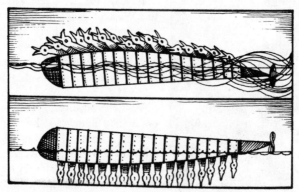

Above: McMenamy's Improved Duck Tandem .0005 seconds after launching.
Below: McMenamy's Improved Duck Tandem .05 seconds after launching. (The ducks, though not yet drowned, have been killed by the shock.)

In terms of human achievement, McMenamy's duckboat ranks with Leonardo Da Vinci's helicopter which was designed four hundred years before the engine which could have made it fly. Economically it was disastrous. Deprived of her ducks, McMenamy's Granny was compelled to knit faster than ever. She sat in her rocking-chair, knitting and rocking and rocking and knitting and McMenamy sat opposite, brooding upon what he could do to help. He noticed that the muscular energy his Granny used to handle the needles was no greater than the energy she used to rock the chair. His Granny, in fact, was two sources of energy, one above the waist and one below, and only the upper source brought in money. If the power of her *legs and feet* could be channelled into the knitting she would work twice as fast, and his crankshaft made this possible. And so McMenamy built the world's first knitting frame, later nicknamed 'McMenamy's Knitting Granny'. Two needles, each a yard long, were slung from the kitchen ceiling so that the tips crossed at the correct angle. The motion was conveyed through crankshafts hinged to the rockers of a cast-iron rocking-chair mounted on rails below. McMenamy's Granny, furiously rocking it, had nothing to do with her hands but steer the woollen coils through the intricacies of purl and plain. When the McMenamys came to display their

stock of caps and mufflers on a barrow in Glasgow's Barrowland that year, the strongest knitters in the West of Scotland, brawny big-muscled men of thirty and thirty-five, were astonished to see that old Mrs. McMenamy had manufactured twice as much as they had.

An engraving by Shanks in Glasgow People's Palace Local History Museum. It amply demonstrates the decadence of the medium before the advent of Bewick. It is impossible to tell whether it portrays Provost Coats or McMenamy's Granny.

Vague, however, was modest enough to know that his appliance was improvable. The power generated by a rocking-chair is limited, for it swings through a very flattened arc. His second knitting frame was powered by a see-saw. His Granny was installed on one end with the needles mounted in front of her. Hitherto, Vague had avoided

34

operating his inventions himself, but now he courageously vaulted into the other end and set the mighty beam swinging up and down, up and down, with a velocity enabling his Granny to turn out no less than eight hundred and ninety caps and mufflers a week. At the next Glasgow Fair she brought to market as much produce as the other knitters put together, and was able to sell at half the normal price and still make a handsome profit. The other inhabitants of Cessnock were unable to sell their goods at all. With the desperation of starving men, they set fire to the McMenamy cottage and the machinery inside it. Vague and his Granny were forced to flee across the swamp, leaving their hard-earned gold to melt among the flames. They fled to the Burgh of Paisley, and placed themselves under the protection of the Provost, and from that moment their troubles were at an end.

In 1727 Paisley was fortunate in having, as Provost, an unusually enlightened philanthropist, Sir Hector Coats. (No relation to the famous thread manufacturers of the following century.) He was moved by McMenamy's story and impressed by his dedication. He arranged for Vague to superintend the construction of a large knit-ting mill containing no less than twenty beam-balance knitting frames. Not only that, he employed Vague and his Granny to work one of them. For the next ten years Vague spent fourteen hours a day, six days a week, swinging up and down on the opposite end of the beam from the woman who had nourished and inspired him. It is unfortunate that he had no time to devote to scientific invention, but his only holidays were on a Sunday and Sir Hector was a good Christian who took stern measures against workmen who broke the Sabbath. At the age of thirty Vague McMenamy, overcome by vertigo, fell off the see-saw never to rise again. Strangely enough his Granny survived him by twenty-two years, toiling to the last at the machine which had been named after her. Her early days in the rocking-chair had no doubt prepared her for just such an end, but she must have been a remarkable old lady.

Thirty is not an advanced age and Vague's achievement was crowded into seven years between the ages of twelve and nineteen. In that time he invented the paddle boat and the ironclad, dealt a deathblow to the cottage knitting industry, and laid the founda-tions of the Scottish Textile Trade. When Arkwright, Cartwright,

Wainright and Watt completed their own machines, McMenamy's crankshaft was in every one of them. Truly, he was the crank that made the Revolution possible.

McMenamy's tombstone, Paisley High Kirk, engraved for the 1861 edition of Samuel Smile's Self Help. *(This corner of the graveyard was flattened to make way for a new road in 1911.)*

ALASDAIR GRAY

The Spread of Ian Nicol

❖❖❖❖❖

ONE day Ian Nicol, a riveter by trade, started to split in two down the middle. The process began as a bald patch on the back of his head. For a week he kept smearing it with hair restorer, yet it grew bigger, and the surface became curiously puckered and so unpleasant to look upon that at last he went to his doctor. 'What is it?' he asked.

'I don't know,' said the doctor, 'but it looks like a face, ha, ha! How do you feel these days?'

'Fine. Sometimes I get a stabbing pain in my chest and stomach but only in the morning.'

'Eating well?'

'Enough for two men.'

The doctor thumped him all over with a stethoscope and said, 'I'm going to have you X-rayed. And I may need to call in a specialist.'

Over the next three weeks the bald patch grew bigger still and the suggestion of a face more clearly marked on it. Ian visited his doctor and found a specialist in the consulting room, examining X-ray plates against the light. 'No doubt about it, Nicol,' said the specialist, 'you are splitting in two down the middle.'

Ian considered this.

'That's not usual, is it?' he asked.

'Oh, it happens more than you would suppose. Among bacteria and viruses it's very common, though it's certainly less frequent among riveters. I suggest you go

37

into hospital where the process can complete itself without annoyance for your wife or embarrassment to yourself. Think it over.'

Ian thought it over and went into hospital where he was put into a small ward and given a nurse to attend him, for the specialist was interested in the case. As the division proceeded more specialists were called in to see what was happening. At first Ian ate and drank with a greed that appalled those who saw it. After consuming three times his normal bulk for three days on end he fell into a coma which lasted till the split was complete. Gradually the lobes of his brain separated and a bone shutter formed between them. The face on the back of his head grew eyelashes and a jaw. What seemed at first a cancer of the heart became another heart. Convulsively the spine doubled itself. In a puzzled way the specialists charted the stages of the process and discussed the cause. A German consultant said that life was freeing itself from the vicissitudes of sexual reproduction. A psychiatrist said it was a form of schizophrenia, a psychoanalyst

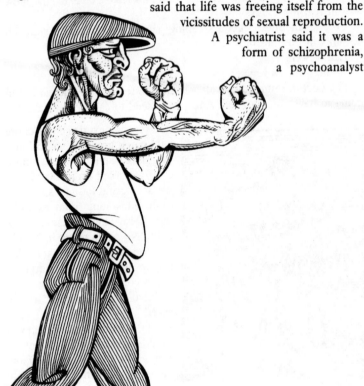

that it was an ordinary twinning process which had been delayed by a severe case of prenatal sibling rivalry. When the split was complete, two thin Ian Nicols lay together on the bed.

The resentment each felt for the other had not been foreseen or guarded against. In bed the original Ian Nicol could be recognised by his position (he lay on the right side of the bed), but as soon as both men were strong enough to walk each claimed ownership of birth certificate, union card, clothes, wife and National Insurance benefit. One day in the hospital grounds they started fighting. They were evenly matched and there are conflicting opinions about who won. On leaving hospital they took legal action against each other for theft of identity. The case was resolved by a medical examination which showed that one of them had no navel.

The second Ian Nicol changed his name by deed poll and is now called Macbeth. Sometimes he and Ian Nicol write to each other. The latest news is that each has a bald patch on the back of his head.

ALEX HAMILTON

Moonlighting

◇◇◇◇◇

KNOW ma brurr Johnny? Well, e wiz orr it oor hoose fur iz tea lass night, n wait tull Ah tell yi thi story e cum away wi.

Know how Johnny's sel-fimployed, odd joabs, cleanin windae zan daein gerdin zan that? Aye, well wan ae iz regulir ziza hoose orr oan thi South Side, jiss tintae Newtin Mearins. Beautifull place, e says. Ditacht, big gravil drive, dubbil garidge inaboot a nacre a grunn. Amazin, e says. Soanlie aboot two minnits walk fae thi shoaps, bit wance yir inside thi gate sit's lik livin right away oot in thi middil a thi country; n fae thi kitchin windae yi kin see nuthn bit grass an tree zan bushiz an flooirs. An that's how it's wan ae iz regulirs kiz, iz yi kin amadgin, a place that size need za lotae attentiun, so e's up therr aboot wan ina hauf tae two day za week.

So enihow, thi hoose bilangs tae a cuppil in thir fifties, n thiv goat wan boay aboot nineteen ur twinti thit's hardli ivir it hame seein e zaway it collidge sumwherr nInglin. Thi aul man's rakin it inin sum kinna import/export bizniss uruthir, n thi wife keep sursel gaun wi good causiz—Oxfam shoaps, charity bizaar zinaw that—bit nae hoosework, mine. Iz well iz Johnny fur thi gerdin, thiv goat a wummin thit cum zin ivri moarnin tae low dup thi autamatic washin machine, swit choan thi autamatic tumbil dryir, start aff thi autamatic dishwashir, n tidy oot thi hoose wi aw thi hunnir za uthir gadgits they hiv stow daway.

That's thi generil setup eniwey, n yi need tae know a bit aboot it afore yi kin appreciate Johny's wee story. NAh'll tell yi this, thir wiz sumdi else thit knew thim back tae front inaw, relse nane a this could ivir a happind.

Noo, iz yi might ixpeck, wir talk naboot a two-caur fameli. He hiz Rovirs thit e gets new ivri year, n thi wife run zaboot ina wee Mini—two-year aul, Ah think. Well. A coupla week sago, ur mibbe three it might a been, thir gaun oot fur dinnir wan night n, see niz how thi Rovir's pretty low oan petril, they dicide thill take thi Mini so's thill no hivtae stoap ita fulln statiun. Thi aul boay's loack inup thi cassil, n when e turns roon thi wife's stauninin thi middil a thi driveway scratchin ur perim n lookn genarilli kinna biwildirt.

'Hullo, hullo,' e says tae izsel, 'here trubbil.' An e pits thi keys cerrfulli intae iz wallit n walk sorr tae ur.

'Whit sup, hen,' e goes, 'firgoat wherr yiv lef thi motir?'

'Well,' shi says, fumblin fur wurd zan knowin shizin fura right shirrickin, 'well dear, Ah'm afraid tae say thit . . . eh . . . well . . . Aye. That is, naw! That is, whit Ah mean is, Ah hivnae *firgoat* wherr Ah pitit, it's jiss thitit sno sittin therr eni merr.'

'Aw naw!' e ixplodes. 'Whitdji mean, *sno sittin therr eni merr*! A motir hisnae goat leg zan feet a it sain thitit kin jiss get up n tay ka walk tae itself whinivir it feels lik a wee daunir doon thi toon! Yi lee vit wherr yi lee vit; yi pit oan thi haunbrake; yi loack thi door—n when yi cum back it's sittin jiss wherr yi walk taway fae it. UmAh right urumAh no right, ih? UmAh right urumAh wrang?'

'Well,' shi goes, 'aye, yir right, bit Ah *did* lee vit jiss here oan thi drive . . .'

'Aw aye,' e says, jiss taboot risign tae it bae noo, 'so yi jiss lef tit oan thi driveway, didji? No in its wee hoose, naw? No in thi extra bit garidge yi insistit Ah goat pit up kiz yir motir widnae start oan thi wintir moarnins? No in thi cosy wee kennil thit coast near inuff a grand tae arect? No in thi liabiliti thit's stuck wir rateable value up that much thit ma accountint hisnae manidge tae dream up a tax dodge tae covir it yit?'

Course, thirz nuthn shi kin say tae this kiz—accordion tae Johnny, eniwey—it saw true, n shi wiz gey stupit tae lee vur caur ootside wi thi keys keek noot thi ignitiun fur aw tae see. Howanivir, eftir thiv phonet thi pleess, they get thi Rovir oot, drive doontae thi petril statiun n gie it its twinti gallin zur whitivir it is they things drink, naway tae thir pals' fur thir dinnir ina right good buckit. Ah sippose thi main topic a convirsatiun wida been aboot how thir no very likeli ivir tae see thi thing agayn see niz how a Mini za dead commin wee motiran how easy it is tae respray wan, cheinge thi registratiun plate san stick a new nummir oan thi ingine casin. Frankly minedji, fae whit thi brurr says, it wid be merr a mattir a pride nannoyince get nit thi aul filla aboot thi wife. Whit Ah mean is, Johnny reckin ziz how if wanae us hid hid a caur nickt, it widnae be jiss thit yi nivir get thi full value back fae yir insurince cumpni, bit thit whit wi loassin yir no claim bonis n that, yi probbli widnae be able tae afford tae pit anuthir wan oan thi road—evin if yi could scray pinuff thigithir tae may kup

diffrince in thi compinsatiun an thi price ae anuthir motir. Sumhin
tae dae wi tax fiddle zan that agayn—how ca caur plus insurince gets
wrote doon tae necissri ixpenses, this gets pit oantae thi cumpni bull,
n thi odds jiss saves thi aul boay fae slip nintae that supirtax brackit an
stoap sim fork noot nineti pence, ur whitivir it is, in thi poun.

So, e get siszel tank tup enihow n, eftir drownin iz sorrow zaboot iz
wife n how shiz no fit tae owe na motir, e histae get ur tae drive thi
baith ae thim hame, see niz how e's that foo e kin hardli staggir fae thi
hoose tae thi caur.

An here, when they tur nintae that driveway—whit's thi furss thing
they see bit thi wee Mini.

'Heh,' e goes, 'umAh slosh tur is that your motir therr, hen?'

'Well,' shi says, pull noan thi haunbrake n get na bitae ur ain back
fur thi doin shiz been get naw night. 'Aye—an aye agayn. Aye, yi *ur*
slosh tan, aye, that *is* ma motir. Thi pleess iv goat aff thir mark quick
this time, hivint they?'

'True,' e goes, faw nowir iz feet iz e firgets tae unclip thi safeti belt
when e's get noot his seat. 'It's funny how they nivir phone duzup it
Jackie's but, see niz how wi lef thim thi nummir n says wid be orr
therr aw night.'

'Aye, bit lookit this, but,' says thi wife, dae na wee bit ditective wur
kursel. 'Here how they nivir phone duzup—they doant know nuth
nabootit.' An shi haun zim owir a bit a papir. 'That wiz stuck atween
thi wipir blade zan thi winscreen.'

'Whit?' e goes, ludgin iz bum agayns thi drivir's door n fumblin wi
iz spec case in thi hope thit pit noan iz glessiz ull sobir im up inuff tae
read thi writin. 'Whit izit? A parkin tickit ur sumhin?'

'Aw, giezit back,' shi goes, 'ya drunk naul bum . Ah'll read it oot n
let yi hear it—if that space atween yir ear zan yir brain ziznae droont
in Islay Mist!'

Your wife ivir tay kidvantidge a you when yir no feeln jiss mibbe
quite uptae thi mark?

'Yi lissnin?' shi goes. 'Right, here whit it says, well.'

Dear Mini Owner,

*Please excuse the worry and inconvenience to which I must have put
you. Late this afternoon, my wife went into labour with our first child
and, as I was rushing her to hospital, our car stalled just at your front
gates. I discovered that the trouble was due to an easily rectifiable fault
in the ignition system (a small, high-tension insulated wire had
severed), but the hour it would have taken to collect and fit a replace-
ment would also have meant my wife's giving birth in the back seat of*

our car. I should, of course, have knocked at your door and begged you to drive us to the maternity hospital, but panic seized me and, I am afraid that, when I tried the door and found it open, I turned the ignition key and made off with your Mini.

I am glad to say that, thanks to your car, my wife and new son are both well and, as I am too embarrassed to see you face to face, I have taken the liberty of filling up your tank by way of recompense. Please find enclosed two Dress Circle tickets for Scottish Opera's production of 'Cosi . . .' for the evening of Tuesday next. If you are free and able to attend, I am sure you will enjoy the production as much as I have myself.

Once again, my deepest apologies and sincerest thanks.

Andrew Smith

'Aaaw,' goes thi wife when shiz finisht readin thi note, 'aw, izat no nice?'

'Aw aye,' grunts thi aul boay, 'helluva nice—tull yi fine doot jiss tixackli whit damidge e's did tae thi motir.'

'Ach, see you,' shi says, 'yiv nae ramance in yir soul neethir yi hiv, nane ataw. Wid you iv did that fur me when wee Billy wiz boarn?'

'Ah wiznae here,' e goes, gettin doonoan iz hunkirz tae hiva good lookit thi undirneath. 'Ah wiz doonin thi Brum fyi rimembir—earnin wee ramantic pennies so's yi could buy a wee ramantic hoose wi a wee ramantic extra garidge fur yir wee ramantic extra motir—thit yi could lee voot fur a big ramantic chancir tae nick n dry vaway fur iz ain kinveniunce!' An e pull zissel tae iz feet n dusts thi gravil affiz knees. 'Well, nae thanks tae you, thir diznae seem tae be nuth nup wi it. Ah've goat a heavy day thimorra—goat tae fly doontae Lundin fura meetin—so yi bettir mine dan phone thi pleess in thi moarnin an tell thim aboot yir thief in shinin armour—an doant firget tae low kup ma Rovir!'

Thi nix Chuesday night—that's tae say, Chuesday therr—they get back hame in much thi same state iz they wir in thi night a thi note. He diznae like opra an e's been guzzlin away in thi baur, an a course thiv took hiz motir see niz how that's thi kinna statis symbil thit goes doon well it penguin suit doo zin thi Theatir Royil.

They coass tintae thi drive, stoap ootside thi garidge wherr shiz been cerrfull tae low kaway thi Mini this time, n press thi elactronic gadgit oan thir dashboard thit makes thi door swing up autamaticlli.

'Heh,' shi goes, dig nim in thi ribs, 'heh! Way kup, gonnae!'

'Ih?' e says. 'Whit? Srang? Ma wife is stone, cold sobir, officir. Nivir touchiz enihin strongirn . . .'

'Aw, shut up, ya fool! Wir no oot oan thi road—wir hame in wir ain garidge. Noo, look kaboot n see fyi kin see enihin diffrint.'

E rub ziz eyes, dead groggy.

'Enihin diffrint? Less see . . . therr thi sperr jack, ma wellies, coupla canza antifreeze . . .'

'Naw,' shi goes, aw impatiunt gettin. 'Naw, naw. No sumhin *diffrint*, mibbe—sumhin *missin*.'

'Heh, here, hen!' e goes, sit inup suddinli sobir, n jiss missin bangin iz heid aff thi paddit roof a thi limazine. 'Doant tell us yiv went n loass yir motir *agayn*!'

Shi ignore zim, get soot thi caur, pit soan thi nein strip in thi garidge n swit chizaff thi headlight san ignitiun.

'Naw,' shi says, 'Ah've no loass tit. Thing kAh'm stupit ur sumhin, get nit nick tagayn eftir aw thi boathir an your tantrim za thi lass time? Aw naw, Ah lef tit in thi garidge, loack tit n pit thi key in ma purse—see?' An shi stick sit upiz nose jiss tae may kim realise shiz no hiv nim oan.

'Awright, hen,' e goes. 'Sorry, sorry. Ah didnae really think yidivir be that daf tagayn—it's jiss thit yi kinna loass yir tempir, know whit Ah mean? An yi olwiz seem tae tay kit oot oan thi wan yi kin shoutit, n no get arrestit fur breach a thi peace fur dae nit.'

'Hm,' shi says, 'my, my. Furss tapology Ah vivir heard yi makin tae us—dead gracius nAh muss say, thang kyou very much.'

Bit e's goat orr iz wee bit chivalri bae noo, an e's pace nup n doon, gaun orr thi poassability zin iz heid.

'Right,' e goes. 'Wull jiss lee ivrihin thi wey it is, naway n phone thi pleess. Thir zoanlie three weys yi kin get intae this garidge when it's shut: thi elactroanic swit choan thi Rovir, thi key ur bustin thi low kin. Moan orr tae thi hoose n wull get thi fuzz oot. Mibbe thill kin get fingirprint sur *sumhin* thit'll gie thim a clue.'

Dae Ah need tae tell yi thi ress?

Yi know, fur sumdi iz big a kinnivin chancir iza nexport/import agint—daein custim zoot thir excise, fox niz wey roon tax riturn zinaw that—this bloke muss be gey innacint in sum weys. Ah mean, thirza phone boax jiss doon thi road fae thir hoose, apparintli: who in thir right mine's gonnae risk knoack inaff a motir tae take thir wife intae hoaspitil tae hiva wean? Certinli no when aw yiv goat tae dae is pick up thi ricivir, dial three nines free a charge n get a nambalin soot in minnits, see niz how labour zan Al amerginci?

They walk orr thi dry vinup tae thi hoose, get oot thir key, opin thi door, swit choan thi loabby light an—zilch!

Nuthn.

No a squerr a linoleum.

No a thread a carpit.

No a hem a curtin.

Nuthn, nuthn, nuth nagayn.

No a singil, solitri thing iz faur iz thi eye kin see, thi length n breadth a thir fifti fit hallway.

E look sit hur.

Shi look sit him.

Lip trimmlin, e go zup thi sterr, swit chizoan thi light sinaw thi room zan cums back doon tae fine dur baeside wherr thi telaphone table use tae be.

'Here,' shi says, 'doant boathir gaun intae thi kitchin ur naewherr. Jiss read this afore wi phone.'

An shi haun zim a wee note.

'It wiz wedge datween thi telaphone an thi dial. They muss tiv broat a rimovil van.'

'Aye,' e goes, pit niz spec soan an bend norr thi bit a papir.

The baby needed a few odd and ends. Once again, I find myself much obliged to you. I do hope you enjoyed the show.

Andrew Smith

See taw kaboot a moonlight flit?

MARGARET HAMILTON

Jenny Stairy's Hat

◆◇◆◇◆

NEIGHBOURS had often seen the bowler hat as they stood at the door, waiting for Jenny to bring a morsel of sugar or marge, to be paid back out of next week's rations. Jenny kept herself to herself, and never would ask you in, though her house must be tidy enough, old maid that she was, with never a man or bairn coming in to mess things.

'I see you've your young man in, Jenny,' they said, winking at the hat hanging up in the lobby.

On the way downstairs they would laugh at the idea of Jenny Stairy with a man—her in that old coat that fitted where it touched her because she had got it second-hand from a customer. Somebody had once said the coat came out of the Ark and Jenny came with it—as the female ostrich.

There was no doubt in anyone's mind that the hat had belonged to one of Jenny's brothers and she kept it to scare off burglars.

But Jenny, owning nothing of value, was not afraid of thieves, and the hat, ancient and curly-brimmed, would have deceived no one.

The hat belonged to a time when Jenny was not a stairy, but young Jenny McFadyen, selling pipeclay and pails to other people from behind the ironmonger's counter. It was not a shop where lads had much reason to come in for chaff, but somehow they found their way there.

'I'll cairry up ma mither's paraffin, Jenny.'

'Whaur's your bottle?'

'Ach, I'll hae to come back wi' it the morn.'

Then, her slenderness had not turned to gauntness, and her hair, now so thin and scraped, was a soft light crown above her face. It was a peaked, inscrutable face, with brown eyes which made men try to follow her at night if they caught a glimpse of her in the gaslight of the street. And, with it all, she was a douce-looking creature whom

46

you could take home to your mother and be sure of a welcome for her as your intended.

But none of the young men who came about the shop was ever allowed to take Jenny home, or even walk out with her. They were too much like her own brothers—and besides there was Peter Abercromby.

Peter worked in a lawyer's office. He had spoken to Jenny at the corner one night, asked her the way to somewhere in such a refined voice that she answered. While he was seeing her home, she discovered that he lived with his mother only a few blocks away.

Every Saturday night after that he was waiting for her when the shop closed. Minnie Walker from the draper's next door used to tease half-jealously if Jenny and she came out together.

'My, some folks is fair gettin' up in the world—I'll need to tell the chaps they've nae chance wi' their bunnets an' dungarees!' she would cry a shade too loudly, so that Jenny, going forward to take Peter's arm in his navy-blue suit, would be certain he had heard.

But he never gave any sign. Precisely he raised his bowler hat and said, 'Good evening, Jenny. What's your news?'

There was never any. At least, she couldn't tell him what old McNair the ironmonger had said yesterday to the woman who was buying a chamber-pot, or how the other night, washing the window, she had been so afraid that . . .

So she always said, 'Oh, nothing much, Peter. What's *your* news?'

He would set off primly on an account of how something had gone missing in the office and he, Peter, had miraculously been able to find it.

Then the inevitable: 'My mother's been not so well.'

Jenny had never seen his mother, but she came to know her as a woman always at death's door, but never quite being pulled through. Peter was her only child, and Jenny sometimes wondered how she would get on, looking after his mother, when, if . . . Or would theirs be one of those courtships which went on for years, waiting for the man's mother to die?

Because of his bowler hat and navy suit, Jenny could never be sure of anything. Walking with him through the streets, she would feel sick with waiting for the moment when he judged it dark enough to put his arm round her.

Sometimes she edged him towards a doorway, but he steered firmly away, talking all the time.

'I was reading in the papers. About this Irish home rule . . .'

When he talked of what he read in the papers, his mouth became a peashooter, sending out the words in self-righteous little bursts. It was a firm thin mouth that could kiss rather well, except that he took it away too soon.

In winter Jenny took him home for his supper. The McFadyens lived on the top flat, in a room and kitchen—Tom and Jim and Jenny and their father and mother. With them all in the kitchen it was a crush for supper, because Tom and Jim were big loud men, and Peter used to turn pale and a little shrewish, sitting with his tea in his hand.

Once they almost came to blows over Irish home rule, because Jim and Tom had Irish mates in the shipyard where they worked and they wouldn't believe what Peter had read in the papers.

'A lot of ignoramuses!' Peter was saying, with angry foam on his lips.

'What did you say, mister?' Jim got to his feet, putting down his cup.

From the other side Tom lumbered over, and Peter, smallish at the best of times, looked like a midge between two bulls.

'Peter—your tea's out!' Jenny plunged in at the more dangerous side, which was Jim's, and by questions about milk and sugar, to which she knew the answers, created a diversion long enough to save the peace.

She got her mother to 'speak to' Tom and Jim, and they began to go out on Saturday nights. Jim had a girl called Isa Bain, and Tom could always find pals at a street corner.

'Is Lord Muck awa'?' they would ask, coming in on pretended tip-toe. 'Can a chap get into his ain hoose?'

With Jim and Tom out, Peter talked away happily. Jenny, gripped by a merciless longing for the few minutes when she would have Peter to herself, saying goodnight on the stair, had less than usual to say. Her mother ignored Peter, as she did everyone, because she was too tired to notice. But her father would listen, smiling now and then with a strange sweetness behind his moustache. His smile was a sign of weakness, but you loved him for it—or Jenny did.

'Ach Faither, you're hopeless!' was the worst you could ever say to him, and sometimes only the fact that he was there made life in the cramped flat seem worth while.

'We'll need to get you out of all this,' Peter murmured one night on the stairhead.

'Him and his *all this!*' thought Jenny, too indignant to feel exalted by this near proposal.

Then he kissed her and she forgot everything except the hope that he would kiss her again. But he never did, and tonight as usual he withdrew his arm and pattered down the long stairs. She listened to hear the last of his rubber soles on the two front steps of the close.

Jenny did most of the housework because her mother was often in bed. She did not suffer from 'nerves' as Peter's mother did. Her body had been distorted at the birth of Jim, her second child; she had gone on to have a third and fourth, who died, and a fifth, Jenny, who miraculously lived.

Jenny minded none of the work except the windows. Sometimes, if Jim were out, she could get Tom to wash them. But, if both brothers were in, they would sit, one on each side of the fire, with their feet on the hob, and Jenny would grit her teeth as she sat or stood on the window-sills, not daring to look down, yet doing it in case she would forget how high she was.

She enjoyed washing down the stairs, moving down the long flight on her knees, with her pail and clayey water. When she was almost finished she liked to look up and see the top steps already dry and clean, except for the footmark which was certain to have been left by a Docherty child, slithering up to the house next door.

Sometimes her father would come up, unsteady because he had been drinking. Jenny, hearing his first dragging steps in the close, would leave her pail and go running to help him.

'You're a good lass, Jenny,' he always insisted all the way up.

Neighbours, though they heard, thought little about it, for old McFadyen was a painter—a trade that gave you a thirst if anything did. But they wondered what his daughter felt about it, her that was supposed to be making such a good match for herself.

Jenny was used to it as part of her father, the weakness that made her love him. Cleaning the stair lavatory after he had been sick, she would grow angry, and resolve to give him a tongueing, but when she came in and saw the bowed man, looking so miserable, with the thin streaks of hair across his head, it would all boil down to 'Ach Faither, you're hopeless!'

Peter Abercromby was a teetotaller and Jenny respected him for it. But she sometimes wondered whether a dram wouldn't make him more—well . . .

Peter's mother died at last. Jenny saw the notice in the paper and knew that this, more than any kissing on the stair, would bring matters to a head.

He did not come to meet her that Saturday. It was not to be wondered at, since it was the day after the funeral. All through the following week, by an effort of will, she kept herself away from his house. It was not her 'place' to go unless he asked her, but she had sent a letter of sympathy with an offer to 'perform any service whatsoever within my power to assist you in bearing this grievous burden of sorrow which had descended upon you (and yours)'—copying it word for word from a book in case she would make mistakes.

On Friday night he came to see her. She was dusting in the room and it was Jim who went to the door.

'Here's Lord Muck!' he called loudly, but Jenny, her fingers plucking feverishly at her apron strings as she rushed to bring Peter in, was not at all bothered.

They sat on the sofa, inches apart. Peter was nervous and played with his hat, suspended awkwardly between his navy-blue knees. She ought to have taken it from him, she . . .

'Thank you for your letter, Jenny.'

'Your mother, did she . . . ?'

He told her about it. The sudden pain, the doctor, the ambulance. The operation but it was too late. Appendicitis. To think it should have carried her off after the years of suffering she had had with other things.

There seemed to be nothing more to say. Of course he would not have had time to read the papers since . . . But he was beginning as usual:

'I was reading in the papers. About an Archduke who's been murdered. It may mean war for France. But it would be foolish for this country to . . .'

He went on in normal peashooter fashion. She could hear Jim's and Tom's voices raised angrily, then the slam of the kitchen door. The two of them slept in the parlour and they had an early rise in the morning. If only Peter would hurry.

She knew what he had come for. It was not very decent so soon after his mother's death, but what was a man to do with a two-room-and-kitchen house and no woman to clean and look after him?

At last he was saying: 'Jenny, we've . . . ep . . . been going steady . . . ep . . . for two years now. I was wondering . . .'

Jenny waited. Surely tonight he would kiss her twice, surely now she would be free of the doubt that made her afraid to open her mouth in case an uncouth word would shatter everything between them.

'So, Jenny, I thought maybe . . .'

Jim and Tom burst in without knocking.

'Coortin's feenished fur the nicht, mister!'

'Awa' hame to your bed an' we'll get to oors!'

Jim caught him under the oxters and Tom seized his feet.

His voice beat punily against their muscular strength. Jenny caught at his arm as it clutched the air.

'Jim an' Tom . . . pit him doon . . . are ye no' ashamed o' yoursel's . . . pit him doon!'

Tom dropped his feet for an instant to open the outside door but Peter could not get his balance in time and he was lifted again and dumped on the mat outside.

'Oh, Peter, you'll need to mind they're rough craters—no' like you. They didny mean ony hairm . . .'

Peter picked himself up, dusted his trousers and mopped his mouth for a high-pitched parting shot:

'You'll hear from my solicitors!'

Afterwards they found his hat on the parlour floor and they hung it in the lobby in case he would come back for it.

Jenny told Minnie Walker about it. She had to tell someone, for it got worse with bottling up. This was Monday, and Peter hadn't shown up on the Saturday and there had been a long dead Sunday between.

Minnie was sympathetic. She was a squat, dark girl, and, although her mother owned the draper's shop where she worked, it didn't seem likely that she would ever get a husband.

'Thae men!' she said vehemently. 'Oh my God, Jenny, is it no' terrible whit they can dae to ye?'

Then the cut meant as comfort:

'Ach, ye're weel rid o' him if he doesny think enough o' ye to come back.'

That was what her mother said, it was what any decent girl ought to feel especially if she had plenty of boys eager to take Peter's place. But Jenny felt only part of it: he hadn't cared enough to come back.

The next Saturday, before shop closing time, she thought she saw him outside, pacing on the pavement as he always did. She hung back, afraid yet eager to go out. When at last she did, it was as if the blow had fallen all over again on a place already tender. The pavement was wet and empty. Even Minnie had closed her door early and was gone. Jenny walked home alone in the rain.

Things happened in the next few weeks. War began. Jim, having got Isa Bain into trouble, married her. Tom joined the HLI and was sent to England.

Jenny lived through it, a little remote, none too hearty at Isa's wedding, but outwardly almost the same Jenny, steeling herself to wash the windows, and choking off the lads who came into the ironmonger's. Once she went for a walk with a boy in new khaki, but he was so shyly passionate and so like Tom that she ran away from him.

She took to washing the stairs on Saturday nights, and would pause, wringing her cloth, every time a rubber-soled foot fell on the close. Only when a downstairs door had banged or the inevitable Docherty child had slipped up past her, did she begin again, wiping in skilful semi-circles.

When she had finished each step, and before it was dry, she would take her pipeclay and at each side trace a row of loops, like a child's first attempt at writing. Mrs Docherty across the landing had no time for such fancywork, and every time Jenny's turn came round she had to trace her whirligigs afresh. But in the mornings she liked to see them gleaming, white against the grey stone, like a promise of something the day never brought.

Jim came up one night, alone, the stairs being too much for Isa with her time so near. He lifted Peter Abercromby's hat from its peg in the lobby and birled it into the kitchen.

'Ye needny be keepin' that ony mair.'

'How?'

'He can get yin oot o' stock. He's marryin' Minnie Walker next week.'

It must be true enough, because Isa's mother lived next door to the Walkers.

Jenny went to wash the stair. It was not her turn, but the stair was the only place where she could be alone

Savagely she slapped her cloth back and forward. Minnie Walker with her 'You're well rid of him . . .' She remembered the night when she had seen Peter outside and Minnie had been away so early . . . probably chaffing him as she locked the door, talking of Jenny and saying, 'You're well rid of *her*,' till he believed it and went with Minnie.

Minnie need never be unsure of Peter, because of her mother's money.

Far below in the close, feet were stumbling up the first few steps. Neighbours heard, and knew it was Willie McFadyen again, with a drop over much. But they listened in vain for Jenny coming down to help him.

He crept up, making a long slow job of each step. He stopped behind Jenny, but her cloth moved ruthlessly on.

'*Fule!*' she muttered tensely, thinking of that dirty job, tonight of all nights.

But he shuffled on past the lavatory and into the house.

When she went up there was no sign of him in the kitchen. She emptied her pail and, after a gurgle of water in the sink waste came Jim's voice saying to his mother: 'It's no' oor war—Tom wasny needin' to fash himsel'.'

Then the banging on the door . . . somebody screaming . . . 'Mrs McFadyen . . . your man's fell ower the windy!'

He was lying at the edge of the pavement with the empty pail a few yards from him and water trickling down the gutter.

'It was the pail I seen first,' said Mrs McLean, one stair up. 'An' then the puir man cam' efter it . . .'

Other neighbours were muttering something about 'a dirty shame, letting a drunk man wash a windy'.

They put a cushion under his head, and Jenny's mother was weeping stormily. She had been tired and silent for so long that it was a wonder to discover she could weep.

Jenny's tears gushed suddenly as they lifted him and his arms fell helplessly. He had done this for her because she had been angry and he loved her.

'Aye, it was the pail I seen first,' Mrs McLean was beginning for more of the neighbours.

'Could he no' have minded,' thought Jenny, lashing against her sobs, '*I washed it masel' last nicht!*'

Jenny came home one day and found her mother selling Peter Abercromby's hat to a rag woman at the door. Angrily, Jenny hung it up and sent the woman away.

'We're takin' nothin' frae him, d'ye hear?'

Her mother shrugged. 'Whaur's the money to come frae?'

There was good money in munition work, but the hours were long when you had housework to do as well.

So one evening, after she had finished at the ironmonger's, Jenny made her way to a part of the town where there were clean red tenements, occupied mainly by professional and business men with their families. She chose a close at random and climbed the first stair. Her feet longed to run back down the stair and all the way home. But she went on and chapped at a stained glass door.

'Were you wantin' anybody to wash the stairs?'

The woman came out . . . a full-bosomed personage, chewing the last bite of her tea, so that you could not read the expression on her face. Jenny shrank, but held her head up.

'D'you mean it, my girl?'

'Y-yes.'

'Oh, thank *goodness*! I was beginning to think I'd have to wash them myself.'

It was easy. The whole stair dropped like a plum into her lap, at threepence per landing, twice a week. Soon she had the close on either side as well. Charwomen had gone to munitions, and she could have had more work if she had been able to do it.

At first she pretended that people passing would think she was washing her own stair. She always said 'Good evening,' and gentlemen especially were profuse in their apologies for marking her steps.

One evening a little boy came calling, 'Jenny Stairy, Jenny Stairy!'

She turned as if to ward off a blow. But he was a nice little boy, whose daddy was fighting in France, and he only wanted to know why the stair dried white after she had made it black with her wet cloth.

Soon afterwards Jenny gave up her work in the shop, and became a full-time stairy. Her mother had taken a shock which left her paralysed down one side, and Jenny could not be away from her for more than a few hours at a time.

Jenny Stairy became a familiar figure in her own street and in the district where she worked—a skinny creature with her hair pulled back, because she had no time for frizzing, and hands and feet made ungainly by the chilblains which were a result of washing stairs and closes in all weathers.

She had a routine rather than a life: getting up in the morning, attending to her mother, going to work, coming back to attend to her mother, going to work, coming back. Sometimes people wanted her to clean house for them, but she would not do it in case she would not please them or they would ask her to wash windows. She stuck to her routine, day in, day out, for years.

Once at New Year she put whirligigs on a close, but the lady asked her not to do it again, it made the place look so common. On Jenny's own stair the whorls still gleamed in the morning, like symbols of hope not dead.

There was a man called Ibbets, whom she saw every Tuesday and Friday. He was a foreman carpenter who had strayed into that quarter because of war wages and the scarcity of houses, and there had been quite a sensation at the time, because the 'tone' of the place was supposed to be lowered. But as tenants the Ibbets were peaceful enough, and it was not long before a neighbour was handing Jenny the pail and pipeclay for Mrs Ibbets, who was said to be 'not too well', with a significant tap of the forehead.

Because he lived so far from his work, John Ibbets was in for his dinner and out again in the short time it took Jenny to wash the stair.

'It's indigestion you'll get,' she said one day, moving aside for him the second time. 'You should carry a piece.'

'Ach no, I come hame for the pleasure o' seein' you.'

She coloured at that, and the next time she was silent, letting him pass. But he caught her waist with his arm, and she saw that his smile was sweet, as her father's had been.

He was tall, too, like her father, with thinning hair and restless eyes. She found herself thinking about him often, as she had not done with a man, Kemp, who sometimes spoke to her when she was working.

He said he remembered her from the old days in the ironmonger's.

'Ach, come on, ye mind me fine,' he said persuasively, standing in her way, so that she had almost to wash over his square-toed boots.

She thought it likely enough, although she did not remember him. He was exactly the type that had come about the shop—broad and clumsy like her brother Tom, now married since the war, and living in the Midlands.

Kemp was doing well for himself in the building line. He was a widower and he wanted Jenny to come and clean for him.

'No . . . I couldna.' That was all she would answer, and by and by his sister came to keep house for him.

But every Tuesday and Friday Jenny watched for John Ibbets, twice in a quarter of an hour. Always as he passed he put his hand on her and called some pleasantry to which she replied as he raced up or down the stair.

One evening on her way from work she met him, and he turned back with her. He did not seem to read the papers, or, if he did, he did not tell her what was in them. Neither of them talked very much, but when they reached the close he came inside and kissed her.

It was a melting experience, and he left his mouth where it was till she took her own away. She would have done anything for him.

'Jenny,' he said, his arms still round her, 'Jenny, would you come and clean for us whiles?'

She had to go at night when he was there, because his wife hated women and might do her an injury. It was only once a week, and Jenny arranged for Isa, Jim's wife, to look in and make sure her mother was all right. In return, Jenny kept the children for a night to let Jim and Isa go out.

It was a queer exchange—a night at the cinema for two hours' scrubbing under the eye of a woman who never relaxed. Mrs Ibbets had once been pretty in a dark way, but now she was a wizened creature, with an air of knowing something more terrible than anybody else could imagine. Her husband stroked her shoulders and talked to her continually.

'Ach, Martha, she canny get me when you're here. Nobody can get me . . . d'ye no' ken that, ye daft lassie?'

She would giggle, with a distortion of her face like lightning tearing a small stubborn rock.

Once Jenny asked John Ibbets as he passed up the stair: 'What made her like that?'

He could not stop to answer, for his wife watched at the window, and was always waiting for him behind the door.

On his way down he muttered: 'Once away our holidays . . . a girl . . . there was no harm in it, but she caught us . . . she tried to do hersel' in.'

Jenny knew it was a lie. At least she knew there was more. His mouth was weak like her father's and he did not drink. A woman would always be tortured by doubts if she were fool enough to love him. Unless he were tied to another woman whom he could not love because she was wrong in the mind.

Twenty-five years later the Abercromby drapery stores (three branches) had sold out at a big price to a combine firm. Jenny was still washing stairs.

Her mother had died, and she might have taken a job, but she made no change in her life except that she cleaned at the Ibbets' twice a week instead of once. She took no other cleaning, although Kemp had asked her again and again.

The depression years had hit John Ibbets hard, but he gave Jenny more money than he need have done for two nights' cleaning. She put some of it in the bank, because she thought she might need it if ever . . .

But Mrs Ibbets lived on. People said sympathetically, 'Why doesn't he put her in a home?' But Jenny thought he ought to let her be.

Since the war began again, John Ibbets had been making good money, but he was a tired man whose voice had dwindled from constantly talking to his wife.

On the twenty-fifth anniversary of the night when he had first kissed her in the close, Jenny finished her scrubbing and left the Ibbets' as usual. He rushed after her, banging the door behind him.

He was sixty-five and she was over fifty, a gaunt woman whom neighbours had compared with an ostrich. But they walked home, and up the long stairs to her house, and were happy together.

The next day she went out with a firm step; the chalky curls on the stair were bright, and she thought she did not need their comfort any more.

She went to start her work, but as she passed the Ibbets' close there was a crowd gathered round. The district had 'gone down' since the days when it was full of teachers and businessmen. The wives of tradesmen and minor clerks were Jenny's employers now, and a few of them stood in a knot about the close.

'It was wee Jean says to me, *"Mammy, what's the funny smell? . . ."* '

Mrs Ibbets. Mr Ibbets had gone out and left her. Poor man, he'd paid for it now. He came in . . . they must have gone to bed.

She'd got up, turned on the gas, put her head in the oven. He must have been dead beat, he never wakened. The policeman could hardly go in, it was so thick.

'Jenny . . . you're not to take it like that. Aye, it's a shock . . . an' you've lost a good job . . . but there's plenty more. She's better away, poor soul, an' he . . .'

'It was wee Jean says to me, *"Mammy, what's the funny smell? . . ."* '

She had been alone in her own house for a long time. It must have been evening when she heard feet come up the stair. Heavy feet, but dulled with rubber soles. Then a thumping at the door.

She went at last. He had been turning away, but he came back. It was Kemp, the widower.

'Jenny . . . they're away now . . . you'll be needin' work . . . if there's nobody else before me . . . would you come an' clean for me?'

He was pathetic, knowing he should not have come so soon, but not knowing how else to make sure of her.

Jenny had always been quiet about things. Her brothers had cheated her out of marriage with a man who loved her less than his dignity. She had been left alone to bear the burden of her mother's helplessness. She had been indirectly to blame for the death of the two men she had loved. And now a man was asking something from her.

Gently she closed her door against him.

But a neighbour, coming up the stair half an hour later, saw something black whirling past her and out through the close. Before she could reach it, the missile had rolled away under the wheels of a lorry in the street. She recognised it, crushed as it was. It was Jenny Stairy's bowler hat.

J. F. HENDRY

The Disinherited

◆◇◆◇◆

A RAY of sun, from behind a cloud, opened out on a small figure in a suit of blue Harris tweed, hastening desperately along the empty streets, between the shadowing tenements, to reach the haven of church before the bell stopped ringing. A pale ghost, with bloodless lips sailed past the dark-blue windows of Templeton's the Grocers, Benson's the Newsagents, and the Hill Café, now and then, as it ran, staring backward, appalled, at a reflection in their window-blinds. A cap bit deep into the brow, and a spotted bow-tie pointed to five past seven. There was no time to adjust them.

——Dong! Ding-dong! Ding-dong!——sang the chimes, their echoes washing in waves of monotonous warning up the High Street, where a yellow cat stood lazily stropping itself against a chalk-fringed wall.

——Dong! Ding-dong!——and then, surprisingly, in a sudden giddy recoil, stopped altogether. Sawney broke into a run as he tackled the cobbled hill.

'What's the hurry?' called Big Sneddon, the policeman, from across the street. 'Ye're awfu' religious all of a sudden, or are ye off to a fire? The Bad Fire?——'

He broke down into raucous laughter at his own wit, but the face which was turned on him was so full of savagery, and something else besides, that it would have silenced anyone, let alone Big Sneddon, the handcuff-king. The angular blue figure straightened at once, and gazed thoughtfully after Sawney, now racing uphill, but it was not the expression alone in the latter's face that had sobered him. 'Poor Devil,' he said aloud, 'he's for it all right.'

Panting as he arrived at the door, Sawney paused for a moment or two, feeling as breathless as the bells. He turned to the east, but only for the wind, and, taking off his bonnet, waved it once or twice before his face, to dry the sweat.

'Late! Curse it,' he coughed, then plunged, like a man in a dream, through the open portals of the kirk.

In their pew, the family were sitting waiting for him. He walked down the aisle, conscious of their hostile stares, and saw his mother's face grow slowly purple. He was wearing high, narrow boots of red ox-hide, which creaked as he walked, and now seemed about to crack, though this was hardly a cause for anger. His father, however, to his surprise, blew his nose loudly in his handkerchief, and Jimmy, his brother, sniggered outright, in the aisle. It was just like Jimmy to snigger. He had neither tact nor sympathy. He needed a doing!

Grinning sheepishly to several of his mother's stairhead acquaintances, he took his place beside her on the cushion, and a long and vicious hair entered his leg. He squirmed.

'How dare ye,' hissed his mother. 'Sawney, how dare ye drag me doon like this! Never, never, will I be able to live doon the disgrace ye've brought upon me this day!'

Why this should be so was not immediately clear to Sawney, since, just then, in a river of robes, the Minister entered through a side-door and flowed up the stairs that led to the pulpit. You would have thought he was going to his execution, the majestic way he walked up.

These ruminations were cut short by a fierce dig in the ribs. 'Ye're finished, dae ye hear? I want no part of ye from now on! Oh, wait till I get ye outside,' his mother moaned in whispering, inarticulate rage, one eye on the pulpit where the Minister was opening the Book—'I'll skivver the liver out o' ye, ye impiddent young deevil! Look at ye, look at your face!'

His father's impassive stare, Jimmy's noble contempt, his mother's passion and the amused glances of young girls, peeping over the tops of their hymn-books, at last forced Sawney actually to feel his face, which had in fact, now that his attention had been drawn to it, begun to seem slightly puffy.

Only then, as the congregation, without warning, stood up like a forest to sing the opening hymn: 'Be Strong in the Fight!' did it dawn on Sawney's horror-stricken conscience that he had come to church, to attend morning service, with two black eyes.

They swelled up till he could scarcely see. Miserably he sat as though in a cage, exposed to amusement, curiosity and scorn, his hands thrust between his knees, out of sight, to still their convulsive bird-like movements of escape.

Whenever he turned to look at her, he met the fixed glare of his mother, or heard the words: 'Vagabond! Scamp!——'

He grued when he thought of the end of the service, when he would have to face her tigerish wrath, out there in the bright sunlight. Surely this enforced silence would do something to calm her down? Instead, it only served to deepen her shame.

'The disgrace!' she said, drawing her breath, and looking round, her back stiff.

Sheepishly, he grinned again and looked at his father, who pushed forward his white moustache and stolidly gazed at the pulpit.

Once more, he was in disgrace. He had always been in disgrace ever since, a boy in striped pants, called 'Zebra' by his unfeeling friends, he had left school for the last time and kicked his books high in the air over the wall into Sighthill Cemetery. The only prize he had ever had in his life, was a book called *No and Where to Say It*, and that was for regular attendance at the Highland Society School. It was a good book. It told you about the perils of life for a young man, and how easy it was, after the first weak 'Yes' to evil companions, to go on saying 'Yes', and end up gambling, drinking, going with women and spending your substance, or breaking your mother's heart.

'You'll break my heart!' she hissed now. 'You and your wild hooligan freens!——'

He had learned to say 'No' from that book. Surely *he* could not be breaking his mother's heart? He did not drink. He did not gamble. All he did was box every Sunday morning in the stables behind Possil Quarry.

He was not, Sawney told himself, in the habit of grousing, but what chance had he ever had? Instead of meditating now on his sins, as he should have done, or trying to remember exactly what it was that Joseph had taken with him from Pharaoh's palace, he began to think of his own upbringing. An old man, who had once been an agricultural labourer, wearing a lum hat wanting a crown, had stood like a clown in the cobbled backyard of the house in Grafton Street when he was born, his patron saint, an industrial troubadour, singing in beggared chivalry. In token of the day of infinite jest it was, he played on a flute that through his mother's dreams had drowned the sound of the traffic, and now and then quavered a thoroughly commercial chorus:

Balloons and windmills for jelly jars!

Amid the great conglomeration of city streets, blocks of tenements, unsightly factories, and engineering shops, intricate as the network of railways imposed on the town without so much as a by-your-leave, without planning of any sort, and with no principles at all save those of immediate and substantial gain, there was no one to suckle the child except the midwife, a stout buxom woman, timeless as one of the Furies, as it lay blinking in the bed on the wall.

Outside his room lay the rampant scenery of loch and mountain, but Campsie and Lennoxtown were as far away, for the child, as the life his ancestors had once led among these former fields. Their miles had been transformed into money. Nearer were the forests of poverty broken down into the fuel and ash of coal-depots and yards. Nearer were the foliage and sky of hoardings, blossoming enormous letters and pictures, a mythology of commerce, whose gods and demons waited to invade his fairyland. Nearer were the woodland paths of tramlines and railways. An iron song of bells and sirens stilled the birds. He had been born into a cage.

Nomadic crime had settled on these steppes. Where once the total police force had consisted of Sergeant Oliver and Constable Walker, now twenty-six officers and men were required to keep what they called 'the peace', a force larger than that of other equally populated areas further south—such as Ayr.

His self-pity was cut rudely short.

A thunder of shuffling presaged the 'skailing' of the kirk. The congregation relaxed and allowed itself the luxury of starched smiles.

Sawney rose, and filtered slowly and shamefully, out into the bright sunlight, feeling more forsaken, more forlorn than ever.

Outside, little groups stood discussing the sermon, waiting for friends, inspecting each other's dress, or gossiping. Mrs Anderson sailed past them, her ears burning, imagining that behind her she could hear suppressed laughter, scandalous allegations and even criminal threats.

She waited until she had reached the comparative neutrality of the pavement, then she spun round on her son, who had been dragging behind like an unwilling puppy.

'How did it happen? Who did it to ye? It serves ye right!' she said in one breath.

'It wasna my fault, honest! He hit me first.'

'Who? I'll never, *never* forgive ye for this, I swear!'

'Dukes Kinnaird. He was sparring. He's to fight the English champion tomorrow. They asked me to go a couple of rounds with him.'

'Did ye?' asked the white-haired old man who was his father, stuffing thick black down into his pipe and trying to look angry, in support of his wife.

'It was only supposed to be a spar,' pleaded Sawney, 'but all of a sudden he hit me right between the eyes. I saw he was coming for a knock-out, the dirty dog.'

'Don't dare use that language in front of me. On a Sunday, too!'

'What happened?' his father asked.

'I let go with my left and crossed with my right. He went back over the ropes into a bath of hot water.'

The old man laughed. His wife turned on him. 'That's enough of you! Well, I'm for no more of it. Ye can come hame and pack yer things. I don't want ye in my hoose. Ye'll end up on the end of a rope one day, I tell ye.'

For all his waywardness, Sawney was genuinely appalled. Leave home? Where would he go? He'd be a laughing stock. He knew his mother, the auld wife, was hard, but only now was he beginning to realise just how hard. She seemed to have no affection for him left.

'Ye'll pack your things and away this very night!' she said.

He looked at the auld wife to see if she meant it. Her collar stood high on her scrawny neck, and her hat, with one feather on it, made her seem a comical figure, in her anger.

'Why can't you be liker your brother?' his father asked in a low voice. 'He never gets into any scrapes.'

'We canny all be in the Post Office,' said Sawney.

'He's a well-behaved lad. It's a pity ye werena liker him. He'll do weel for himself.'

Sawney did not doubt it. He had never denied that his brother was a very worthy man, a gentleman, and different altogether from himself. It had seemed natural to him, even as a boy, that he should have to fight Jimmy's battles, although Jimmy was older than he was, in the days when fights really were fights. Many a 'jelly-nose' he had awarded boys at school to save his brother's reputation and the family honour, but it never occurred to him to talk about it, or to think there was any particular merit in it. Jimmy was the meritorious one. He never got into scrapes, never fought, never squabbled. Such things were beneath him. He read books until they wafted him into the Post Office, and now he was a Sorter—to Sawney, one of the intellectuals.

As they walked down Hillkirk Road, Mrs Anderson bowing in enforced silence, and screwing up her eyes in what she imagined to be a smile to her neighbours, he had to step on to the pavement to avoid a horse and cart, which with a great grinding of the brake was proceeding downhill. It reminded him of early escapades, which really, he thought, had been enough to break even his mother's stout heart. Had he been younger, he would almost certainly have jumped on the back of that same lorry. He had always done so, until the fatal day when he slipped and the wheel went over his leg, breaking it. He had then had to spend six weeks in bed. What a delight it had been to get out again!

He could still remember that afternoon as clearly as this one. It had been such heaven to run about with his leg out of plaster of Paris, that he must have gone slightly mad. Another lorry passed, and forgetting his mother's injunctions, he had darted after it as soon as he was out of the close-mouth. Leaning on the back with his stomach, he heaved himself up, putting one foot on the rear-axle as he did so. To his horror, his foot slipped and slid through between the spokes. He had howled, for the bone was broken, for the second time. Then, far more scared of his mother than of what had happened to his foot, he had limped upstairs into the close, and sat for three-quarters of an hour on the stairhead lavatory seat, white and sick, gazing at the blood on his leg and hoping somehow it would heal before he had to go in. It did not heal, and he had had a thrashing on top of the ordeal.

Now they were in Springburn Road and Mrs Anderson could give something like full vent to her fury.

'I've a good mind to belt yer ear!' she said. 'If you were half a man you'd dae it!' she concluded to her husband.

'But he's a man!' protested the latter. 'He's past that!' Then, seeing the ruthlessness in his wife's features, he came to a firm resolve.

'All right,' he said, 'I'll take him in hand myself.'

'You will,' she repeated, 'and he'll go this very night, don't forget!'

'How could you do it? To me? Your own mother? Don't I work and slave for ye? Haven't I always worked and slaved to bring you up in decency?'

She was working herself up into a frenzy, starting a 'flyting', and Sawney sought for a way of escape, any way of escape.

'You told me to come to church, so I came!' he parried.

'You came! You came did ye? Do ye know what the neighbours will be saying this verry meenit? Do ye?'

'Excuse me, mither,' he said, 'there's Rob across the street. I want to talk to him. See you later!'

As he dashed across the roadway to Rob, he heard his mother's last few words hurtle after him.

'Ye can come and fetch yer things when ye're ready!'

It was late when Sawney finally arrived home, having put off the evil hour as long as he possibly could. The door was locked. But it was not the first time he had been locked out, and he knew what to do. Prising open the bedroom window, he climbed up and firmly grasped the aspidistra plant he knew stood there, so that it should not fall over. Then, stepping in, he advanced with it in his arms, through the darkness, into the middle of the room. There was a loud crash.

He had walked bang into the half-open door. Now the fat was in the fire! For a second there was silence, then:

'Come here!' thundered his father's voice from the kitchen.

Walking awkwardly through, the plant still in his hand, he saw the old man standing firmly by the gas-bracket, in his shirt-sleeves, with his cap on.

'I've come to get my things,' he said sullenly. '——are they up-stairs?'

'A fine time to come in I must say! Yer things? I've done all *your* packing, my lad! There's nothing left for you to do. It's all here for you to take!'

He had never seen his father so determined before. It was an unpleasant shock. He had no idea where he would go in the middle of the night, unless to Rob's. He saw his father peer forward, as though to read his mood, and an unreasoning anger took hold of him:

'I'm not going to give up boxing because of her,' he said defiantly. 'Where are my things?'

'Ye can do whatever ye like. It's up to you,' was the answer. 'Your things? How many things dae ye think ye've got, beyond what ye stand up in, ye pauper? There's your things, the lot of them!'

He nodded towards the mantelpiece. Sawney's eyes followed.

'There's only a matchbox there!' he said.

His father's features relaxed. 'I ken that,' he answered, knocking out his pipe, 'but it's big enough to hold a' *you* own!'

They stared at each other, and ruefully smiled.

His father put his fingers on the gas-bracket.

'Try not to upset your mother again!' he said. 'Are you a'right?'

'All right,' said Sawney, about to speak, but his father had already turned down the gas and the little kitchen was in complete darkness.

By the red glare of the fire they made their way to bed.

JAMES KELMAN

Remember Young Cecil

❖❖❖❖❖

YOUNG Cecil is medium sized and retired. For years he has been undisputed champion of our hall. Nowadays that is not saying much. This pitch has fallen from grace lately. John Moir who runs the place has started letting some of the punters rent a table Friday and Saturday nights to play Pontoons, and as an old head pointed out the other day: that is it for any place, never mind Porter's.

In Young Cecil's day it had one of the best reputations in Glasgow. Not for its decoration or the rest of it. But for all-round ability Porter's regulars took some beating. Back in these days we won the 'City' eight years running with Young Cecil Number 1 and Wee Danny backing up at Number 2. You could have picked any four from ten to make up the rest of the team. Between the two of them they took the lot three years running; snooker singles and doubles, and billiards the same. You never saw that done very often.

To let you know just how good we were, John Moir's big brother Tam could not even get into the team except if we were short though John Moir would look at you as if you were daft if you said it out loud. He used to make out Tam, Young Cecil and Wee Danny were the big three. Nonsense. One or two of us had to put a stop to that. We would have done it a hell of a lot sooner if Wee Danny was still living because Young Cecil has a habit of not talking. All he does is smile. And that not very often either. I have seen Frankie Sweeney's boy come all the way down here just to say hello; and what does Young Cecil do but give him a nod and at the most a how's it going without even a name nor nothing. But that was always his way and Frankie Sweeney's boy still drops in once or twice yet. The big noises remember Cecil. And some of the young ones. Tam!—never mind John Moir—Young Cecil could have gave Tam forty and potting only yellows still won looking round. How far.

Nowadays he can hardly be annoyed even saying hello. But he was never ignorant. Always the same.

I mind the first time we clapped eyes on him. Years ago it was. In those days he used to play up the YM, but we knew about him. A hall's regulars kind of keep themselves to themselves and yet we had still heard of this young fellow that could handle a stick. And with a first name like Cecil nobody needed to know what his last one was. Wee Danny was the Number 1 at the time. It is not so good as all that being Number 1 cause you have got to hand out big starts otherwise you are lucky to get playing, never mind for a few bob—though there are always the one or two who do not bother about losing a couple of bob just so long as they get a game with you.

Wee Danny was about twenty-seven or thirty in those days but no more than that. Well, this afternoon we were hanging around. None of us had a coin—at least not for playing with. During the week it was. One or two of us were knocking them about on Table 3, which has always been the table in Porter's. Even John Moir would not dream of letting anyone mess about on that one. There were maybe three other tables in use at the time but it was only mugs playing. Most of us were just chatting or studying form and sometimes one would carry a line up to Micky at the top of the street. And then the door opened and in comes this young fellow. He walks up and stands beside us for a wee while. Then: Anybody fancy a game? he says.

We all looks at one another but at Wee Danny in particular and then we bursts out laughing. None of you want a game then? he says.

Old Porter himself was running the place in those days. He was just leaning his elbows on the counter in his wee cubby-hole and sucking on that falling-to-bits pipe of his. But he was all eyes in case of bother.

For a couple of bob? says the young fellow.

Well we all stopped laughing right away. I do not think Wee Danny had been laughing at all; he was just sitting up on the ledge dangling his feet. It went quiet for a minute then Hector Parker steps forward and says that he would give the young fellow a game. Hector was playing 4 stick at that time and hitting not a bad ball. But the young fellow just looks him up and down. Hector was a big fat kind of fellow. No, says the young yin. And he looks round at the rest of us. But before he can open his mouth Wee Danny is off the ledge and smartly across.

You Young Cecil from the YM?

Aye, says the young fellow.

Well I'm Danny Thompson. How much you wanting to play for?

Fiver.

Very good. Wee Danny turns and shouts: William . . .

67

Old Porter ducks beneath the counter right away and comes up
with Danny's jar. He used to keep his money in a jam-jar in those
days. And he had a good few quid in there at times. Right enough
sometimes he had nothing.

Young Cecil took out two singles, a half quid and made the rest up
with a pile of smash. He stuck it on the shade above Table 3 and Wee
Danny done the same with his fiver. Old Porter went over to where
the mugs were playing and told them to get a move on. One or two of
us were a bit put out with Wee Danny because usually when there
was a game on we could get into it ourselves for a couple of bob.
Sometimes with the other fellow's cronies but if there was none of
them Wee Danny maybe just covered the bet and let us make up the
rest. Once or twice I have seen him skint and having to play a money
game for us. And when he won we would chip in to give him a wage.
Sometimes he liked the yellow stuff too much. When he got a right
turn off he might go and you would be lucky to see him before he had
bevied it all in; his money right enough. But he had to look to us a few
times, a good few times—so you might have thought: Okay I'll take
three quid and let the lads get a bet with the deuce that's left . . .

But no. You were never too sure where you stood with the wee
man. I have seen him giving some poor bastard a right sherricking for
nothing any of us knew about. Aye, more than once. Not everybody
liked him.

Meanwhile we were all settled along the ledge. Old Porter and
Hector were applying the brush and the stone; Wee Danny was
fiddling about with his cue. But Young Cecil just hung around
looking at the photos and the shield and that, that Old Porter had on
full view on the wall behind his counter. When the table was finally
finished Old Porter began grumbling under his breath and goes over
to the mugs who had still not ended their game. He tells them to fuck
off and take up bools or something and locks the door after them.
Back into his cubby-hole he went for his chair so he could have a
sit-down to watch the game.

Hector was marking the board. He chips the coin. Young Cecil
calls it and breaks without a word. Well, maybe he was a bit nervous,
I do not know; but he made a right mess of it. His cue ball hit the blue
after disturbing a good few reds out the pack on its way back up the
table. Nobody could give the wee man a chance like that and expect
him to stand back admiring the scenery. In he steps and bump bump
bump—a break of fifty-six. One of the best he had ever had.

It was out of three they were playing. Some of us were looking daggers at Danny, not every day you could get into a fiver bet. He broke for the next and left a good safety. But the young fellow had got over whatever it was, and his safety was always good. It was close but he took it. A rare game. Then he broke for the decider and this time it was no contest. I have seen him play as well but I do not remember him playing better all things considered. And he was barely turned twenty at the time. He went right to town and Wee Danny wound up chucking it on the colours, and you never saw that very often.

Out came the jam-jar and he says: Same again, son?

Double or clear if you like, says Young Cecil.

Well Wee Danny never had the full tenner in his jar so he gives us the nod and in we dived to Old Porter for a couple of bob till broo day because to tell the truth we thought it was a bit of a flash-in-the-pan. And even yet when I think about it, you cannot blame us. These young fellows come and go. Even now. They do not change. Still think they are wide. Soon as they can pot a ball they are ready to hand out JD himself three blacks of a start. Throw their money at you. Usually we were there to take it, and we never had to call on Wee Danny much either. So how were we supposed to know it was going to be any different this time?

Hector racked them. Young Cecil won the toss again. He broke and this time left the cue ball nudging the green's arse. Perfect. Then on it was a procession. And he was not just a potter like most of these young ones. Course at the time it was his main thing just like the rest but the real difference was that Young Cecil never missed the easy pot. Never. He could take a chance like anybody else. But you never saw him miss the easy pot.

One or two of us had thought it might not be a flash-in-the-pan but had still fancied Wee Danny to do the business because whatever else he was he was a money-player. Some fellows are world beaters till there is a bet bigger than the price of renting the table then that is them—all fingers and thumbs and miscueing all over the shop. I have seen it many a time. And after Young Cecil had messed his break in that first frame we had seen Wee Danny do the fifty-six so we knew he was on form. Also, the old heads reckoned on the young fellow cracking up with the tenner bet plus the fact that the rest of us were into it as well. Because Wee Danny could pot a ball with a headcase at his back all ready to set about his skull with a hatchet if he missed. Nothing could put the wee man off his game.

But he had met his match that day.

And he did not ask for another double or clear either. In fact a while after the event I heard he never even fancied himself for the second game—just felt he had to play it for some reason.

After that Young Cecil moved into Porter's, and ever since it has been home. Him and Wee Danny got on well enough but they were never close friends or anything like that. Outside they ran around in different crowds. There was an age gap between them right enough. That might have had something to do with it. And Cecil never went in for the bevy the way the wee man did. In some ways he was more into the game as well. He could work up an interest even when there was no money attached whereas Wee Danny was the other way.

Of course after Young Cecil met his he could hardly be bothered playing the game at all.

But that happened a while later—when we were having the long run in the 'City'. Cleaning up everywhere we were. And one or two of us were making a nice few bob on the side. Once Cecil arrived Wee Danny had moved down to Number 2 stick, and within a year or so people started hearing about Young Cecil. But even then Wee Danny was making a good few bob more than him because when he was skint the wee man used to run about different pitches and sometimes one or two of us went along with him and picked up a couple of bob here and there. Aye, and a few times he landed us in bother because in some of these places it made no difference. Wee Danny was Wee Danny. In fact it usually made things worse once they found out. He was hell of a lucky not to get a right good hiding a couple of times. Him and Young Cecil never played each other again for serious money. Although sometimes they had an exhibition for maybe a nicker or so, to make it look good for the mugs. But they both knew who the 1 stick was and it never changed. That might have been another reason for them not being close friends or anything like that.

Around then Young Cecil started playing in a private club up the town where Wee Danny had played once or twice but not very often. This was McGinley's place. The big money used to change hands there. Frankie Sweeney was on his way up then and hung about the place with the Frenchman and one or two others. Young Cecil made his mark right away and a wee bit of a change came over him. But this was for the best as far as we were concerned because up till then he was just too quiet. Would not push himself or that. Then all of a sudden we did not have to tell him he was Young Cecil. He knew it himself. Not that he went about shouting it out because he never did that at any time. Not like some of them you see nicking about all gallus and sticking the chest out at you. Young Cecil was never like that and come to think about it neither was Wee Danny—though he always knew he was Wee Danny right enough. But now when Young Cecil talked to the one or two he did speak to it was him did the talking and we did not have to tell him.

Then I mind fine we were all sitting around having a couple of pints in the Crown and there at the other end of the bar was our 1 and 2 sticks. Now they had often had a drink together in the past but normally it was always in among other company. Never like this—by themselves right through till closing time. Something happened. Whenever Young Cecil went up McGinley's after that Wee Danny would be with him, as if he was partners or something. And they started winning a few quid. So did Sweeney and the Frenchman, they won a hell of a lot more. They were on to Young Cecil from the start.

Once or twice a couple of us got let into the club as well. McGinley's place was not like a hall. It was the basement of an office building up near George Square and it was a fair sized pitch though there was only the one table. It was set aside in a room by itself with plenty of seats round about it, some of them built up so that everybody could see. The other room was a big one and had a wee bar and a place for snacks and that, with some card tables dotted about; and there was a big table for Chemmy. None of your Pontoons up there. I heard talk about a speaker wired up for commentaries and betting shows and that from the tracks, but I never saw it myself. Right enough I was never there during the day. The snooker room was kept shut all the time except if they were playing or somebody was in cleaning the place. They kept it well.

McGinley and them used to bring players through from Edinburgh and one or two up from England to play exhibitions and sometimes they would set up a big match and the money changing hands was something to see. Young Cecil told us there was a couple of Glasgow fellows down there hardly anybody had heard about who could really handle a stick. It was a right eye-opener for him because up till then he had only heard about people like Joe Hutchinson and Simpson and one or two others who went in for the 'Scottish' regular, yet down in McGinley's there was two fellows playing who could hand out a start to the likes of Simpson. Any day of the week. It was just that about money-players and the rest.

So Young Cecil became a McGinley man and it was not long before he joined Jimmy Brown and Sandy from Dumfries in taking on the big sticks through from Edinburgh and England and that. Then Sweeney and the Frenchman set up a big match with Cecil and Jimmy

Brown. And Cecil beat him. Beat him well. A couple of us got let in that night and we picked up a nice wage because Jimmy Brown had been around for a good while and had a fair support. In a way it was the same story as Cecil and Wee Danny, only this time Wee Danny and the rest of Porter's squad had our money down the right way and we were carrying a fair wad for some of us who were not let in. There was a good crowd watching because word travels, but it was not too bad; McGinley was hell of a strict about letting people in—in case too many would put the players off in any way. With just onlookers sitting on the seats and him and one or two others standing keeping an eye on things it usually went well and you did not see much funny business though you heard stories about a couple of people who had tried it on at one time or another. But if you ask me, any man who tried to pull a stroke down McGinley's place was needing his head examined.

Well, Young Cecil wound up the man in Glasgow they all had to beat, and it was a major upset when anybody did. Sometimes when the likes of Hutchinson came through we saw a fair battle but when the big money was being laid it was never on him if he was meeting Young Cecil. Trouble was you could hardly get a bet on Cecil less he was handing out starts. And then it was never easy to find a punter, and even when you did find one there was liable to be upsets because of the handicapping.

But it was good at that time. Porter's was always buzzing cause Young Cecil still played 1 stick for us with Wee Danny backing him up at Number 2. It was rare walking into an away game knowing everybody was waiting for Young Cecil and Porter's to arrive and the bevy used to flow. They were good days and one or two of us could have afforded to let our broo money lie over a week if we had wanted though none of us ever did. Obviously. Down in McGinley's we were seeing some rare tussles; Young Cecil was not always involved but since he was Number 1 more often than not he was in there somewhere at the wind up.

It went well for a hell of a long while.

Then word went the rounds that McGinley and Sweeney were bringing up Cuddihy. He was known as the County Durham at that time. Well, nobody could wait for the day. It was not often you got the chance to see Cuddihy in action and when you did it was worth going a long way to see. He liked a punt and you want to see some of the bets he used to make at times—on individual shots and the rest of it. He might be about to attempt a long hard pot and then just before he lets fly he stands back from the table and cries: Okay. Who'll lay me six to four to a couple of quid?

And sometimes a mug would maybe lay him thirty quid to twenty. That is right, that was his style. A bit gallus but he was pure class. And he could take a drink. To be honest, even us in Porter's did not fancy Young Cecil for this one—and that includes Wee Danny. They said the County Durham was second only to the JD fellow though I never heard of them meeting seriously together. But I do not go along with them that said the JD fellow would have turned out second best if they had. But we will never know.

They were saying it would be the best game ever seen in Glasgow and that is something. All the daft rumours about it being staged at a football ground were going the rounds. That was nonsense. McGinley was a shrewdie and if he wanted he could have put it on at the Kelvin Hall or something, but the game took place in his club and as far as everybody was concerned that was the way it should be even though most of us from Porter's could not get in to see it at the death.

When the night finally arrived it was like an Old Firm game on New Year's Day. More people were in the card-room than actually let in to see the game and in a way it was not right for some of the ones left out were McGinley regulars and they had been turned away to let in people we had never clapped eyes on before. And some of us were not even let in to the place at all. Right enough a few of us had never been inside McGinley's before, just went to Porter's and thought that would do. So they could not grumble. But the one or two of us who would have been down McGinley's every night of the week if they had let us were classed as I do not know what and not let over the doorstep. That was definitely not fair. Even Wee Danny was lucky to get watching as he told us afterwards. He was carrying our money. And there was some size of a wad there.

Everybody who ever set foot in Porter's was on to Young Cecil that night. And some from down our way who had never set foot in a snooker hall in their lives were on to him as well, and you cannot blame them. The pawn shops ran riot. Everything hockable was hocked. We all went daft. But there was no panic about not finding a punter because everybody knew that Cuddihy would back himself right down to his last penny. A hell of a man. Aye, and he was worth a good few quid too. Wee Danny told us that just before the marker tossed the coin Cuddihy stepped back and shouts: Anybody still wanting a bet now's the time!

And there were still takers at that minute.

All right. We all knew how good County Durham was; but it made no difference because everybody thought he had made a right bloomer. Like Young Cecil said to us when the news broke a week before the contest: Nobody, he says, can give me that sort of start. I mean it. Not even JD himself.

And we believed him. We agreed with him. It was impossible. No man alive could give Young Cecil thirty of a start in each of a five-frame match. It was nonsense. Wee Danny was the same.

Off of thirty I'd play him for everything I've got. I'd lay my weans on it. No danger, he says: Cuddihy's coming the cunt with us. Young Cecil'll sort him out proper. No danger!

And this was the way of it as far as the rest of us were concerned. Right enough on the day you got a few who bet the County Durham. Maybe they had seen him play and that, or heard about him and the rest of it. But reputations were made to be broke and apart from that few, Cuddihy and his mates, everybody else was on to Young Cecil. And they thought they were stonewall certainties.

How wrong we all were.

But what can you say? Young Cecil played well. After the event he said he couldn't have played better. Just that the County Durham was in a different class. His exact words. What a turn-up for the books. Cuddihy won the first two frames then Young Cecil got his chance in the next but Cuddihy came again and took the fourth for the best of five.

Easy. Easy easy.

What can you do? Wee Danny told us the Frenchman had called Cecil a good handicapper and nothing else.

Well, that was that and a hell of a lot of long faces were going about our side of the river—Porter's was like a cemetery for ages after it. Some of the old heads say it's been going downhill ever since. I do not know. Young Cecil was the best we ever had. Old Porter said there was none better in his day either. So, what do you do? Sweeney told Young Cecil it was no good comparing himself with the likes of Cuddihy but you could see it did not matter.

Young Cecil changed overnight. He got married just before the game anyway and so what with that and the rest of it he dropped out of things. He went on playing 1 stick for us for a while and still had the odd game down McGinley's once or twice. But slowly and surely he just stopped and then somebody spoke for him in Fairfield's and he wound up getting a start in there as a docker or something. But after he retired he started coming in again. Usually he plays billiards nowadays with the one or two of us that are still going about.

Mind you he is still awful good.

JAMES KELMAN

The Hon

❖❖❖❖❖

AULD Shug gits oot iv bed. Turns aff the alarm cloak. Gis straight ben the toilit. Sits doon in that oan the lavatri pan. Wee bit iv time gis by. Shug sittin ther, yonin. This Hon. Up it comes oot fri the waste pipe. Stretchis right up. Grabs him by the bolls.

Jesis Christ shouts the Shug filla.

The Hon gis slack in a coupla minits. Up jumps Shug. Straight ben the kitchin hodin onti the pyjama troosirs in that jist aboot collapsin inti his cher.

Nevir know the minit he wis sayin. Eh. Jesis Christ.

Looks up it the cloak oan the mantelpiece. Eftir sevin. Time he wis away ti his work. Couldni move bit. Shatird. Jist sits ther in the cher.

Fuck it he says Am no gon.

Coupla oors gis by. In comes the wife in that ti stick oan a kettle. Sees the auld yin sittin ther. Well past time. Days wages oot the windi.

Goodnis sake Shug she shouts yir offi late.

Pokes him in the chist. Kneels doon oan the fler. He isni movin. Nay signs a taw. Pokes him wans mer. Still nothin bit. Then she sees hes deed. Faints. Right nix ti the Shug fillas feet. Lyin ther. The two iv them. Wan in the cher in wan in the fler. A hof oor later a chap it the door. Nay answir. Nothir chap. Sound iv a key in the door. Door shuts. In comes the lassie. Eywis comes roon fir a blethir wi the maw in that whin the auld yins oot it his work. Merrit hersel. Mans a bad yin bit. Cunts nevir worked a day in his life. Six weans tay. Whin she sees thim ther she twigs right away.

My Goad she shouts thir deed. Ma maw in ma da ir deed.

She bens doon ti make sure.

O thank Goad she says ma maws jist faintit. Bit da. Das deed. O naw. Ma das deed. Goad love us.

JOHN LAVIN

By Any Other Name

◇◇◇◇◇

I was always hungry in that slum where I was born and where my parents died. Even in my sleep I dreamt I was hungry. The only well fed things I knew were the bugs that ruled in their myriad might during the sultry summer months, swarming from house to house, up and down the woodwork, through the peeling walls; unconquerable, all devouring. In winter they retired to previously prepared positions and trained huge reserves for their annual spring offensive.

All the year round in that slum were rats and whippets, drunks, bawds and faction feuds. Disease and death and want stalked through the rotten, sunless hovels; and party tin whistles and asthmatic melodeons wheezed or piped their accompaniment to all the crimes in the calendar.

It wasn't a long street, but it had a notoriety that spread far and wide, and the added distinction of a 'Hansard' quotation to the effect that more misery existed in a square yard there than in any other selected square mile in the land.

The Hon Mem wasn't talking through his hat.

It boasted a beautiful name that slum where I was born and where my parents died. It could be deciphered, through my uncle Matt's telescope, on the blue, perpendicular strip of tin swinging on one nail above the pub at the east corner, where on windy nights it contributed its feeble note to the cacophony of slumdom.

At the other end, past flickering lamp posts and dimly lit, buttressed closes where hovered a perpetual smell of cats and sickness and primitive drainage, the sign of the three brass balls marked its western limit. Through all the industrial crises and depression cycles, the pawn shop prospered. Regularly on Monday mornings I used to join the queue at the door, labouring under as many parcels as I could possibly manage, all belonging to neighbours who regularly pawned the breadwinner's weekend clothes which were regularly lifted again on Friday evenings. I supplemented that meagre income by selling newspapers at night.

The pub flourished even more, and most of my father's wages contributed to its upkeep. He was always drunk just as I was always hungry. I can't remember him sober.

And regularly as the pawn shop queues on Monday morning and the Saturday night brawls at the pub, the factor called and was more or less regularly paid. He called to collect money for the privilege of being eaten alive in his vermin-ridden property, and once, supported by the might and majesty of law, he carried out an eviction at number 88.

My uncle Matt, from his open window three stairs up, levelled his red painted telescope at the Law, and thundered his denunciation, but nobody paid any heed; it was well known he was queer. I joined in with other semi-starved urchins and some women in loudly booing the shame-faced men who carried down the miserable sticks of furniture to the pavement, and when the police broke up the demonstration, the urchins scurried through the pens screaming the obscenities of the gutter. I learned a lot of them in that slum.

We lived at 88, three up, in the heart of it all, in a room and kitchen that suggested the aftermath of an iconoclastic orgy. The pawn shop was our cold storage.

My uncle Matt occupied the room. He was a remote connection of my father's and a shell shock case from the last war. A stooping, white-haired man with fear-haunted eyes, he affected a style of dress reminiscent of a Cruikshank illustration in Dickens. He existed on a small government pension eked out by coppers he collected ranting in back courts, warning the people of approaching Armageddon.

Of course, nobody paid any heed. They smoked and drank and blasphemed and pawned and fornicated and procreated and went hungry; they fought bitterly over their party colours, over Celtic and Rangers, King William and His Holiness the Pope; the men kicked their wives, the police beat the men, the children beat the police and the slum beat them all.

He kept to his room, where he would sit for hours at a time staring silently into the fire, then suddenly begin to talk to himself as if rehearsing speeches; or shaking his white head, ask himself all the questions that had no answer: 'What is God? What is genius? What are dreams? What is it that wind out there and why does it stir such atavistic yearnings in my soul? What is the soul?'

Sometimes he would sit at the window, gazing long and earnestly at the south-eastern sky through his red painted telescope, and one day I asked him what he saw there.

'The trail of the horror yet to come,' he replied. 'Oh, why did man aspire to fly?'

I looked curiously through the telescope.

'What do you see?' he asked.

'Clouds,' I informed him. 'Like big loafs. And ships sailin' in funny seas. Imagine a sea a' orange an' red . . . Imagine seas and ships up there, uncle Matt . . .'

'Where does imagination and reality part?'

'Ah don't know, uncle.' I trained the telescope on the street below. Like a creeping tentacle of Dante's *Inferno* the slum came to life, gigantic, monstrous . . . A familiar figure, gigantic too, staggered from the east corner, in his dock labourer's clothes.

'Ma faither,' I said, and reversed the telescope.

'Unhappy man,' said my uncle Matt.

My father came in and sat down on the bug ridden couch, beneath the solitary picture of 'Arran in the Autumn'; his elbows on his knees and his face hidden in his cupped hands; but still facing the bed in the corner where my mother lay She was consumptive and spent most of the time in bed.

They seldom spoke. They asked nothing from each other; in their understanding they had no need of words; they neither upbraided nor accused, and their terrible silence was worse than the most violent scenes I ever witnessed in the street; the silence of a dream long dreamt, a faith that is dead, a hope that has for ever vanished.

Presently he rose and made as if to stroke the rich, gleaming hair spread over the bedclothes—she lay with her face to the wall—then went out without a word.

My mother had the loveliest hair I ever saw; luxuriant, flaming red it was. I used to comb it at night as she lay gasping for breath and trying to ask me things . . .

'Where dae ye go at nights, son?'

'Oot,' I would reply.

'Ah ken that, Peter . . . But where?'

'Doon tae the corner.'

'Whit dae ye dae there?'

'Nothin'.'

'Did ye see yer faither?'

'Aye.'

'Wis he . . . ?'

'Aye . . . Whit did ye go an' get mairrit tae him for, onywey, maw?'

'Ah kent him long afore you, son . . . when he wis young . . . an' guid tae me.'

A spasm of coughing would interrupt the hair dressing for a while, then: 'Did ye get somethin' tae eat the night, Peter?'

'Aye. Did you, maw?'

'Uncle Matt brocht in fish an' chips. Ah left some by for ye in the oaven.'

'That's great, maw.'

'Tired, son?'

'Naw. It's only half past eleeven.'

'Are ye gettin' on a' right at school?'

'Aye. Ah'm the best fighter in the class.'

'Are ye?'

'Aye. Your hair's awfu' bonny, maw.'

'Is it, son?' Then she would suddenly cry and cough all the more.

Home had no meaning for me in those days. I used to wonder why people were always in a hurry to get home. The word to me connoted an atmosphere of dreadful unhapphiness, a place where there was seldom anything to eat, and a smell of booze and sickness—and bugs. I was never in a hurry to get home. Dallying on my way from school or from my street adventures, I would count the two eights fading into the grey stone at the close mouth and wish I were a man of sixteen sailing over distant seas in search of fame and fortune. Then I would slowly climb up the spiral stairway on the outside of the banister, all the way up the serpent-like trail, till I reached the rotten bit at the top facing our door, then vault over.

It was scarcely waist high at our landing, besides being rotten. And far down at the well, the tail of the serpent coiled curiously in perspective, dimly lit by the gas light, unglobed, that burned there night and day.

I recall the night my mother rose from her bed and opened the door. My father lay half over the rotten banister, drunk. He had staggered there after trying to turn the key in the door and had remained in that position, in a drunken stupor, his weight just evenly balanced. Some strange premonition had urged her to rise. She put her thin arms around him and I tugged at his greasy jacket till we both dragged him back to safety.

He roused himself and struck her across the mouth.

She reeled, gasping, into the house. He reeled in after her, and all night long he sobbed.

I lay awake all night, thinking: 'When I'm a man, I'll kill him.' But always I would see his glazed, drunken eyes pleading dumbly for forgiveness, and with the insight that is childhood's I saw the torment behind those eyes and I could not hate the man. Even at this distance of time I still feel the pity I had for him, the only emotion he ever stirred in me.

My mother died when I was ten. It was a Saturday, the end of a grey autumn day, and I had just returned after selling my news-papers. The twisted gas jet protruding from the wall above the bare mantel shelf lit the room and the figure of my father crouched at the bed side, drunk. The rain dripped from the sodden ceiling, drip, drip, drip, into a basin near the bed, and a bug crawled across the white sheet. Somewhere in the building, a melodeon wailed 'Give me a June night; the moonlight and you.' I heard shouting and more music down at the east corner, and a dog whimpering.

Not grief, but a loathing and a hatred inexpressible forced a rebellious cry from me.

Drip, drip, drip.

'Oh give me the moonlight . . .'

She lay there, indifferent silent . . . beautiful in death with her gleaming red hair, framing the white, waxen face.

'As it was in the beginning, is now, and ever shall be . . .' My uncle Matt stood at the door of his room, looking down upon us. 'Anguish is the lot of man. The tears shed by humanity since creation could swamp the universe; the accumulated force of his joy but rustle like a zephyr wind across an autumn cornfield . . .'

My mother lay there, silent, indifferent.

'. . . the moonlight and you . . .'

Drip, drip, drip.

'Whence to birth? Whither in death?' My uncle's voice still sounded from the room where he had retired again. 'Beyond the entry and exit of mortal life lie mystery unfathomable, and all life itself is encompassed by question marks forming an unassailable blockade which truth cannot pierce. What is truth? What is happiness? Why do grief and sadness prevail?'

There was nothing to eat in the house. I was hungry. I whimpered like the unseen dog outside.

My father was drunk all the time. He had to be assisted into the coach behind the hearse, and there was a murmur among the sight-seers at the close, women mostly, that almost amounted to a hostile demonstration. I heard a faint hiss as we drove off.

He drank even more after that; drank whatever was left of the insurance money; pawned the clothes bought for the funeral and drank that too. I roamed the streets at night, ragged, unhappy, often hungry and always alone. I developed the cunning of the slum arab and a knowledge of life beyond my years, and always in my heart was a burning bitterness against things and people and God that has not yet completely gone.

Conspicuous in his living misery where misery predominated, my father's end two years after my mother's death, seemed a natural climax. He crashed against the rotten banister opposite our door one night and toppled over; whether a frenzied act of despair or really accidental will never be known.

He lived for several minutes, with one leg doubled up beneath him like a broken doll, beating the ground feebly with his hand. I happened to be near that night. He saw me. His eyes had the same dumb, pleading look as on that night he had struck my mother. But in my sullen, unmoved gaze was his last agony; he read the silent accusation of his ragamuffin child who had no pity, no forgiveness. And presently his hand stopped beating the ground; his head lolled round in a half circle and stopped too.

They covered the mangled thing with bags and sprinkled the bloodstains with sawdust.

So died my parents in that slum with the beautiful name. I continued to live at 88, with my uncle Matt, who still preached in the back courts and came home to sweep the sky with his telescope, or sit by the fire asking his eternal questions.

We never bothered with each other. Our closer relationship now did not strengthen any bond because none had ever existed. Only once during the whole time I continued to stay with him, did a glimmer of normality illumine the dark wastes of his mind. It was when I asked him thoughtfully, one more than usually depressing day: 'Were ye ever awfu' gled, uncle Matt?'

'What about?' he asked, in a strange, low voice.

'Onythin',' I said. 'Onythin' at a'.'

'Yes. A long time ago.'

'Afore ye . . . Ah mean . . . afore the war?'

'Yes.'

'Whit did ye dae . . . afore the war, uncle?'

'I dreamt great dreams. And the thoughts of youth were mine . . . and the courage of Conrad's "Youth".'

'Whit's that?'

'A story by a great writer of the sea.'

'The sea . . .'

'Your element . . . the sea . . . You want to go to sea, don't you?'

'Aye, when Ah leave school.'

'That won't be long now.'

'Were ye never mairrit, uncle?' I asked him, after a moment.

'No.'

'Whit wey?'

'She changed when I came back.'

'An' so ye settled doon here?'

'I drifted here.'

'An' ye're no' glad ony mair, uncle?'

'I don't know. One forgets as time goes on. And one forgives too.'

'Is that right? Ma faither . . .'

'Yes . . . ?'

'Ah forgied him although Ah let on Ah didnae. Ah wish Ah had jist said somethin' afore he deid.'

'Unhappy man,' said my uncle Matt, and I saw the darkness return to the eyes that stared into the fire. 'Man . . . Creature of slimy depths and vision sublime, hermaphroditic composite of ecstasy and despair, angel and devil . . . man, what is your ultimate destiny?' He raised his hand in an oratorical gesture, and a giant insect danced clumsily on the ceiling. 'Must the war lords beat the drums again and ordain your total destruction? And would that matter very much here in this unhappy plague spot? The drums are sounding. The spirit of Attila breathes again over his ancient kingdom. Wake, Britain . . . Stud the fields and house tops with guns. Horror is coming over the sky.'

The winter wind wailed outside, and it seemed to have a music in it; the music of far away places over the seas where fame and fortune dwelt . . . where happiness was and sadness and hunger were unknown.

And something of the courage of Conrad's 'Youth' stirred in me and the hope that is born in all men. I whistled as I made the meagre tea.

At the age of fourteen I left school. The sea called me and I sailed the oceans of the globe. I saw the far cities I had once dreamed about in the slum with the beautiful name; and tolerance and wisdom came to me in the place of fame and fortune I had once dreamt of too.

I knew happiness beneath the changing skies and in the hush and fury of the mighty deep. I lived as my life had been meant to be lived, and years slipped by. The memories of former days grew vague and far away as objects seen through the wrong end of my uncle Matt's telescope.

And one day the war drum rolled. I came home. As I left so I returned, with nothing, the few possessions I had managed to gather, at the bottom of the Atlantic. A U-boat had singled us out of a large convoy that reached the Clyde, and I was lucky to arrive home with it.

It was early evening when I stood at the east corner, and already dusk had crept around the street where I was born and where my parents died. There was little left of it now.

A swinging sign, blue, creaked on one nail above what once had been the pub; the entire building gaped leeringly, its guts literally torn out, and over it hung a smell of rotten plaster and dust—and the unmistakable aura of fear that had been registered there when death and horror rained from the sky. Further along, standing monumental-like, slender, snake-like, coiling upwards from the devastation all round were the banisters of the spiral stairway of number 88. I knew it by the rotten bit at the top which alone had snapped.

I walked towards the west corner. The three brass balls had vanished. The site was a heap of still smoking rubble, where, they said, people were still lying buried.

Fragments of baffle walls stood like worn and ancient tomb stones in that cemetery of evil and unhappy things, where one day may stand a street as beautiful as the name it bore. That day will dawn when the present dark hour has passed and the war drums roll into dreadful history.

TOM LEONARD

Honest

◆◇◆◇◆

A CANNY even remembir thi furst thing a remembir. Whit a mean iz, a remembir aboot four hunner thingz, awit wance. Trouble iz tay, a remembir thim aw thi time.

A thinka must be gon aff ma nut. Av ey thoat that though—leasta always seemti be thinkin, either am jist aboot ti go aff ma nut, or else am already affit. But yi ey think, ach well, wance yir aff yir nut, yill no no yiraffit. But am no so sure. A wish a wuz.

Even jist sitn doonin writn. A ey useti think, whenever a felt like writn sumhm, that that wiz awright, aw yi hud to say wuz, ach well, a think ahl sit doonin write sumhm, nyi jiss sat doonin wrote it. But no noo, naw. A canny even day that for five minutes, but ahl sitnlookit thi thing, nthink, here, sumdayz wrote that afore. Then ahl go, hawlin aw thi books oootma cupboard, trynti find out hooit wuz. Nwhither a find out or no, it takes me that long luknfurit, a canny be bothird writn any mair, wance av stoapt. An anyway, a tend ti think, if it's wan a they thingz that *might* uv been writn before, there's no much point in writin it again, even if naibdy actually huz, is there?

It's annoyin—a feel av got this big story buldn up inside me, n ivri day ahl sit down, good, here it comes, only it dizny come at all. Nthi thing iz, it's Noah's if a even no what thi story's goany be about, coz a doant. So a thinkty ma cell, jist invent sumdy, write a story about a fisherman or sumhm. But thi longer a think, thi mair a realise a canny be *bothird* writn aboota fisherman. Whut wid a wahnti write about a fisherman fur? N am no gonny go downti thi library, nsay, huvyi enny booksn fishermen, jiss so's a can go nread up about thim, then go n write another wan. Hoo *wahntsti* read a story about fishermen anyway, apart fray people that wid read it, so's they could go n write another wan, or fishermen that read? A suppose right enough, thi trick might be, that yi cin write a story about a fisherman, so long as thi main thing iz, that thi bloke izny a fisherman, but a man that fishes. Or maybe that izny right at all, a widny no. But a do no, that as soon as a

84

lookt up thi map ti see what might be a good name furra fishn village, nthen maybe went a walk ti think up a good name for a fisherman's boat, nthen a sat nworked out what age thi fisherman should be, nhow tall he wuz, nwhat colour his oilskins were, nthen gotim wokn iniz oilskins, doon frae thi village tay iz boat, ad tend ti think, whut duzzy wahnti day that fur? Kinni no day sumhm else wayiz time? Aniffa didny think that ti masell, if a jiss letm go, ach well, it's iz job, away out ti sea, ana big storm in chapter two, ahd tend ti think, either, here, sumdyz wrote that before, or, can a no day sumhm else wi ma time? An in fact, if a came across sumdy sitn readn it eftir a did write it, if a hud, ad tend ti thinkty ma cell, huv *they* got nuthn behtr ti day wi their time?

A don't no that am sayn whut a mean. But a suppose underneath everythin, thi only person a want ti write about, iz *me*. It's about time a wrote sumhm aboot masell! But whut? Ah thought even, ach well, jist write doon a lohta yir memories, then maybe they'll take some kinda shape, anyi kin use that ti write a story wi, or a play, or a poem, or a film-script, or God only knows whut, on thi fly. So that's whuta did. Didny mahtr thi order, jist day eftir day, writn doon ma memories. N ad be busy writn it, thinkin, whut an incredible life av hud, even upti noo. Then ad be thinkin, they'll no believe aw this hapnd ti me. Then a looktitit, najistaboot threw up. It wiz nuthin ti day wi me at all. Nthi other people ad be writin about, thi people ad met an that, it wuz nuthin ti day wi them either. It might eveniv been awright, if you coulda said it was about me nthem meetin, but you couldny even say that. It wiz jis a lohta flamin words.

But that's sumhm else. Yi write doon a wurd, nyi sayti yirsell, that's no thi way a say it. Nif yi tryti write it doon thi way yi say it, yi end up wi thi page covered in letters stuck thigithir, nwee dots above hof thi letters, in fact, yi end up wi wanna they thingz yid needti huv took a course in phonetics ti be able ti read. But that's no thi way a *think*, as if ad took a course in phonetics. A doant mean that emdy that's done phonetics canny think right—it's no a questiona right or wrong. But ifyi write down 'doon' wan minute, nwrite doon 'down' thi nixt, people say yir beein inconsistent. But ifyi sayti sumdy, 'Whaira yi afti?' nthey say, 'Whut?' nyou say, 'Where are you off to?' they don't say, 'That's no whutyi said thi furst time.' They'll probably say sumhm like, 'Doon thi road!' anif you say, 'What?' they usually say, 'Down the road!' the second time—though no always. Course, they never really say, 'Doon thi road!' or 'Down the road!' at all. Least, they never say it the way it's spelt. Coz it *izny* spelt, when they say it, is it?

A fine point, perhaps. Or maybe it izny, a widny no. Or maybe a think it is, but a also a think that if a say, 'Maybe it izny' then you'll turn it over in your head without thinkin, 'Who does he think he is—a linguistic philosopher?' Or maybe a widny bothir ma rump whether it's a fine point or it izny: maybe a jist said it fur effect in thi furst place. Coz that's sumhm that's dawned on me, though it's maybe wanna they thingz that yir no supposed ti say. An thirz a helluv a lohta *them*, when yi think about it, int thir? But anyway, what's dawned on me, or maybe it's jist emergin fray ma subconscious, is, that maybe a write jist tay attract attention ti ma cell. An that's a pretty horrible thought ti emerge fray *emdy's* subconscious, coz thi nixt thing that emerges is, 'Whut um a—a social inadequate?' N as if that izny bad enough, thi nixt thing that yi find yirself thinkin, is, 'Am a compensatin for ma social inadequacy, "by proxy", as it were?' An thi nixt thing, thi fourth thing, that yi find yirself thinkin, is, 'If av committed maself, unwittingly, ti compensation "by proxy", does that mean that a sense a inadequacy, unwittingly, huz become a necessity?' An thi fifth, an thi sixth, an thi seventh thingz that yi find yirself thinkin, are, 'Whut if ma compensation "by proxy" is found socially inadequate?' and 'Ivdi's against me—a always knew it,' and 'Perhaps posterity will have better sense.'

'Thi apprentice has lifted ma balls an cock,' said the plumber. Sorry, that comes later. Am no sayin that these seven thoughts necessarily come in the order in which av presented thim. Ti some people, ahl menshin nay names, these thoughts *never* emerge fray thir subconscious, particularly thi fifth, which is, yi can imagine, thi most terrible thought, of thi lot. Often it turns out that thoughts six and seven are thi most popular, though thoughts one ti five are largely ignored. But thi more yi ignore thoughts one ti five, thi more thoughts six and seven will out. Coz although thought five, 'Whut if ma compensation "by proxy" is found socially inadequate?' never emerges fray yir subconscious, there comes a day when, in a casual discussion about Literature in general, sumdy says, 'Your stuff's a lohta rubbish.' It might not even be so blunt—in fact, what usually happens is, that in the foyer of a theatre or sumhm, an in thi middle of a casual conversation about Literature in general, then sumdy introduces you ti sumdy else, an thi other person says, 'Who?' An although 'Who?' might no *sound* like a literal translation of, 'Your stuff's a lohta rubbish', nonetheless, in the thoughts of a social inadequate, it's as near as dammit. So havin secretly thunk thought six, 'Ivdi's against me—a always knew it,' yi hurry hame ti write sumhm, ti get yir ain back. These ur thi symptoms. Coz yir that fed up wi ivdi yi know, so yi think, that writin sumhm seems about thi only thing worth dayin.Then at least when yir finished yi feel a hell of a lot better, coz whoever it was that was gettin onyir wick before, yi can go upty an say, 'A don't gee a damn *whut* you think about me, coz av jist wrote a poem, an that's sumhm you huvny done. An even if yi huv, albetyi it wuz rotten.' Course you don't actually say all that—you don't *huvti* say it, even if yi could be bothered. An if it's sumdy that *did* say ti you, 'Your stuff's a lohta rubbish,' thirz no much point in goin upti thim anyway, is there? But yi can ey jist look thim in thi eye, in yir mind's eye, an think, 'Perhaps posterity will have better sense.'

'Ahma writur, your only a wurkur,' a said, to thi plumber.

'Fux sake Joe stick wan on that kunt,' said the apprentice.

'Ball an cocks,' said the plumber. 'Ball an cocks. A firgot ma grammur.'

'Gerrihtuppyi,' a said, to thi apprentice.

'Lissn pal yoor tea'll be up na minit,' said the plumber.

'Couldny fuckin write a bookie's line ya basturdn illiturate,' a said, ti the plumber.

'Right. Ootside,' said the plumber. 'Mawn. Ootside.'

Sorry. That comes later.

TOM LEONARD

Mr Endrews Speaks

❖❖❖❖❖

(The following short scene takes place in St Kevin Barry's, a large school in Glasgow. Over the tannoy which has speakers in every classroom, comes the voice of Mr Andrews, the new headmaster. He speaks with a Kelvinside accent.)

THIS is your headmester speaking. This is Mr Endrews, your new headmester. I want to make one thing clear above all. It is my determination to make St Kevin Berry's a school of which the city of Glesgow cen be justly proud. This city of Glesgow, the envy of Europe for its many beautiful perks. Why only the other day in one of these beautiful perks, Kelvingrove, I chenced across a former pupil of this very school, who answered to the name of 'Tem.' Now Tem, I could see, was thinking long thoughts over a small bottle of hair lecquer. Beside him on his bench lay one of his unfortunate pals, who had some hours before shaken off this mortal coil. Rigor mortis was complete, end his right hend was set in what is known es 'a messonic hendshake'. 'Tem,' I said severely, 'hev you been freternising with those of another Faith?' But Tem slid forward from his bench, end went to join his hepless friend in thet lend from whose bourn no treveller returns.

Now Tem was never one to hev known the dignity of a laudable profession with a substantial celery, like my own. It was his own fault, of course. Et St Kevin Berry's he would hev the school motto, 'Porridge end the Tawse' inscribed on all his Eff Two's. But a lack of self-discipline was to prove his downfall in later years. You know, my feather was gerrotted when I was a child end it didn't do *me* any herm. No, I stuck herd et my studies, end in the fullness of time became a gredduate of Glesgow University. End there were no State hendouts in my day, one hed to get by on a seck of oats. *(Clears his throat)*. A seck of oats.

Of course none of you listening to me here this morning will ever go to Glesgow University, I'm aware of thet. Most of you will be in the hends of the Glesgow constebulary before very long, end some of you will no doubt make your appearance in the High Court on a cherge of murder. Now I want you to hev the honour of St Kevin Berry's in mind when you plead guilty, end under no circumstences should you use the glottal stop. I want you all to say, 'Guilty,' in a clear, well-mennered voice, with no trace of slovenly speech.

Teachers. Efter this address, all clesses will prectise saying 'Guilty' for thirty minutes. Tomorrow morning et 9 am sherp I will make a rendom inspection, end any boy who uses the glottal stop in reply to my question, 'How do you plead?' will be for six of the belt. With my new Lochgelly, which can stend on its own.

Finally. You will no doubt be aware thet with the coming of spring, it is no longer derk between the hours of four end five. This means thet I will be doubly severe with those pupils caught urinating in the hedges of local gerdens on the way home from school. If pupils behave like sevages, they will be sevagely dealt with.

Now I want Thomas Meguire end Frencis Lawson of Four Zed in my office et once. Sherp.

FREDERIC LINDSAY

The People of the Book

A TALL thin boy with eyes like a hare too ready to be startled is wound into the corner of a deep window ledge, reading. Since the building has been dedicated to this activity, his reading should be secure from interruption. In a library, however, the librarians are the ones paid to do something else. He listens for the third floor buzzer that signals a reader's request slip; more attentively, he keeps an edge of awareness ready to catch any warning of the approach of one of the senior staff. Nearby, under a single pool of light, a table is scattered with newspaper clippings, the torn blue agency envelope they came in, an open ledger with the left hand page already jigsawed with clippings, a pot of paste (yes, and with a brush to spread it on; remembering, it seems like an archaeological artefact from a lost world).

Thirty years later in a quiet room in a different city, a man turns a stolen book between his hands and studies the library's name rubber-stamped on the first blank page.

In the summer, the window by the boy's side would lie open and sounds of traffic turning off Sauchiehall Street would be carried in on the warm caressive air. Since on this evening it was already dark, the window would be closed and it must have been some time in winter. When the signal came, he jumped down from the ledge and walked by the dark aisles between the bookstacks until he came to the hatch. The shaft ran from the basement to the roof and he pulled on the right side rope hand over hand until the wallet appeared drawn up from below; it was a simple mechanical device with no electricity about it, workable even by thin adolescent arms, and it never went wrong. The wallet was of worn leather, a clumsy capacious affair that might have flapped at the side of a mailman's horse; the books went into it, and on the front were sewn leather pockets just big enough to take the request slips folded.

He put on the lights in the right aisle and located the case from the code on the slip. It was a bottom shelf and he had to hunker down to scan the titles. Because he was slightly and pleasantly drunk, he rocked back and had to steady himself by holding the edge of the shelf. He stared at a large grey book with bright letters on the spine. Dropping his head to one side, he read, *The World Conspiracy Of Rome*; from the blurb inside the cover, 'a world-wide conspiracy . . . the truth about the Church of Rome . . . tentacles . . .' and so forth. Putting the book back, he finds the one he wants beside it.

As a child when he had come back to Glasgow from the country, a tough boy had cornered him in the park and chanted, 'Are ye a Billy or a Dan or an auld (ould?) tin can?' 'Eh?' 'Are ye a Pie or a Cake?' 'What?' The tough boy stared, menace lost in confusion, 'Do you not know *whit* you are?'

From an untroubled household of post-Calvinist pagans, remembering his childhood, the boy on the library ledge would not have believed, back then in the Fifties, in the possibility of someone dying any more for being one kind of Christian in preference to another. It was true even in his simplicity, though, that he had been conscious in the afternoon of a certain tension between those two good friends Jamesie Farrell and Billy Macdonald. Both of them were older than him, in their twenties, with National Service behind them, men of the world. It had been an honour to be invited to join them in the pub in North Street before the evening part of the split shift. Heroically he had managed three pints of Double Diamond.

In the middle of the second one, when it had become easier, Jamesie was saying, 'What do you mean, what did I do? I walked her home—she lived up Garnethill.'

Lifting weights as a hobby had shaped Billy into a cube. He drew his black brows together and brooded, 'What did you do? She was wearing bloody white ankle socks. I mean, she was only about fourteen.'

'Do?' Jamesie pantomimed incomprehension. 'I got her to wank me, and then I came back down to George's Cross and got a fish supper.'

'You are an animal,' Billy said, spacing and emphasising each word.

'And you're an Orangeman,' Jamesie said, smiling.

The boy had seen the girl in the white ankle socks, she had been sitting in the Reading Hall last night, so that was true. On the other hand, yesterday he had heard Jamesie saying to one of the older men, 'Get your wife to stick her finger up your bum when you're coming.

I can recommend it.' That was Jamesie. You could never tell when he was serious, not when you were only eighteen.

About sport, Billy was a fanatic. On the boy's first morning in the great library, this square dark man had glowered on him and asked, 'Footballer?' It was the kind of question you thought to have left behind at last with school. 'No? You won't get on well here unless you're a footballer. I run the team.'

'. . . three years, I've waited three years to get in. And a good social side as well,' Billy said. 'A great bunch. And no four-by-twos, of course—that's guaranteed.'

Four-by-twos?

'The chosen people,' Billy said. 'No Yids.'

'They don't let Jews into Billy's golf club,' Jamesie explained.

He was outraged. Well, it was the Fifties, before Israel had won one war too many; anti-semitism was still out of fashion. Wet behind the ears, he had sat in the old Star cinema and wept inside at American newsfilm—the British, for some reason, refusing to release theirs to the public—of skeletal men in striped pyjamas and trenches piled with asexual nakedness.

'That's terrible,' he blurted, forgetting to be timorous. 'That's why we fought the war—I mean, that's wrong.'

'My best friend was *killed* in Palestine,' Billy snarled. 'By the Stern Gang.'

And Germans? The boy's father had been ruined by an anti-personnel mine, full of nails and shards of metal, left behind by the Master Race for him to step on come D-Day plus twelve. How did they feel about Japanese in Billy's golf club? But then, how many Japanese lived in Giffnock? (Thirty years later, it might have a colony of them, polite middle managers in glasses, with daughters at private schools, and nice wives who claimed to like the city and did their best to hide a certain culture shock at the dog shit on the pavements.)

His moment of courage over, he could not bring himself to say anything but smiled placatingly.

Jamesie, who had been turning his glance from one to the other, set down his glass and said, 'Will I tell you who the Holy Ghost was? A big Roman soldier out to get his nookey in Palestine. It's not generally known.'

Although he was a Catholic, Jamesie had no respect for anything.

The ring of a step on the iron stair galvanised the boy. In a moment, he had scrambled off the ledge and was sitting with his head bent at the work table. Reading swiftly, he discarded some of the newspaper clippings into the waste basket and set the others in order, mostly by date, occasionally by some juxtaposition that struck him as funny. That done, he began the task of pasting them into the big ledger, which was the latest in a series going back he had no idea for how many years; ledger upon ledger full of Burns Suppers reported from Scotland, England, the United States, Africa, Hong Kong; the Immortal Memory proposed by retired colonels, patronised by industrialists, deprecated by clergy; and every ten years or so some self-publicising clown from Nottingham or Chelmsford would turn up with a translation into Standard English so that the poems might be more widely read. When towards the end of that year (or at the beginning of the next?) he read MacDiarmid's 'A Drunk Man Looks at the Thistle', that tide of platitude and confused sentiment counterpointed the prophet's rage.

It would take about twenty minutes to get through what the boy could represent as an evening's work, and he was leaning back stretching the crick out of his neck when the buzzer shrilled again. This time the slip in the pocket of the wallet had been sent up to him in error. It was for a book from the Chief Librarian's corridor. Things had been so quiet on the third floor that he decided he would fetch it anyway. The iron stair wound down from floor to floor and turned the building into a lighthouse. As he descended, he passed tables like the one he had left, each one deserted under its single lamp, so that it felt as if he had all of behind the scenes entirely to himself.

In the first floor toilet, however, old Benny O'Connell rested his forehead against the tiles and groaned as he struggled to empty his bladder. Beside him the boy unbuttoned and at once the stream jetted from him poker straight and steaming where it splashed on the wall. It was a fine thing to be young.

'O-o-oh, dear God,' Benny complained softly. He was so old that he had joined the service at fifteen before you needed any certificates from school; and in all the years between he had never sat a library examination. He was a relic of the past, and they had given him the job of bundling and storing the readers' slips. He took the task very seriously and when detectives came in January, he was able to retrieve the slips of those who had taken too much interest too recently in the lay-out of Westminster Abbey. With Benny's help, the youngsters who had taken the Stone of Destiny from under the King's chair in London were caught. People said they were stupid to have filled in their names and addresses on those slips; but then they were students, and the library was a place in which students put an unthinking trust and affection.

And so old Benny, groaning and pulling hopelessly at himself, had helped to write another page of Scotland's history.

If it wasn't that evening, it must have been round about then. Certainly, it was when he had gone to fetch a book from one of the cases which lined the high-arched corridor that led to the Chief Librarian's office. There were round windows set at floor level and light came through them into the shadowy corridor from the Reading Hall below. It was with that light over his shoulder that he sat down cross-legged to glance at the book when he had found it. Which book was it? Hemingway, Henry Miller, Neil Munro, Bergson, Lawrence, Frank O'Connor, Gide, Thurber, Cocteau, Thomas Mann, the collection of prints in the locked cabinet showing men, women and dogs intertwined, J. G. Frazer and Agnes Mure Mackenzie—and Dashiell Hammett—and the books about relativity; and all of them for all of those three years that came pell mell, unplanned, not a course but a wandering.

It was like starting awake after being wrapped in sleep. The book was open in his hand and he had read more than half of it. More than an hour had passed! This time the boy knew he had gone too far; he would be thrown out, fired, dismissed. He scrambled round on to his knees and stared down into the Reading Hall. A small man in a long raincoat was waiting by the serving counter. Head bowed, there was something so submissive and uncomplaining in the little man's stance that it seemed he might wait for ever. Stamped in the memory, he remains as a furtive ikon, a seeker after proleptic punishment, and so perhaps the book the boy was holding had a nude illustration after all. Stimulation in the Fifties was hard to come by.

'I wondered where you were,' Jamesie said, mild and ironical, when he tumbled back on to the third floor, panting. 'I've served a couple of slips for you.'

He too had been reading, reclined against the wall by the square opening of the shaft. 'That's good stuff,' Jamesie said. 'By God! but we pull out the cultural stops.'

The boy stuffed the book he was carrying into the wallet and sent it down towards the patient little man. Catching his breath, he asked, 'What stops?'

'Joyce,' Jamesie said, tapping the book, 'and Yeats and O'Faolain and O'Flaherty and O'Casey and—'

Oh, Jesus, the boy thought, and he was born and bred in Glasgow

94

just like me and has the same broad Scots accent. Still, there was no way of telling where Jamesie went for his holidays.

But the buzzer rasped again and it was Jamesie who drew up the wallet and took out the slip. 'I'll fetch this one, while you get your breath back.' He grinned. 'You're not what I'd call a drinking man just yet.'

He liked Jamesie, and Billy, and little Tommy (who became a professor of English at Oxford), and Mr Barnett who told his aunt about the job in the first place, and even Billy Macdonald. They were all servants of the truth, for a library was the place in every city where the truth lived or hid and tried to survive.

Jamesie came back still carrying the slip. 'It's not there,' he said. 'I've written that it's missing.' And he handed over the slip and the boy glanced at it and put it in the right pocket and signalled.

Left alone, he knew that it couldn't be right. Working from memory, he made a mistake the first time, and even when he found the aisle started at the wrong side. It was a bottom shelf and he found the slip put in to mark the place where he had taken out the book requested earlier; the gap there was wider than he remembered and when he groped in behind the other books he felt it there, shoved away out of sight. It was a large grey book with vivid lettering sideways on the spine. Dropping his head to the side, he read the title.

Long before he had encountered Borges, the man at the desk in the quiet room had understood the great libraries, their shells and content, as being like a human skull and what it held. No university attended later could replace that image, left with him unexamined as the paradigm of what it was to be civilised, for he had made it part of himself as a boy wandering from the shadowed basement to the morning roof with its smoke-obscured vision of the distant hills. 'A Sanatorium for the Mind' was what those old Greeks had written at the entry to the Library of Alexandria before the birth of Christ; the man had seen that 'Spiritus Nutrimentum'—food for the soul— was inscribed above the portal of the Royal Library in Berlin. Yet in Alexandria, light of the ancient world, the last librarian was torn apart by a mob of religious fanatics howling for darkness; and about Berlin, divided monument to both megalomaniacs who had unleashed the dullard sadists on their betters, a smell of burning paper still hung on the air. Like a mind, Borges said, and if a mind then doubt and bigotry, lust and betrayal, had to walk its corridors and it would sometimes happen that they burned the place down.

The man closed the book he had borrowed (stolen) when he was a boy and set it back in its place. It could never belong to him, but he had kept it by him half a lifetime, which made it a familiar possession.

The people of the book were not worthy of it—but, after all, when had they ever been? They kept trying. Even now when it was so late, there was a little hope, while they did not tire of trying.

HUGH McBAIN

Supper on the Wall

❖❖❖❖❖

GEORGE was proud of his wallpaper. He regarded it as a work of art. Such regard, indeed, had a certain substance to it, for George had long been a regular member of the City Corporation evening class at the School of Art where he was looked upon as a promising student, despite the fact that in his sixtieth year he was by far the senior member of the class and could give even his instructor twenty years or so.

He had put up the wallpaper himself, with a fond care, to decorate the single room he rented from a city factor for £2 a week. The furniture of gas cooker, small table, two chairs, divan bed, clothes chest and carpet square, together with curtains, napery and cooking utensils, was all his own. As a widower for some fifteen years now, doing for himself when he came home in the evening from his clerical duties in the export company, he was proud of a place which showed no sign of intrusive female hand, a place which he had called his own from the time when he had given up the other house on his wife's death. An only son had not survived his tenth year, and George had lost touch with any other remaining relatives. With that urge to self-expression which possesses all of us in varying degrees, he had put his whole life into his wallpaper.

It was no ordinary wallpaper. None of your floral patterns, twittering birds, formal designs; nothing of your contemporary stuff with one wall red, another green, a third in pink stripes and the fourth virgin white. None of that. Not that at all. It was a very special kind of wallpaper.

On occasion, getting quietly drunk in The Vaults, the big pub at the Cross, George would confide to the nearest ear the superlative fact of his treasure at home, just, perhaps, as Michelangelo, in his cups, would have boasted about the Sistine Chapel to the boys in the pub in Rome—these precious walls, murals worked to his own conception, according to the artistic cunning of his own shaping hand, which no one but himself had ever seen.

The owners of the ears reacted variously. Some, his drinking cronies, nodded indulgently, some bought him a drink, some stared at him hard, some moved away quietly, some said that he was as nutty as a bloody fruit-cake. The regulars, in general, were kind, for they knew George to be an inoffensive creature, of whose background they were aware, who was a little bit not quite, but who was never quarrelsome, was good-hearted with his money when he had it, and who would last a fair time yet before the booze finally got him. He earned a fair wage as a long-service clerk, enough for his simple needs, enough to get him as drunk as a puggy several times a week, and that not always on the best stuff.

Friday and Saturday were his favourite evenings at The Vaults. It was on a Friday evening in the winter of his sixtieth year that George was to have the experience he had worked and waited for all his life.

It was strangely like any other Friday. He arrived home from work at 1800 hours, prepared himself a meal of sausage, ham and egg on his own gas cooker, washed up after the meal, and after a sprucing at the swan-neck tap, was ready to go off down to the Cross.

Before he went out, however, just as he put his hand on the door knob, he was suddenly seized by an odd sense of tension in the room. He had felt this dimly before, but it was so strong now that he almost staggered under the impact, stone cold sober as he was. And all at once, as he looked around the four walls, he knew. It had been a long time coming, but now he knew.

In The Vaults, as usual, he greeted the barmen cheerfully, was given his order without his having to ask, and joined his drinking cronies in their favourite corner. With a large whisky and a pint of heavy in front of him on the table, George smiled around the group of his two-three friends, who were already well supplied, raised his whisky glass in a toast and drank it straight off. Upending the glass, then, he trickled the last drop of whisky into the brimming pint, raised it to his lips and at a single draught reduced the level by a third. The boys in the corner then got down to the serious business of drinking, which they pursued for a space of two and a half hours, the talk ranging variously over the football matches to be played next day, that day's form at Kempton Park and Epsom, the very near miss in last Saturday's pools, the goddam carry-on of the wife and the snot-nosed kids, the bastard of a foreman, the sneaky wee rat of a chief clerk, the cotton runt of a supervisor, the cost of living at 16p a nip. There were jokes too, mostly of a bawdy nature, a great deal of belly laughter and rib-digging; but as closing time approached, the hour appointed by the city fathers when they thought the burgesses had had enough, the essentially sober business of drinking progressed to its graver aspects until it was time for the ritual which George's friends had learned to observe gathering on his portentous features.

Jake, the most indulgent of his cronies, was already smiling in anticipation as George leaned over to a total stranger who had taken a seat for a moment, and in a highly confidential manner said for the hundredth time, but yet with some difficulty, 'Y'oughta see my wallpaper.'

The stranger, still in possession of most of his faculties, looked suspiciously at George's grave countenance and at Jake's smile. 'What's that, Mac?' George looked around carefully before he spoke again to the stranger, 'Oughta see it. Psychological!'

With a slightly anxious glance, the stranger appealed to Jake who nodded knowingly and waited for George to continue.

'Did it mysel'. Whole bloody lot. Should see it.'

'How 'bout it, then, Geordie,' Jake's smile was broader. 'When we gon get a chance to see this marvellous goddam wallpaper o' yours?'

George put a finger in the corner of his eye, against his nose, and said mysteriously: 'T'morra, Jake. Not t'night. Somethin' special on t'night. I know. I know now.'

Jake's eyes widened. He'd been hearing about the wallpaper for as long as he could remember, but this was new. This was definitely new. 'What's on t'night, Geordie? What d'ye know?'

But with the finger still at his eye, George glanced secretively at Jake, smiled slowly, nodded his head, and said nothing. The bell for closing time was ringing and there was general hoarse demand for carry-outs. Like a host preparing for a party to which he knew the guest-list in detail, George ordered for carry-out a bag of little strong ales and a half-bottle of whisky, gave a cheery goodbye to his wondering friends, and set out from the Cross back to his single room on the ground floor of the tenement block.

Halfway there he turned in at the entrance to a fish-and-chip shop, took his place in the queue, and in a moment, without his having to ask, was being served. Chris the proprietor, who always served George not only as a customer but as a personal friend of long standing, wiped globules of sweat from his fleshy, slightly harassed face, as he set the fried haddock and chips down for a liberal sprinkling of salt, vinegar and sauce, for he had long known George liked the whole works with his fish supper.

'Big party, Georgie?' Chris glanced with some surprise at the bulging carrier bag in the crook of his customer and friend's arm.

'Somethin' special on t'night Chris. Put plenty on. Big night this. Gimme another dozen.'

With the sauce bottle poised in his hand, Chris stared at George. 'What! What did ye say?'

'For God's sake Chris,' George was a little annoyed, perhaps because of the drink, perhaps for another reason. 'Are ye corned beef? I said gimme another dozen.'

Chris blinked through the sweat trickling over his eyes. 'You trying to take the—'

'The fish suppers, for Chrisake. Are ye gon' gie me them or . . . ?'

Something in George's eyes arrested Chris from further question. In complete silence, then, while the queue grew impatiently larger, Chris prepared twelve more fish suppers, while George watched him with a curiously satisfied smile. When the suppers were bestowed in the carrier bag, George paid willingly and smiled as Chris continued to stare at him in obvious bewilderment.

'Special night, Chris. Big night. I know now.'

The fleshy face behind the counter puckered in rolls of beading fat.

'What . . . What d'ye know?'

The finger was at George's eye again and the slow smile was on his face as he nodded down at the carrier bag. 'The boys are coming up for the night. Must have something in for them.'

Chris stared at him. 'Boys! What b— What you givin's man? Heavy jag t'night, or what?'

'Oughta see it, Chris.'

'Uh . . . Oh, you mean——'

'Oughta see my wallpaper. Psychological.'

Quite bewildered by now, Chris had a strong, concerned desire to press George further, but the queue was growing much too impatient. 'Geordie, are ye feelin' okay? Are ye sure ye——'

'Ta, Chris. There's a big mob ahint me. Gie my best regards to Ella. Tell her . . .' George faltered, and then with an effort he smiled again, before he wheeled to walk out of the shop. A little alarmed, Chris watched him go, in half a mind to pursue him, but insistent voices were claiming him and he was forced to turn aside to meet the clamatory demands for fish suppers, single chips, single fish, and pudding suppers.

Clasping his heavy but precious burden to his breast, George continued along the road in a remarkably straight line, for, as everyone knew, he could hold his liquor with the best of them.

With steady step he came into the tenement entrance, with steady hand he found the yale key and let himself in to the tiny lobby giving on to the single room which remained, as he knew it would remain, exactly as he had left it. He put the carrier bag in the centre of the small table and with ordered method began to lay out the greasy newspaper packages and the strong ales, one of each together, along the edges of the table. When twelve places had been so set, he put the bag on the floor and laid in the centre of the twelve a thirteenth package along with the half-bottle of whisky and a bottle opener for the strong ales. The table was now completely full, and though there did not seem much room to accommodate the party of guests for whom George had prepared his table, this obviously did not concern him at all, for now he took off his shoes and put on his slippers, replaced his jacket with a cardigan, and sat down in his old easy chair to puff contentedly at a cigarette.

Easily, happily he puffed, glancing abstractedly at the glowing electric fire he had switched on, lost in some wholly compelling reflection. When the cigarette became a butt he stubbed it out, hunched deeper into the chair and crossed his legs indolently, but his attitude beneath the apparent ease, was one of waiting, of eager anticipation. The alarm clock on the mantelpiece ticked on evenly, but it, too, seemed somehow to be impatiently expectant.

All at once, then, George switched his glance upward to the wallpaper, his tired body came erect in the chair and his grizzled head began to revolve slowly from wall to wall.

The background of each side of the single apartment was a richly dark blue, like the colour of the sky when night retains the azure flush of a brilliant day. On one wall there was pasted in cut-out drawing paper the life-size figure of a woman swathed from head to foot in a wrap of royal blue, her head slightly inclined, with features of a certain, reserved beauty; around her feet gambolled a fleecy lamb, while directly above her there was the disembodied head of a very old man with piercing eyes and a long flowing beard, set at the centre of a cumulus cloud formation. The whole wall was crowned by three large capital letters in gilt paper—KBS.

The other three walls formed the background for a group of men seated on stools at a long refectory table, the two side walls carrying four men apiece, the centre one, at which George was now steadfastly gazing, containing five figures, the middle one of whom was dressed in a white robe, distinctive among the other dark habits, his head also halo'd in cumulus, his arms extended in some all-embracing gesture. Looking fixedly at the man in the centre, George now began to speak, as if resuming an interrupted conversation.

'. . . so I thought ye might like a bit bite and a snifter afore . . . One and nine for the suppers and one and five each for the wee heavies, that's wi' tuppence on the bottles, ye ken. Hech, bet you never had to pay tuppence for your bottles. Ye've no idea what that Chancellor bloke gets up to.'

The sadly beautiful features of the figure at the centre of the table on the wall suddenly breathed into life. 'Fine I ken Geordie. Fine I ken what that mannie's after. But as I keep tellan the boys here, gie Caesar what's his ain and gie my faither what belongs to him.'

'Aye aye,' cried George. 'That's it Jee, boy. That's it. The Caesar bloke gets far too much out o' us. Fags, beer, the cratur, purchase tax, income tax, pension tax—ach, ye're just workin' for peanuts. What would ye do wi' that bloodsucker?'

The sad man on the wall looked down compassionately on the appealing grey face.

'You'll mind, Geordie, how I had to put up wi' them Pharisees and publicans. Took their taxes, their rent, profit and interest, right intil my faither's house. Imagine! But ye ken weel enough, I gied them the whup, Geordie, I gied them the whup.'

George was nodding triumphantly. 'Fine I ken ye did, Jeez, fine I ken. I on'y wish ye'd gie me a lend o' it to go down to Lunnon and gie that publican o' ours a good workin' owr.'

'Mebbe I'll do just that, Geordie. I maun be about my faither's business. Right, faither?'

The speaker appealed straight across the room to the disembodied, cloud-blown head, which inclined gravely.

'Fine ye ken, son. You do weel for yirsel and you'll do weel for me.'

George had turned round in deference to the flowing beard, and now nodded his own head in keen approval.

'How's things, faither?'

'Canna complain.'

George suddenly remembered something, and his face was lined with concern. 'Ye'll no mind, will ye, faither. I brought hame a bit supper for Jeez and the boys, but I forgot—'

'That's aa right, Geordie,' said the head in a kindly tone. 'Just you go ahead. I have enough o' my ain. Just you see Jeez and the boys aa right.'

'I maun say, Geordie, it's real decent o' ye to think o' us,' continued the man in the white robe, turning now to the others at the table. 'Is it no', boys!'

There was a chorus of assent from the assembled diners, all of whom, excepting one with a darkly troubled face, seemed to be enjoying themselves. The president of the table again looked across the room.

'How about yirsel, mither?'

The woman with the features of reserved beauty smiled delicately. 'Na, no for me, son. Ye ken I'm no a big eater. Like faither here says, just you go ahead wi' Geordie. I'm quite happy to listen.'

The fleecy lamb at her feet bleated happily, and now all the eyes on the wall were fixed on George, as if waiting for him to continue the conversation. George smiled at them all expansively.

'I was hearan that . . . that ye were thinkan o' coman down to see us again. Is there any . . . I mean . . . ?'

'I dinna rightly ken, Geordie,' said the president, with a troubled countenance. 'What wi' yir bombs and yir inhumanity o' man to man.' The speaker glanced for an uncertain moment at the cloud-blown head across the room. 'I sometimes wonder if it was aa worthwhile, the whole . . .'

'Na na, ye maunna speak like that,' George broke in with an excited urgency.

'We aa want ye to come again and wash away the sin o' man wi' yir bluid. We . . . I've been waitan a long time mysel, ever syn the day, ye'll mind o' it, when I took ye to be my very ain per'nal Saviour. I want ye to come down and get rid o' aa they bombs, aa this bitterness in the herts o' men. Will ye no, Jeez? Better lo'ed ye canna be. Will ye no come back again?'

The president's face was shadowed in an infinite sadness as he looked down at the old grey man. 'I will be coman down, Geordie, I will. Mebbe no in the way ye——'

'Man, but that's great, that's just the doddles,' George broke in excitedly. 'We're aa right pleased to hear that. Now mebbe we'll get somewhere on this forfochen bit o' ground they caa the earth. But tell me Jeez, how's Jeannie?'

The white-robed man nodded faintly. 'Fine. Just fine.'

'And wee Geordie?'

'He's fine as weel.'

'Jeez that's great. Aa body thegither again. Just like . . . Eh, look, a brought ye a wee snifter,' George held up the half-bottle of whisky.

'If ye think, mebbe, just the now for a minute ye could come down and I'll gie ye . . . the best stuff, set me back mair nor a quid. Are ye for a bit drappie?'

The president did not reply. He simply gazed down at the host for several long moments that might have been a silent eternity. Slowly then, the sad eyes travelled along the faces at the table, resting for a longer moment on the dark, troubled one; then they gazed across the room at the withdrawn, beautiful woman, and at the cloudblown, bodiless head. It seemed presently that the eyes had found some answer to a deeply pondered question, for now they were fixed resolutely on the man below—softly, with infinite compassion came the voice.

'Ye know now, Geordie, don't ye?'

George's eyes were shining, his whole face was transfigured as he stood up with the whisky bottle held at arm's length.

'I know, Jeez. I know.'

The white-robed man rose from his seat at the long table. 'I'm coman down, Geordie.'

Even as he spoke, without any physical effort at all, he was gliding from his place on the wall, outwards and downwards, to stand a few feet from the tenant of the single apartment. With one hand, then, he took a chip and a piece of fish from the supper lying in the centre of the tiny table, put them in his mouth and chewed slowly; with the other, he took the bottle, from which the cork had already been removed, and took a long draught of the best Vaults whisky. Wiping his mouth, then, he replaced the bottle on the table and stood silently gazing deep into George's sparkling eyes. The room was filled with an unearthly silence as he reached out and took George's hand.

The ground floor neighbours suspected nothing for a whole week for George was a man who kept himself to himself. Only then did they become curious and try to find out where George had got to. Only then did they finally summon the police. They found George sitting upright in his good easy chair. They stared at the fish suppers, the strong ales, and the half-empty whisky bottle. And then they saw the wallpaper.

CARL MacDOUGALL

A Small Hotel

❖❖❖❖❖

I CAN attribute my pessimism to the fact that I spent my formative years in Glasgow where youthful success often leaves middle-aged casualties working as waitresses or night porters in the small, unlit hotels off Bath Street. It has become difficult to ask, 'Haven't I seen you somewhere before?', especially if you are liable to find the barmaid played Hedda Gabler in her final year at drama college, that the window cleaner danced on Broadway or the hopeless drunk in the corner taught classics at Oxford. I believed the most obvious axiom occurred when Falstaff offered all his fame for a pot of ale, yet in a small, unknown hotel I found I had been mistaken.

I'd lost my way and didn't know where I was going. Driving through the night, I needed rest and though I wondered where I was, I seldom slowed down to find out.

I don't know why I drove up the avenue. I'd passed dozens of hotel signs, so why I picked that one is something of a mystery. If I was a Buddhist I'd believe the hotel picked me. I am not even sure there was a sign at the foot of the driveway, but I suppose there must have been something.

The building wasn't special, hundreds like it are scattered across the country, houses that used to be a place out of town for a Dundee jute baron, an Edinburgh banker, an Aberdeen fish merchant or a Glasgow bailie—a two-storeyed sandstone square with a turret on each corner, steps to the front door, which was made of oak and a carved lintel, all closely modelled on Balmoral.

I remember a drystane dyke, then a cluster of trees and bushes. The drive swept upwards from the roadside with a grass ridge in the middle marking the way. There was a verge where I imagined daffodils and bluebells in the spring and beyond the ridge rhododendrons, laurel and gorse.

The drive spread into an open, tarmaced area with a crowded car park by the side of the house. The smell of flowers lifted the cold, wet evening air and above the door a small yellow, red and blue sign exploded the word HOTEL into the darkness. By the neon moonlight I could see we were on a raised piece of land, surrounded by good, tall trees.

I asked where I could get a cup of tea and was told to go upstairs. I thought I recognised the woman I'd spoken to in the hallway and as I climbed the stairs there were other people who looked familiar. Then I realised I had imagined them to be victims of some kind of misfortune, having based their proneness to fail on my pessimism. As I sat in the lounge I became aware that most of my youthful heroes were walking past me; the greatest sportsmen and women, the finest writers and actors, the politicians, musicians and sexual escapologists of a generation ago were all here, perhaps a little fatter, but certainly more contented and less troubled than I remembered them.

I met wee Bobby Simpson, the winger responsible for more artistry than any player I ever saw. Fellow Scots hacked him, but he survived to make them look lumpish. He was a product of the back streets and never lost that appearance, small and muscular; he looked as if he had biceps in his head. Fielding him was a moral victory against a foreign opposition, who had never seen anything like him. Managers and players would stare, some of them even laughed as he hunched his shoulders and tucked his hands into the sleeves of his strip as though to protect himself from the cold. They praised him across Europe and revered him in Lisbon and Moscow, Sofia and Milan. In Buenos Aires they sang his name on the streets and he was an honorary Brazilian citizen. He was ignored in England where journalists favoured a drunken Irishman whose lifestyle was more in keeping with the times.

Betty Riley was there, she who used to sing in Glasgow ballrooms. Dancers followed her from hall to hall. When lights were low and mirrors glittered, when the band played softly as the darkness lifted and she Dah-rah-dah-dahed her first few phrases you knew your search was over. She sings occasionally, at socials on a Saturday night, a little huskier, but her voice is full of memories.

Bookies and trainers, jockeys and punters crowd the place, drinking fruit juice in the bars and eating oysters in the restaurants. I was never a gambling man, but I had heard of Swifty Thomson, ghost who walks, the man the bookies feared, who cleaned up continually till they caught him basking in the Bahamas beside a bank of teleprinters, evidence of ante-post betting and various forms of financial jiggery-pokery. He was extradited to Glasgow. His trial was a cause célèbre in the city, largely because of Swifty's wonderfully dry, pungent humour and the glamour of his witnesses. Film stars, millionaires and socialites, the prominent names of a generation were called to Swifty's trial. His mistress turned out to be the current sex symbol. All the lonely men and a few women loved her, dreamed and desired her, only to learn she was Swifty Thomson's mistress and about to renounce her career to devote herself to him. 'Not bad for a boy from the Cowcaddens,' said Swifty. And that was his downfall. The judge admired his entrepreneurism, his individuality, business flair and acumen. He did not admire his cheek. Swifty's sentence was reduced on appeal, but he came out to find his fortune gone. He sold his story to the papers, which just about paid his divorce costs. I last heard his name when he was done for resetting two hundred yards of Royal Stewart tartan material. When asked to plead, he told the judge, 'Not kilty, your honour.'

He's well. And she's there too, still wonderful; when she turns her head and shakes her curls, you can see a trace of youth and the stare that once was Melissa Morgan. Swifty spends a lot of time talking to journalists, who seem to enjoy his company, and she joins them in the evening.

I spent a fair amount of time swopping stories with Sandy Allison, a legend from the time when newspapers all had Glasgow offices and there was competition for who got which story, when a murderer's nearest and dearest would sell to the highest bidder or if found Not Guilty or Not Proven could have their story written by journalists who used headlines such as My Agony is Over! and ended their piece with something like, 'Now all I want to do is forget about the nightmare I've been through and start living a normal life again.'

Sandy Allison was a maverick in a profession which prides itself on individuality and a legend in a profession devoted to building legends. He would have been notable no matter what he did. He had style, flair and could produce copy as fast as you could type. Copy takers hated to hear his whisky-stained voice tell them, 'I'm working from notes, so bear with me.' He never learned to type and didn't know shorthand.

As we sat drinking tea, he was resting after lunch, I asked if the story of how he got Albert Smith's confession was true. Smith typified the sexual and social predilections of the time. He had demanded absolute devotion from his eight mistresses and when he didn't get it he murdered them. The fact that he encouraged them to be unfaithful was a clinching factor in denying his request to be considered insane.

Smith was arrested in a small village outside Glasgow which Allison knew had a police station with only one cell. While other reporters were bribing policemen, annoying neighbours and associates, and even trying the local minister rather than prepare themselves for a long and fruitless stake out, Allison threw a brick through the post office window and waited to be arrested. He spent the night with Smith, who gave him exclusive rights to his story, much of which was sub judice, unprintable and generally not very nice. When Sandy Allison became a blethering drunk that escapade and others like it stood by him, even though he was retired early and rather ignominiously. He still smokes too much. His hair is grey and he's grown a moustache. He is working on his memoirs and is a great raconteur. He spends his time with a contemporary from the world of sport, Jumping Joey Joy, the jockey they said had more winners than dinners. He's still got his gold tooth and parts his hair in much the same way as Sammy Sullivan.

That's right: Sammy Sullivan, champion of the world, a man with nothing in the way of sophistication, other than as a fighter. When he was feted and adored, desired and worshipped, he submitted. When the man who was raised on fish suppers was dining at the Ritz, sleeping at the Dorchester and shopping on Bond Street, he didn't train and twice had to spend hours before a weigh-in skipping in a boiler room to make the weight. His wins were glorious. It was an American writer who coined Sammy's favourite phrase, that he punctured himself with women and drink. He tried to get his titles back and was beaten ignominiously; he who had seemed invincible crumbled, his right cross and left hook inactive because the younger man made him work, made him chase and get frustrated. Sammy Sullivan ended where he'd begun, taking on all comers in the booths, fighting for a bottle of cheap wine. He talks lightly of those days and is very popular. Everyone wants to know him because he seems to have stretched himself to the absolute limit, sunk lower and risen again. The assumption is that he's learned something he's willing to pass on and in his case the assumption is correct.

Several of yesterday's novelists, playwrights and poets like to be seen with him. Jackson Melville is different. He always was, it's true, but it's reassuring to know he's pretty much the same as ever. The first poetry reading I attended, or even wanted to attend, was him and his slim volume. He was incoherent, slobbering and stammering.

That seemed the start of it all and for years we expected he would blow his brains out. He seems fine. He's jolly, still with the same boyish energy, bald now and clean shaven.

Of the theatre crowd I will mention Maisie Miller, one of the many who went to America and disappeared. She cropped up on television from time to time and the papers annually ran a feature about her. Then nothing. She tells me she's resting at present. She hangs around with Luigi Cilento, who was sent to London to prepare dessert for the Royal Wedding and finished drinking himself out of fish supper shops.

It won't surprise you to learn that all the great chefs, restaurateurs and barmen are here. Every Saturday night they and the musicians prepare suppers with a musical accompaniment—chili con carne with the Dixieland jazz band, a Schubert quartet followed by prawn vinaigrette, a renaissance wind band whose concert was followed by petit fours, sugar sticks, meringues and doughnuts. Everyone enjoyed that night. You wouldn't believe how many were there and you wouldn't believe how many lost faces had been rescued, those you imagined as publicans, shop keepers or baptist ministers, those you imagined were pursuing their vanished splendour crucified on drink and drugs were living it up in this comfortable hotel.

Some of the great prostitutes are here, stouter and gaudier than ever before, but still regal, private people. I saw Olga Williamson, the mulato soubrette who broke her ankle and became the most famous prostitute of her time. She was holding the hand of R. Smillie Saunders, who used to be major domo at the Scottish Office and secretary to the Secretary himself. He looked happy and seemed to be enjoying the music.

My stay was so short, yet so memorable. I couldn't tell you all the wonderful people I met, the boyhood dreams and fantasies I fulfilled. I keep thinking about this place for heroes. It pleased me to know the world takes care of them and if you suffer from a congenital sadness, I thought it might please you too.

FARQUHAR McLAY

Headlines for Whitey

❖❖❖❖❖

THE albino boy with the aerosol worked away quietly unknown to all the world save one. The same meticulous regard in the shaping of each letter and the spacing of each line. Nothing slipshod permitted. The gable-end of the spinsters' flats will have less scrupulous beautifiers. The paint-spray chronicle ran thus:

uzz toon
rule toon
rule the universe

joe-n
mak
westy
goucho
rule

brighton pony
mugs

tiny
spike
dan
derry
mugs

baltic torch
mugs

sunny
tam
gus
sinky
mugs

HEADLINES FOR WHITEY

cumbie
mugs

scrapper
pie
monk
swiftie
mugs

nunny
mugs

young young nunny
rides
for
grunchie
jake
donaboots

fleet mugs

young young fleet
wanks
for
alky
doc
mushy

uzz toon tongs
real
OK
mental
OK

joe-n
mak
westy
goucho
kill

toon tongs ya bas
kill

OK little gents

Abe turned the focusing wheel till he got the correct readjustment. The boy stood on an upturned ash can. Abe knew Whitey. Habitué of Fun Land and lure for pederasts. A bad article. Carried two golf balls in a woollen sock. Burgled the spinsters' flats. Tied up old May Crawford and peed on her. Half-blind little scrunt. Night-hawk. Had his eye on Abe's flat. That time Abe going down to empty the bin caught him prowling about in the back. Sussing the place out. Looking where the roan pipe ran: next to whose window. After that night Abe always left his window open. Abe hoped he would chance it. Jesus, a one-legged man. You could handle a one-legged man, Whitey. Abe waited patiently each night. That guff on the walls didn't scare Abe. Kids' phantasies. Even if he had a gang he was at liberty to bring them. Goucho sounded a bit ferocious but who could he be? No matter. All the others Abe could identify. They could all come. In for a rude awakening in tackling Abe. Bring your chibs: Abe needs no chib. At karate since he was eight years old. Has all the belts with the single exception of the black. Would have won the black but for the leg crush in McNiel's forge. OLYMPIC HOPE LOSES LEG. Let them rush in screeching with their claw hammers and meat cleavers. It wouldn't work with Abe. Abe would just shriek back at them, only louder. He had been famous for that, the way he used to shriek at opponents. Then a kick with the old gammy and a couple of chops. He would scatter the tongs all right, no danger. Has every colour of belt save only black. ABE IS SO SAD. Could have gone right to the top. He was a natural was Abe. Even the Japs had to admit it after he knocked out their champion. Turned down an all-expenses-paid trip to Tokyo for special coaching. Japs know a fighter when they see him. JAP PROMOTERS WOO ABE. Then there was his reputation as a citizen. KARATE STAR FOILS RAIDERS. The Shakespeare Street payroll snatch. 'This brave man . . . grappled with and over-powered two masked and armed men . . . as a security guard lay dying . . . and terrified passersby cowered in doorways . . .' Watson and White, ex-pugs, two of the hardest men up the Gaspipe Road. White had an air-gun and Watson a bayonet. Detective Chief Inspector Finlay MacLaren, head of Maryhill CID, said 'Abe was magnificent. I will be recommending that he be honoured for his outstanding bravery.' HAVE-A-GO-ABE GETS GALLANTRY MEDAL. The Chief Constable's Commendation for Brave Conduct is framed and hangs on the wall above Abe's bed. 'This brave man . . .' Abe would like to show Whitey that Commendation. Poor disadvantaged boy. They could sit together on the bed and study the lettering: a work of art. The sort of thing Whitey would appreciate. Sit close together and be friends.

Whitey moved out of view, the graffiti message completed to his satisfaction. An able propagandist, you had to admit. Sexual vituperation of rival gangs his speciality. Whitey knew all about sexual kinks. A war-time must in any chronicler. Two golf balls in a sock inside his shirt. When they least suspect it he lets fly. The dull thuds. Likes making dents in bald shiny skulls. Takes their jackets and trousers away with him, plus any jewellery and cash. Will provide you with a gold watch or signet ring at low cost any time: just give him an hour's notice. Never short of dough. Playing with spray-paint his only relaxation.

Abe let the binoculars drop on to his amplitude of waistline and hang there. He shook out and straightened the *Daily Record* yet again. MINI THUG ROBS GRAN (80). It had to be Whitey. What that boy needed. First: the boot with the gammy in the crotch. That would sicken him right. Then a punch in the throat. No coming back after that. And then. And then?

Abe was thinking how he would go about reassuring Whitey afterwards. A man with Abe's reputation. Scourge of the hard men. A man Whitey would respect. All a matter of names. Abe knew all the names, all the hard men, past and present. He had fought with them and drunk with them. Kemp, Russo, Scout O'Niel, Algie, Sankey, Maxie Klar, Fitch & Bros, Kilna, Tamburini, Ollie Gluck, Peter Manual, Swiftie McCool, Cowboy O'Hara, Cyril Crow. All names to conjure with. And plenty more if needed.

Then Abe could bring out his 32×50 Mark Scheffel Prismatics, the model de-luxe with lanyard and straps. Point out to the boy the 70 mm objectives for increased effectiveness after dark. Ask him if he would like to know who burgled May Crawford and peed on her. Abe was an eye-witness. Or who smashed 244 panes of glass, shattered four giant skylight windows, set ablaze 400 text books and wrecked a grand piano in St Xavier's primary school only two weeks ago. Someone was watching. Whitey would be won round all right. A boy like that would soon cotton to where his best interests lay. First Abe would relieve him of the cosh. Very important that. Feel in his shirt till you come on it and pull it out. Abe knows it all. Abe's no mug. Hold on to it for safe keeping.

Examine it under the lamp with the door locked. Traces of human blood, particles of bone. Get his confidence. Let him feel the power of the gammy. That quietens them.

Abe rolled himself a fag out of his Old Holborn tin. He rolled a Barlinnie special, thin as a matchstick, the way he liked them. Nothing moving in the spinsters' flats? A last quick look.

Abe eased himself gently on to the bed. He loosened down his trousers and the waistband button went away with the buttonhole. Abe would sew it back on, but further out this time. Needed more room for the pot. It was Guinness and meat pies doing that to him, down in the Burnt Barns at the dominoes. Whitey's old man is there a lot. At the ponce most of the time. A big man, stooped, alcoholic most likely.

Have to get needle and thread next. Abe liked sewing. Put him in mind of the days, in Barlinnie. Abe the hooligan in 14 Party. That was the mail bag section. Before Abe lost his leg and saw the light. That's where the learnt to roll fags nice and thin. Rubbed shoulders with some big names: Jack Toe Riley, Louis Dugella, Harry Crown, Colley Mair. A fine bunch of lads. Friends still. Come in Burnt Burns from time to time. Kip on the Talbot Centre. That's them down for keeps, on the bel-air, done right this time.

Talk about the Beehive and Whitey will listen. It's the lore of gangs that grips them. It's all posturing these days, just words stuck up on a wall, but it was real once. No gangs any more. A lonely boy with an aerosol. Talk about the gangs and Whitey will listen. It's what he craves in his black little heart. Talk about Beehive, the defenestration squad. A hard team that. Lineal descendant of Johnny Stark's gang that hung about Wellington Street. Tim Rilly the leader-off in Abe's time. That was in Abe's svelte youth, before he donned the mantle of active citizenship. Ran with a bad crowd, he did. Aldo the baker's boy that had the plookie face was second-in-command. Too much cream of tartar brought his face out. Turdie McCarron was another. Turdie attended Black Street to get the umbrella needle for VD: the barbed needle to scour out the rot. A bad reputation Black Street had. Tim said poor Turdie had nothing left but a vein with hair on it. Could be quite witty when he wasn't propelling people out of high windows. The Beehive in Abe's day always eschewed the stand-up fight. They waited till they got you at a party, plied you with wine till you couldn't stand up, then bundled you out of the window on the quiet. A lot of people took flying headers in the old Gorbals. Come and have a dekko at the moon and the stars. Old Walaski the cobbler paid Tim protection. Eduardo Fabrizzi in the chippie paid up as well.

Abe could talk about even further back: the first Beehive. No need for writing on walls in them days. The street battles said it all.

Marauding mobs two-thousand-handit. They had Ghurka knives, bayonets, swordfish spears, spiked cudgels, hatchets, grapnels, bicycle chains, studded belts, machetes, fireside pokers and the ever-popular open razor. Corporation dust-carts took a whole day clearing up after a battle. Lots of fingers and ears, bits of noses and scalp, for the pickers to drool at. Staff reporters always on the spot. Lauder & Lorne, the Exact Details. BATON CHARGE QUELLS RIOT. The constabulary charged valiantly to disperse the trouble-makers. An heroic tale. MR SILLITOE NOW SAYS IT: THEY'RE HEROES ALL. No finer body of men. Fondly remembered is Percy. He was raised to the Order of the Royal Garter. Dang the stoor out of the Reds and hammered the apaches into fealty. A LEGEND WALKS OUR STREETS. The rope, the cat, the birch and Percy: all sadly missed. GOD BLESS SIR PERCY. A resonant echo alow and aloft. Gone but not forgotten. Percy the gang-buster, RIP.

Abe scratched a stubbly chin. Should have kept the birch at least. Make Whitey sit up and take notice. Sergeant-at-arms used to lay it on. Then they'd take you away and put stitches in your arse. That was the day shit flew. Whitey's tender loins. In Macarmon's court six strokes. Used to throw fits on the bench. All flushed and frothing at the mouth. 'Make the beggar bleed!' he would yell. One of the old school, always roaring, wig half-down his face. In a glass case in the People's Palace now, that birch. Donated by the PF. Now Brother Bartholomew never shouted at you in the borstal. Twenty with the heavy-duty tawse after a short sermon: his favourite prescription. The sullen and lymphatic sharpened up. Abe the shining example.

Abe ran his fingers over the carrying case on the bed beside him. Genuine chestnut pigskin. Lovely to the touch. He would talk about precision optics to the albino. This superb instrument. Maybe not a Mark Scheffel but astonishingly adaptable. The magnification is infinitely adjustable: $7\times$ to $15\times$. Infinitely variable fields of view. Affords you 102 metres width at 100 metres with $7\times$ magnification. Cracked the Sex Fiend case of 1964 with these. Dig out the headlines for Whitey. Park gates had to stay closed and all public toilets were shut down. THE SQUARE MILE OF FEAR. It lasted a year before Abe finally spied out the fiend. A pitiful figure by the pole in Seaward Street. You wanted to go to his aid, you wanted to offer him money. The face a mask of anguish with the eyes shut tight. Had kidded millions but not Abe. Standing there, bent almost double, clutching at himself. Abe saw through him at once. The day the squad led by Sergeant Leonard went to get him he made a bolt for it. He disappeared into a back close, hurled himself down railway embankments, went splashing across canals, leapt spiky railings, climbed drain pipes, scampered along narrow ledges and was finally apprehended on the roof of Templeton's carpet factory. In the back of the Land-Rover they forced the fiend to open his eyes. 'There! Do you see?' Abe cried triumphantly. With the eyes open, spread over that face was a grin, a huge lascivious grin. 'This is indeed the fiend,' Sergeant Leonard said at last and he shook Abe's hand. A TOWN SAYS THANK YOU, ABE. It was a besmirching sort of grin which made the squad very angry. The contents of the fiend's pockets were as follows:

Cash: nil.

Yellow Card: Department of Employment and Productivity. Day: Fri. Time: 4.20. Signing box number 7. Disabled section.

Packet of 10 Woodbine, seal intact.

Intimation from the Social Security: An officer will be calling.

A Notes for the Guidance of Accused Persons poster eased off a cell door in Tobago Street police station.

A public library ticket expired ten years.

In pouch of above ticket a clipping from the warrant sales column of the Evening Times: Christie, 2 Moir Street, Calton, at 10 a.m. Thursday 14 October, furniture and household effects.

Crumbling and faded Sheriff Court citation dated 1952. Lewd and libidinous.

Two pawn tickets. One for a wristwatch, the other for pair of flannel trousers, each pledged for £1.50 two years ago, never redeemed.

Postal Order counterfoil. £4 payable to the Clerk of Court, Brunswick Street.

An official poll card for last parliamentary election but one.

A white shirt. It was stuffed into his pocket by one of the minor philanthropists of this town as he stood by the pole one day in 1959.

Packet of Victory-V lozenges (for when you wish it was warmer), three remaining.

Book of postage stamps, none remaining.

In the back of the Land-Rover the fiend crouched on the floor with his back to them. Sergeant Leonard reached under the seat and pulled out a banjo.

'You into Folk, Abe?' Sergeant Leonard asked. Abe admitted he was. 'Well,' Sergeant Leonard said, 'I'm going to write a song about how you helped us capture the fiend. I'm going to make you famous.'

And that was how their friendship began. A TOWN SAYS THANK YOU, ABE. Whitey ought to know about a thing like that, having Sergeant Leonard for a friend.

Abe went back to the window. Whitey was back in view again and this time his pals were with him. It seemed to Abe they were looking straight up at him and even pointing. He would dig out all the headlines for Whitey.

That night Abe put out his light and raised the window earlier than he'd ever done before.

J. FULLERTON MILLER

A Lover of Nature

❖❖❖❖❖

THE urgent cooing of the pigeons bubbled through the long gloom of the loft which ran the length of the great mass of sandstone known as Riverbank Buildings. The evening meal was over in the house immediately below. The birds seemed to know this, for they fluttered against the walls of their pens and pecked woodenly at their feeding boxes.

Toggy McIvor glanced anxiously at the ceiling as his wife continued to natter. Jess was a massive woman with the brows of an Airedale. Her red-brown hair had the coarseness of oakum. By feminine standards she was no beauty, but there was a curious fascination in her ugliness. As a man, Jess would have been a bruiser, but nature botched the sex of the job and made her pugnacity in a jumper.

'. . . and to crown it all you're going out after rabbits the night again. If it's no fish, it's rabbits, if it's no rabbits, it's pigeons.' She thrust her head across the table and glared into Toggy's small brown face. 'You just sit and think and look up at the ceiling as if you can see them damned birds.'

Toggy continued to look overhead. The birds must be starving. He'd have to go up.

Toggy crossed the kitchen and opened the door of a large cupboard set into the wall. It contained nothing but a vertical ladder fixed where the shelves should have been. Toggy grasped the siderails and climbed up through a small hatchway cut in the plasterboard ceiling. He reached for a switch and flooded the corner of the loft with light.

The attic was floored with plyboard set across the beams. The pigeons were penned in adapted egg crates. The dovecot proper was cunningly built into the back of a large ventilator which stood out like a small penthouse from the sloping roof. The rest of the loft, which was common to the whole of the buildings, ran from the perimeter of the lights into a sooty infinity. Toggy's end had brightness and life; it showed the hand and heart of a man.

Toggy dragged a sack of maize from a corner. He stopped at the mouth of the hatch as his wife's voice welled up. '. . . docker, you're supposed to be a docker, but you're a poacher, that's what you are. Imagine telling anybody you're married to a poacher in the heart of Glasgow—they'd think you were cakey!'

Toggy looked down to her upturned face. It looked a flat brown thing at the bottom of the cupboard. If he dropped the sack it might crush it to pulp like a beetle mashed with a stone.

The pigeons fluttered to him when the pens were opened. There was an elemental quality about Toggy as he knelt among the birds. His back was slightly buckled through years of constant stooping at the docks and in the fields. He wore a rough drill shirt with trousers and belt. He seemed to have none of the appendages of the over-civilised, like spectacles, watch, braces, handkerchief. His hair required no combing, being cropped close to his scalp like a pad of steel wool.

When the pigeons were fed, Toggy went to the dovecot and opened the landing board, a device which lowered outwards like a small drawbridge. He leaned on his forearms and gazed out over the city. Glasgow was pink in the evening sun; a hotch potch of steel and stone strewn about a river. Toggy inhaled deeply and put Jess out of his mind.

Toggy kept close watch on a black and white dovecot in the yard of Bell's stable a block away to his left. Presently, two black specks rose and soared in the sky. Toggy followed them with his eyes and smiled. Two cocks by the look of them. Well, they'd soon be on his landing board.

Toggy lifted two of his hen birds. 'Goan, lassies, fetch them two fellas to your faither.'

The birds met in the air and paired. They flew in courting flights of up and down swinging curves. Toggy's eyes gleamed, the glory of the flying took his own soul in flight far from the cares of domestic life.

Jess sat below, cigarette in hand, legs splayed before the fire, her tiny mind lost in the vast vice of *Amazing Confessions*. She sat in a kitchen furnished with evidence of her own incompetence. An expensive dining-room table was ringed with heatmarks. A display cabinet, which must have cost two weeks of Toggy's pay, contained such artistic objects as the Whistling Boy in stucco, a Redskin chief with garish feathers and a chipped nose, a set of tumblers jammed irremovably one inside the other, and a cottage teapot firecracked at the base.

Jess read with her mouth open until Toggy descended from the loft. 'Maybe you'll do the dishes before you go out big game hunting,' she said.

Toggy lit the gas below the kettle. Anything for peace, and besides it was better than getting cups with the tidemarks of a previous meal on them.

An hour later Toggy put on his jacket and lifted a set of wire snares and a sandwich of bread and cheese. 'Oh Jess, if big Bell comes up for his two birds, tell him he can have them at the market price—nine bob each. You can keep the money—help with the housekeeping.'

Jess brightened at this. 'That'll be eighteen bob; but how am I to get up there?'

'Och, let Bell go up; he'll know his own birds best.'

After he'd gone Jess stared at the door for a while. Right enough, he was good with the money whenever he made a capture. Funny, he never bothered much about the cash; it was the catching, the sport he liked. He was good to her in some ways, but he wasn't a man, a real man—he was a wee animal. He was a man once, though, when they got married. It was good at first, the way he kidded and joked about their private life as if talking about birds or beasts. 'Is this you spreading your wings, Jess?' It was funny until she knew she couldn't have any children: then it was horrible, especially that favourite one of his, 'It's time we were nestin'.'

Jess returned to her book. On the glossy cover a woman lay relaxed in the arms of her lover while the giant shadow of her husband reached for them from the background. The title was, 'I Sought Glamour.' That's what Toggy never had—glamour. He didn't know how to treat a woman; that's what her life badly needed, glamour.

It came in the form of big Bell—though not at first apparent, for he was in a foul mood. 'Has that damned eagle you're mairried tae, got my two birds?'

'Oh, it's you, Joe, Come in.'

Joe Bell had a face too smooth for a man of forty. It was a pink thing without bone lines and was topped with flat black hair. To denote his bachelor status he was dressed youthfully in a drape-cut suit and long-peaked shirt. His eyes span round the room. 'Is he no in?'

'No, he's away after rabbits. You've to take your birds yourself, and the price is eighteen bob.'

'Away after rabbits, is he? Does he never sleep?'

'Och, he lies down in barns and piggeries before he comes back. Says he can get his head down anywhere because he knows every byreman in the West of Scotland.'

'Don't know how he does it. And he turns up at the docks every morning fresher than any of us. There's something queer about Toggy.'

Jess looked at him meaningly. 'You're telling me,' she said.

Bell collected his two birds and returned to the kitchen. 'Well, I suppose I'll have to pay up.' When Jess gave him two shillings change, he said, 'I think I'll gie up the pigeons, Jess; I was only keeping them going in memory of my auld faither, him being so keen on them.'

Jess looked at him disbelievingly. Joe and his women troubles had heart-roasted his auld faither to the grave.

'Aw, I admit the auld man and me had many a fa' oot, but you know how it is—yer faither's yer faither.'

'True enough,' agreed Jess.

'Well, I'll be going round now—will Toggy no be back the night?'

'No, he gets the first bus home in the morning.'

'Must be lonely for you.'

Jess half-closed her eyes and nodded. 'Sometimes I feel like a widow.'

'Ay, and no the merry widow, either, eh?' This remark drew simultaneous laughter, and at the end of it an invitation to Joe to stay for tea.

While they sat and talked, Toggy was putting snares along the bottom of a wire fence near the River Lanrick. When the last snare was down, Toggy took the river bank and walked towards McKay's farm where he would get a couple of hours' sleep in the barn.

Toggy slouched along in dew-soaked grass. His wet toecaps glistened in the moonlight. Toggy knew Strathlanrick with the intimacy of a lover, knew every individual tree for at least two miles of the river bank, knew the family of otters at Priest's Pool and was almost pally with the tawny owl who hunted from the big oak at the Lan burn. When a salmon slunged out of the water he knew it was one of the late-runners making for the redds above Gartlynn.

In the pearly mist of dawn Toggy was on his hunkers working at the snares. His small hands worked swiftly. A rabbit's neck was placed in the gusset of thumb and forefinger. His other hand grasped the hind legs, stretched the animal taut, twisted the body and snapped the spinal cord. The rabbit's heart fluttered and stopped. He was a true lover of nature. He killed cleanly and quickly and without compunction.

Toggy's sheath knife thrust and twisted. Blood and guts spilled into a hole cut in the turf. A neatly-cut sod was replaced and tramped down. He liked to obey the rules. It wouldn't do if rats were attracted to the burrows.

When Toggy arrived home Jess was snoring. He made breakfast and carried his wife's to the bed. Jess chewed a thick morning saliva and looked dazedly at Toggy's glowing face.

'Oh, oh, tea—ta.'

Toggy was on his way to work at Shieldhall Dock before Jess had fully recovered from sleep. She was left with six carcases and the smell of rabbit blood.

As usual, Joe Bell met Toggy on the tramcar. 'How do you do it, Toggy? My two best birds.'

'Och, just the luck of the game.'

'No, it's more than that. You've got the feel of animals, just like my faither had. I'll need to do away with the loft: it's a waste of time and money.'

Toggy looked at him in alarm. He couldn't imagine the district without pigeons at Bell's stable. It's all there was left. For years now it hadn't been a stable, only the house remained, and the yard where old Bell used to make pony traps. That small industry died with the old man's skill. The pigeons were reminders to Toggy of the grand days he spent with old Bell.

'I'd maybe hang on to them if you took me up to your place and showed me the ropes, Toggy?'

Toggy hesitated. He was unsure of young Joe Bell.

'I'd hate to part with them without trying, Toggy, for the sake of my auld faither.'

There was something about the phrase 'my auld faither' that Toggy didn't like. Joe's auld faither never liked Joe. They were as like each other as a weasel and a sheepdog. Toggy remembered sitting ankle deep with old Bell, listening to him, watching his bunched fingers manipulating a spokeshave on a shaft. He remembered his broad belt and blue eyes, his cottonwool moustache.

Old Bell was one of those men who had principles to a fault. He despised favouritism and so was stricter with Joe than with strangers.

But when Joe reached manhood there was little anyone could do about his twisted attitude to women. Joe didn't just court girls, he expended them. From girls he graduated to married women until he was openly talked about for the way he was making a clown of Mrs Jessiman, a widow in Greenbank Pend.

The old man put a stop to this affair when he waited in the yard for Joe early one Sunday morning. Toggy saw the whole thing from his dovecot.

He watched Joe advancing to the back door and trying to turn past his father into the house. He was felled by a vicious blow to the side of his face. That first punch just about levelled up the difference in years and made it an even match. Toggy didn't wait to see the progress of the fight, but hurried round to stop it.

It was over when he arrived. Joe lay on the ground and grunted through bruised lips. The old man was leaning against the wall, the breath rasping in his lungs. Toggy helped him inside, then revived Joe who stumbled up to his room.

Old Bell laid his head on his arms for a time. When he looked up his moustache was stained red. 'He's like a bad collie, Toggy; you train it and finish up by shooting it.'

Toggy took another look at Joe. He had a sleekit look about him right enough, but maybe his father had been too hard on him from the start. He seemed to like the birds, though, and it would be a shame if he had to let them go.

'All right, Joe, I'll get you up to the loft back and forrit.'

'Sticking out, Toggy, sticking out.'

The tramcar emptied at the dock. Joe and Toggy were sent to a Blue Funnel liner loading cases of machinery. Toggy got up on his winch platform and forgot pigeons for a few hours.

Toggy liked his job as winchman, snatching loads from the quay, swinging them through the air and dropping them into the bottom of the hold right to the tips of the stowers' fingers. From where Toggy worked, Joe and the rest of the stowing gang were little cloth caps with arms and legs sticking out from them—like beetles. It was dangerous work for the men below. They worked under suspended loads all the time, and fatal accidents were not unknown.

During tea breaks that day and many other days, Joe Bell kept asking about pigeons. He became a visitor to Toggy's loft and got tips on how to capture other men's birds.

But, for all Joe's interest, Toggy continued to trap his birds with a regularity that took much of the pleasure away. On many evenings,

Joe didn't release any pigeons but when he did it was usually two cocks ready for hens. Toggy took these easy captures and put it down to Joe's ignorance. He never thought it strange that it was always on a fishing or rabbiting night that Joe Bell lost birds.

Toggy's friendship with Joe lasted until late November, when one evening Toggy turned back from the bus stance and went home because of a steadily thickening fog. It would have been a wasted night going for rabbits.

Jess was out. Toggy went straight to the cupboard and climbed up to the loft. One of his birds was bad with the feather waste and he wanted to clean it in case it should affect the others.

Toggy took the bird in his hand and with a cloth dipped in surgical spirits began to clean it feather by feather. He was so engrossed in his task that only gradually did he become aware of voices below in the kitchen. He craned his neck over the hatch. There was a sliver of light where the door fitted badly and through the space came the voices of a man and a woman. The woman was Jess. Who was the man? Toggy knew the voice, but it was thickened with drink, then suddenly he knew it was Joe Bell's. Was he up for birds? No, there were none of his here—must have come earlier for them. What was he back for?

A giggle rose to his ears, a giggle from Jess was one of the vulgar noises of the world. The giggling continued and through it Jess cackled, 'Oh, stop it, Joe, oh, Joe, you're a hard man . . . you're a hard man so you are!'

Toggy's grip tightened on the bird in his hand. At first he couldn't feel the urgent throbbing of the pigeon's heart, for his own was pounding in unison so that both man and bird were caught in a pulsating panic. Then he recovered, opened his fist and looked after the bird as it fluttered to a pen. He was sorry if he'd hurt it.

Toggy compressed his lips and listened through the sordid proceedings. He heard the clink of glasses and Jess saying, 'No much for me, Joe—just a wee sensation.'

'Sensation, Jess? I'll gie ye a wee sensation a' right.' They laughed dirtily at this.

Toggy knew that the situation was beyond him. This was a furtive, foul thing which begins in the back rooms of pubs and ends up in the High Court. He had seen it before in Glasgow; he knew the pattern and didn't like the way the law and the gossips dealt with it. One thing he was certain of; he was not going down to challenge big Bell. The shame he felt was bad enough.

Toggy waited until the voices subsided into murmurs, then rose and put out the light. He reached up and gripped a joist, set his foot on a beam and walked slowly into the darkness of the loft. He went down a hatchway three entries along and down a common stairway into the street.

Toggy walked all through the night. He felt no hatred for Jess. She was only the person who gave him his meat and his bed. Any feelings they ever had for each other were lost in childless years which sent him deeper into the world of animals he had loved since boyhood.

It was Joe Bell who enclosed his whole being like the fog he walked in, not so much for seducing Jess as for the sleekit way he went about it. And he used the pigeons as an excuse for getting into the house, used Toggy's birds to help him in a long prepared plan for lust. There was something unnatural about that. Maybe it was true what Joe's father once said: 'You and me's that close to animals, Toggy, that sometimes I think we're oot o'touch with men.'

Toggy had a wash-up in a street lavatory and went home for breakfast. Jess looked no different from usual. 'What's up this morning—nae rabbits?'

Toggy pulled on his dungarees. 'No,' he said, 'rabbits have more sense than men—they lie low in the fog.'

He spoke with a deliberation which made Jess uneasy all day while Toggy was at work. Her conscience bothered her so much that she cleaned the house as never before.

Toggy returned from the docks and noted the shining kitchen with his eyes. He sat down and ate steadily through his meal. Jess watched him mopping up gravy with little pieces of crust. The habit finally convinced her that everything was normal. Then, as Toggy walked towards the cupboard, he said, 'Bad accident at work today, Jess.'

Something bunched in her stomach. 'A—an accident?'

Toggy put a foot on the ladder. 'Ay, poor Joe Bell, case of machinery fell on him—hadnae a chance.'

Toggy ascended to the loft and took out the bird with the feather waste. Jess called up the hatch. 'But what happened? Did you see it?'

'Ay—the load came off my winch.'

Toggy thought he heard a moaning sound in the kitchen. The infected bird was worse, it would smit the others. Toggy threw its neck with a quick movement of thumb and forefinger. A true lover of nature, he killed cleanly and quickly and without compunction.

WILLIAM MONTGOMERIE

Daft Jenny

❖❖❖❖❖

DAVID walked up Dalmarnock Street in a very stilted manner, head down, left foot in a space, right foot on a line, left foot in a space, right foot on a line, saying the rhyme over and over to himself under his breath, emphasising the accents:

> Fraser's sausages are the best,
> In your belly they do rest;
> Simpson's sausages are the worst,
> In your belly they do burst.

He knew that if he could say the rhyme five times before reaching the draper's shop at the corner he would be lucky, and if he could reach it before the tramcar coming up the road stopped at the tramstop he would be doubly so. The tramcar unluckily stopped just as he reached the factor's office, but he was able to say the lines seven times and a half.

Then he ran round the corner to Fraser's ham-shop in Great Eastern Road. Daft Jenny was already in the shop, waiting patiently three yards away from the counter, holding her infant in a green plaid wrapped also round herself, as if the small sleeping face were another pale bud on the same green stem. The boy gazed at them intently, puzzled by a mother and child without a father.

Three weeks ago he had passed Jenny. She was walking along the pavement near the tenement wall, as if afraid of leaving the shadow of it. There was no infant then, but the same green plaid sheathed her forehead and cheeks, crossed below her chin, and was clutched in both her hidden hands. Underneath her shapeless grey skirt she walked on the outsides of her feet, so worn were the heels of her black boots. David had called after her:

'Jenny! Jenny! Jenny!'

But when she turned slowly round and looked at him the sadness in her dark eyes had made him ashamed, so that when he heard other boys calling after her he repeated to them his mother's words.

'Leave her alone! She's harmless.'

The manager of the shop, a stout man in white overalls, served him first, pulling the heavy round of bacon from the row of hams on the shelf at the back of the window. David liked to watch him unspike the bacon from its handled board, remove the enamelled price ticket and the label with 'Delicious' in black letters; to listen to the wheep-wheep of the broad hamknife on the whetting steel hanging, when not in use, from the man's belt, and the hiss of its edge keenly cutting the thin slices that fell one by one on the greaseproof paper. The man's eyes rested once or twice on Daft Jenny. He lifted a hambone from the counter, wrapped it up in paper, and laid it without a word beside the quarter pound of funeral ham his girl assistant was preparing for Jenny. The girl nodded slightly, and placed the two packages together on the front of the counter.

Then she walked round the end of the counter and raised the edge of the plaid from the infant's forehead. The other girl followed her, and the two of them peered together at the sleeping child.

'I wonder where you come from?' said the second girl. It was a rhetorical question, and she expected no answer.

'Ah dinny ken,' said Daft Jenny.

The manager began to cough, and coughed so long that he recovered only when Jenny had put out her white hand with the blue veins and clutched the two packages from the girl who had picked them off the counter, withdrawn her hand under the plaid like a small carnivorous animal retreating into its burrow, and left the shop.

David saw that the man's face was wet with tears, yet he was laughing.

'Ah dinny ken,' said the man.

'It's a crying shame,' said the girl who had wrapped up Jenny's ham, and she was smiling.

'I'm crying,' said the manager, wiping his eyes with his wrist, for his fingers were greasy from the bacon slices he arranged neatly on the paper. Then he pushed the paper package across the counter, and dropped David's half-crown into the till.

'He should get ten years,' said the other girl.

'He should be made to marry her,' said the first one.

'A life sentence,' said the manager, spiking the boiled bacon on its board, and sticking on a new word 'Superfine' instead of the one he had taken off.

'Up ye go!' he said, heaving the heavy board up to the gap in the row of hams in the window.

'I wonder who he is,' said one girl, as if she were trying to identify the accused in a line of men stretching from the door of the shop to the end counter.

'*Ah* dinny ken,' said the manager, emphasising the first word. Then he looked at David who was still standing there.

'What do you want, sonny?' The three of them looked at the boy, as if he had overheard something he shouldn't have heard.

'You've forgotten my change,' said David.

'So I have,' said the man, finding it on the edge of the counter.

David told the story to nobody, but turned it over and over in his mind. He felt that he had learned something new about adult life, but was not quite sure how much.

'Daft Jenny's got a baby,' said his mother to his father a few days later, and his father said the same thing as the girl in Fraser's.

'I wonder who he is.'

He said it in the same tone as the girl in the hamshop, and very slowly, as if he were looking into his mind at all the men in the district.

'I can't understand some men,' said his mother, and then his father looked at his mother, and nodded slightly in David's direction. They changed the subject.

This knowledge that there were things they did not tell him, nor even discuss in his presence, planted in the boy's mind one very curious illusion which, because of the limitation of his experience, he could neither prove nor disprove.

'Suppose my father and mother are German spies. They wouldn't tell me. Suppose my father is a German spy. Maybe he wouldn't tell even my mother.'

He couldn't ask them, because they would either refuse to tell him or, if they were not German spies, they would only laugh at his silly notions. The boy could think of no way out of the suspicion, except by watching them very carefully in case they would give themselves away by some chance remark, but they never did.

When David met Jenny next she had no infant, and no green plaid. Her arms were folded under her breast as if she did not know what else to do with them. She was walking along close to the tenement wall, and anyone looking out from behind the lace curtains of the ground-floor windows of the tenements would not have seen her eyes, nor did she look into the face of anyone who passed. Perhaps her head was a little more bowed than usual as though she were looking for something on the ground or at the bottom of her own mind.

David's mother heard in the grocer's that detectives had called at Jenny's house and questioned her about her baby, but all she had answered had been:

'Ah dinny ken.'

'It wiz better deed onywey,' was the general verdict.

Daft Rab brought the news that they were dragging the river, 'wi' boats, an' ropes, an' a'thing'. He stopped everyone he knew, or half-recognised, and told them in broken phrases that were always difficult to understand. David heard the rumour, and went down in the evening to the River Clyde, past the place where the gambling school met on the coup near the fever hospital. There was a boat he had never seen before, moored across the river to a new post. He looked into the water as if he might see something where the police had failed.

A young man, wearing a brown muffler, came along the path at the top of the high riverbank, carrying a young white dog. He laid it down on the greasy grass very carefully, and when David looked at the animal he saw that its hind legs were broken. Then the man took a brick from under his oxter, and a hank of string from a pocket of his blue serge suit, tied the string twice round the brick with a firm knot, and twice round the dog's neck. He looked at David and said:

'Ah canny dae onythin' else wi' him. Can ah?' He stroked the animal's head, and it licked his hand. Very gently he picked up the dog and the brick together, and threw them into the air. They swung round each other as they rose, and fell to strike the water together. The brick sank fast and dragged the white terrier head first to the bottom, where it swayed like a pale green weed anchored to the ground, its broken hind legs pointing upward to the light and air, its forefeet pawing blindly down.

STEPHEN MULRINE

A Cold Coming

◆◇◆◇◆

MELTING snow announcing its arrival through socks, winter weight, at the ankles. Most unpleasant. And the extremities, naturally, extremely cold. Fur-lined boots the answer. Pair of heavy-duty ex-RAF officers'—if he (or they) could be prised out of them. Very tired joke. Wouldn't go in this area anyway. Capitalist opulence. Different a car, though. Impressive evidence of medical skill, awarded for two thousand bronchitis prescriptions or one liver transplant. Yea though I walk through the valley of the shadow I will make tired jokes.

The Keogh girl nearly nubile, God help her. Running ahead in the snow, splashing as high as her navy-blue knickers.

Guttering gaslight and vintage drains on ice. All it needs is a gypsy fiddler to make the moment eternal. Bringing forth in pain up a Glasgow close. Parturitioned off, as it were.

No nameplate. Not even a GPO Keogh pencilled on the wall. Utter anonymity. Come to sunny Glasgow, get away from it all in miles of golden slums.

Rags, a steamie pram jammed against the door. Wet clothes in it stiff with soap. Or frozen. God, what a place to be born on a winter's night. Pulpit joke, very Presbyterian.

Small boy taking gradual shape in the lobby darkness next door. Shoeless, a wide gap between liberty bodice and trousers. Scratching, holding out doorkey on a string looped round his neck.

'Mah mammy's in bed.' Waiting to be released from the key.

'Ah've tae stey wi Missis Shaw while she's hivvin it.' Fade apparition back into the lobby darkness, embassy carried out to the letter.

Forward into Anonymity Hall. Unlit, more wet clothes on a pulley, located by touch. The unmistakable fragrance of cimex lectularia—bedbugs to you, Mrs Keogh. A large pot heating water on a gas ring, blue nimbus of the gas around it. Madonna colour suggesting its purification role in the business to come, as it were. White sheets would be nice, never mind hot water. Playing hunt the

130

grey woman in grey blankets in an unlit kitchen. Can you come back next week?

'Have you no lights, Mrs Keogh? This is the right house, I suppose.' Grey face against grey, highlights of sweat on unhandsome sad brow. Two shillings for the meter. And it doesn't last. No, nothing lasts, Mrs Keogh. Not even this. Envoy despatched to the unfailing Mrs Shaw, the fourth Keogh, recklessly clawing still in the gap between vest and trousers.

'Still with us, Mrs Keogh? Not arrived yet, has he?' Fiat lux. About forty watts of it. Wallpaper coming or going? Pelts of slaughtered cimex fastened to the wall. No dates. White frozen breath like muslin over the bed. Fingers numb with cold, probably drop it when it comes.

'Haven't you another basin, Mrs Keogh?' Knowing damn well she hasn't.

'Couldn't your daughter take care of these things?' Avalanche, clothes, shoes, bottles, tins from a cupboard.

'What about your maternity grant, Mrs Keogh? You can't expect these to do. Do you want to poison the child?' For my own peace of mind. Nappies and a shawl. Zinc and castor oil. No talcum. No matinee coat, bootees, broderie anglaise. Don't you take the women's magazines. Mrs Keogh? Dear Marje, What do you suggest I do about bedbugs, a cracked sink, no coal in the house, and a husband who forgets my birthday? Dear Fed-up. Remind him.

'Where is your husband, Mrs Keogh? Doesn't he know you're like this?' Shrug. Meaning paralytic drunk on cheap white, wetting its reluctant head.

'What's it to be this time, Mrs Keogh, boy or a girl? You'll be able to feed it anyway.' Never think it, under that peaky face.

'The Green Lady'll be here first thing in the morning. Not as if it was your first, eh, Mrs Keogh?' God, the warm bedside manner—very nice at a warm bedside.

'No, lie back, Mrs Keogh. Just take it easy now. Just relax. Easy now. Easy. Nearly there, Mrs Keogh. Easy now.' God knows it looks anything but. Keogh should see this, the drunken pig. God, the sweat of her! Amorous on a pint of mammy mine, and here comes . . . the consequence . . . to join . . . the starving . . . millions!

'There we are, Mrs Keogh.' Clouds of steam enveloping one male breidsnapper.

'Think he'll mind cold hands, Mrs Keogh?' First of life's little ironies, one-two! on the backside. And a third muslin breath to hang over the bed.

'Fine hairy wee brute of a boy, Mrs Keogh. Look, see it all down his shoulders. Now you keep this round him till the Green Lady comes. Knock through the wall for your girl. These nappies aren't enough, you know.' In repose an ugly woman. Strange how much finer she looked in labour. Now? Grey upon grey.

'I'll leave this with you, Mrs Keogh. The girl can make you some tea, and then get this prescription. And for God's sake see there's a fire kept on in this room.' Talk to the wall. Her fifth, anyway, fire or no fire. Well, if it isn't the lord of the manor himself. Wonder who scraped him off Gallaher's bar? Pig eyes behind the cheap wine bonhomie. A D.H. Lawrence unpolished diamond, pig the whole way through.

'Just two minutes too late, Mr Keogh. A fine baby boy. More hair on him than Mick Jagger.' Swaying, suspicious. Thinks he's been framed.

'Well, he's all yours, Mr Keogh. I'll be going now. Remember to keep this room warm. Child'll get pneumonia in an atmosphere like this.' Cirrhosis too, if it gets a smell of that breath. Just fancy, thanks to its commendable foresight in having got itself born into a scientific age, it will probably not succumb to infant mortality. God help it.

'Try and sleep as much as possible between feeds, Mrs Keogh. Goodnight. Night, Mr Keogh.' Nubile girl an embarrassed shape in the lobby. Probably got a complex about her navy knickers. And the envoy, finally. Safe conduct to the snow-line and fresh air at the closemouth.

'Missis Shaw says Ah've goat a wee brurra.' Not a question, a flat statement, but he waits to be contradicted. Satisfied.

'Whit's it like?' Clawing incredibly at wrong shoulderblade. Like?

'Mah wee brurra. Whit's it like?'

'Well, he's very small. That size.' Not too convinced.

'Blue eyes. And long black hair. And warm. Yes. Warm, and long black hair. Right down his back, like Mick Jagger.'

ALAN SPENCE

Tinsel

◇◇◇◇◇

THE swing-doors of the steamie had windows in them but even when he stood on tiptoe he couldn't reach up to see out. If he held the doors open, the people queuing complained about the cold and anyway the strain would make his arms ache. So he had to be content to peer out through the narrow slit between the doors, pressing his forehead against the brass handplate. He could see part of the street and the grey buildings opposite, everything covered in snow. He tried to see more by moving a little sideways, but the gap wasn't wide enough. He could smell the woodandpaint of the door and the clean bleachy smell from the washhouse. His eye began to sting from the draught so he closed it tight and put his other eye to the slit, but he had to jump back quickly as a woman with a pramful of washing crashed open the doors. When the doors had stopped swinging and settled back into place he noticed that the brass plate was covered with fingermarks. He wanted to see it smooth and shiny so he breathed up on it, clouding it with his breath, and rubbed it with his sleeve. But he only managed to smear the greasy marks across the plate leaving it streaky and there was still a cluster of prints near the top that he couldn't reach at all.

He went over and sat down on the long wooden bench against the wall. His feet didn't quite reach the ground and he sat swinging his legs. It felt as if his mother had been in the washhouse for hours. Waiting.

People passed in and out. The queue was just opposite the bench. They queued to come in and wash their clothes or to have a hot bath or a swim. The way to the swimming baths was through an iron turnstile, like the ones at Ibrox Park. When his father took him to the match he lifted him over the turnstile so he didn't have to pay.

Unfastening his trenchcoat, he rummaged about in his trouser pocket and brought out a toy Red Indian without a head, a pencil rubber, a badge with a racing car, a yellow wax crayon and a foreign coin. He pinned the badge on to his lapel and spread the other things out on the bench. The crayon was broken in the middle but because the paper cover wasn't torn the two ends hadn't come apart. It felt wobbly. He bent it in half, tearing the paper. Now he had two short crayons instead of one long one. There was nothing to draw on except the green-tiled wall so he put the pieces back in his pocket.

The coin was an old one, from Palestine, and it had a hole in the middle. He'd been given it by his uncle Andy who had been a soldier there. Now he was a policeman in Malaya. He would be home next week for Christmas. Jesus's birthday. Everybody gave presents then so that Jesus would come one day and take them to Heaven. That was where he lived now, but he came from Palestine. Uncle Andy had been to see his house in Bethlehem. At school they sang hymns about it. Come all ye faithful. Little star of Bethlehem.

He scraped at the surface of the bench with his coin, watching the brown paint flake and powder, blowing the flakings away to see the mark he'd made.

The woman at the pay-desk shouted at him.

'Heh! Is that how ye treat the furniture at hame? Jist chuck it!'

He sat down again.

Two boys and two girls aged about fifteen came laughing and jostling out of the baths, red faced, their hair still damp. One of the boys was flicking his wet towel at the girls who skipped clear, just out of reach. They clattered out into the street, leaving the doors swinging behind them. He heard their laughter fade, out of his hearing. For the moment again he was alone.

He stood his headless Indian on the bench. If he could find the head he'd be able to fix it back on again with a matchstick. He pushed the Indian's upraised arm through the hole in the coin, thinking it would make a good shield, but it was too heavy and made the Indian fall over.

He shoved his things back into his pocket and went over to the doorway of the washhouse. The place was painted a grubby cream and lightgreen and the stone floor was wet.

Clouds of steam swishing up from faraway metaltub machines. Lids banging shut. Women shouting above the throbbing noise.

He couldn't see his mother.

He went back and climbed on to the bench, teetering, almost falling as he stood carefully up.

A woman came in with a little girl about his own age. He was glad he was standing on the bench and he knew she was watching him.

He ignored her and pretended to fight his way along the bench, hacking aside an army of unseen cut-throats, hurling them over the immense drop from the perilous bench-top ridge. He kept looking round to make sure she was still watching him, not looking directly at her but just glancing in her direction then looking past her to the pay-box and staring at that with fixed interest and without seeing it at all.

The woman had taken her bundle into the washhouse and the little girl sat down on the far end of the bench, away from him.

His mother came out of the washhouse pushing her pram. He jumped down noisily and ran to her. As they left he turned and over his shoulder stuck out his tongue at the girl.

Once outside, his mother started fussing over him, buttoning his coat, straightening his belt, tucking in his scarf.

'There yar then, ah wasn't long, was ah?' Gentle voice. Her breath was wheezy.

She was wearing the turban she wore to work in the bakery. Today was Saturday and she only worked in the morning, coming home at dinnertime with cakes and pies. He'd gone with her to the steamie because his father was out at the doctor's and he couldn't find any of his friends. They'd probably gone to the pictures.

He had to walk very quickly, sometimes trotting, to keep up with the pram. The snow under his feet made noises like a catspurr at every step. The pramwheels creaked. In the pram was a tin tub full of damp washing which was already starting to stiffen in the cold. It was the same pram he'd been carried in when he was a baby. His mother's two other babies had been carried in it too. They would have been his big brothers but they'd both died. They would be in Heaven. He wondered if they were older than him now or if they were still babies. He was six years and two weeks old. His wellington boots were folded down at the top like pirate boots. His socks didn't reach up quite far enough and the rims of the boots had rubbed red stinging chafe-marks round his legs.

They rounded the corner into their own street and stopped outside the Dairy.

'You wait here son. Ah'll no be a minnit.'

Waiting again.

Out of a close came a big loping longhaired dog. The hair on its legs looked like a cowboy's baggy trousers. Some boys were chasing it and laughing. All its fur was clogged with dirt and mud.

His mother came out of the shop with a bottle of milk.

There was a picture of the same kind of dog in his Wonder Book of the World. It was called an Afghan Hound. But the one in the book looked different. Again the steady creak of the pram. The trampled snow underfoot was already grey and slushy.

They reached their close and he ran on up ahead. They lived on the top landing and he was out of breath when he reached the door. He leaned over the banister. Down below he could hear his mother bumping the pram up the stairs. Maybe his father was home from the doctor's.

He kicked the door.

'O-pen. O-pen.'

His father opened the door and picked him up.

'H'Hay! Where's yer mammy?'

'She's jist comin up.'

His father put him down and went to help her with the pram.

He went into the kitchen and sat down by the fire.

Dusty, their cat, jumped down from the sink and slid quietly under the bed. The bed was in a recess opposite the window and the three of them slept there in winter. Although they had a room, the kitchen was easier to keep warm. The room was bigger and was very cold and damp. His father said it would cost too much to keep both the room and the kitchen heated.

He warmed his hands till they almost hurt. He heard his mother and father coming in. They left the pram in the lobby. His father was talking about the doctor.

'Aye, e gave me a prescription fur another jar a that ointment.' He had to put the ointment all over his body because his skin was red and flaky and he had scabby patches on his arms and legs. That was why he didn't have a job. He'd had to give up his trade in the shipyards because it was a dirty job and made his skin disease worse.

'An ah got your pills as well, when ah wis in the Chemist's.'

His mother had to take pills to help her breathing. At night she had to lie on her back, propped up with pillows.

'Never mind hen. When ah win the pools . . .'

'Whit'll ye get ME, daddy?' This was one of their favourite conversations.

'Anythin ye like, sun.'

'Wull ye get me a pony, daddy? Lik an Indian.'

'Ah'll get ye TWO ponies.' Laughing. 'An a wigwam as well!'

He could see it. He'd ride up to school, right up the stairs and into the classroom and he'd scalp Miss Heather before she could reach for her belt.

He'd keep the other pony for Annie. She was his friend. She wasn't his girlfriend. That was soft. She was three weeks older than him and she lived just round the corner. They were in the same class at school. She had long shiny black hair and she always wore bright clean colours. (One night in her back close—showing bums—giggling—they didn't hear the leerie coming in to light the gas-lamp—deep loud voice somewhere above them—sneering laugh—Annie pulling up her knickers and pulling down her dress in the same movement—scramble into the back—both frightened to go home in case the leerie had told, but he hadn't.)

The memory of it made him blush. He ripped off a piece of newspaper and reached up for the toilet key from the nail behind the door where it hung.

'Jist goin t' the lavvy.'

From the lobby he heard the toilet being flushed so he waited in the dark until he heard the slam of the toilet door then the flop of Mrs Dolan's feet on the stairs. The Dolans lived in the single end, the middle door of the three on their landing. The third house, another room and kitchen, was empty for the moment because the Andersons had emigrated to Canada.

When he heard Mrs Dolan closing the door he stepped out on to the landing and slid down the banister to the stairhead. In the toilet there was only one small window very high up, and he left the door slightly open to let light seep in from the stairhead.

A pigeon landed on the window-ledge and sat there gurgling and hooing, its feathers ruffled up into a ball. To pull the plug he climbed up on to the seat and swung on the chain, squawking out a Tarzan-call. The pigeon flurried off, scared by the noise, and he dropped from his creeperchain, six inches to the floor.

He looked out through the stairhead window. Late afternoon. Out across the back and a patch of wasteground, over factory roofs and across a railway line stood Ibrox Stadium. He could see a patch of terracing and the roof of the stand. The pressbox on top looked like a little castle. When Rangers were playing at home you could count the goals and near misses just by listening to the roars. Today there was only a reserve game and the noise could hardly be heard. Soon it would be dark and they'd have to put on the floodlights.

For tea they had sausages and egg and fried bread. After they'd eaten he sat down in his own chair at the fire with his Wonder Book of the World. The chair was wooden and painted bright blue.

His father switched on the wireless to listen to the football results and check his pools.

The picture of the Afghan Hound had been taken in a garden on a sunny day. The dog was running and its coat shone in the sun.

'Four draws,' said his father. 'Ach well, maybe next week . . .'

'There's that dog, mammy.' He held up the book.

'So it is.'

'Funny tae find a dog lik that in Govan,' said his father.

'Right enough,' said his mother. 'Expect some'dy knocked it.'

Nothing in the book looked like anything he had ever seen. There were pictures of cats but none of them looked like Dusty. They were either black and white or striped and they all looked clean and sleek. Dusty was a grubby grey colour and he spat and scratched if anyone tried to pet him. His mother said he'd been kept too long in the house. There was a section of the book about the weather with pictures of snow crystals that looked like flowers and stars. He thought he'd like to go out and play in the snow and he asked his mother if he could.

'Oh well, jist for a wee while then. Ah'll tell ye what. If ye come up early enough we kin put up the decorations before ye go tae bed.'

He'd forgotten about the decorations. It was good to have something special like that to come home for. It was the kind of thing he'd forget about while he was actually playing, then there would be moments when he'd remember, and feel warm and comforted by the thought.

He decided he'd get Joe and Jim and Annie and they'd build a snowman as big as a midden.

Joe was having his tea and Jim felt like staying in and Annie's mother wouldn't let her out.

He stood on the pavement outside the paper-shop, peering in through the lighted window at the Christmas annuals and selection boxes. The queue for the evening papers reached right to the door of the shop. The snow on the pavement was packed hard and grey-brown, yellow in places under the streetlamps. He scraped at the snow with the inside of his boot, trying to rake up enough to make a snowball, but it was too powdery and it clung to the fingers of his woollen gloves, making his hands feel clogged and uncomfortable. He took off his gloves and scooped up some slush from the side of the road but the cold made his bare fingers sting, red. It felt as if he'd just been belted by Miss Heather.

TINSEL

Annie's big brother Tommy was clattering his way across the road, trailing behind him a sack full of empty bottles. He'd gathered them on the terracing at Ibrox and he was heading for the Family Department of the pub to cash in as many as he could. Every time the pub door opened the noise and light seeped out. It was a bit like pressing your hands over your ears then easing off then pressing again. If you did that again and again people's voices sounded like mwah . . . mwah . . . mwah . . .. mwah . . .

He looked closely at the snow still clogging his gloves. It didn't look at all like the crystals in his book. Disgusted, he slouched towards his close.

Going up the stairs at night he always scurried or charged past each closet for fear of what might be lurking there ready to leap out at him. Keeping up his boldness, he whistled loudly. Little Star of Bethlehem. He was almost at the top when he remembered the decorations.

The kitchen was very bright after the dimness of the landing with its sputtering gas light.

'Nob'dy wis comin out tae play,' he explained.

His mother wiped her hands. 'Right! What about these decorations!'

The decorations left over from last year were in a cardboard box under the bed. He didn't like it under there. It was dark and dirty, piled with old rubbish—books, clothes, boxes, tins. Once he'd crawled under looking for a comic, dust choking him, and he'd scuttled back in horror from bugs and darting silverfish. Since then he'd had bad dreams about the bed swarming with insects that got into his mouth when he tried to breathe.

His father rummaged in the sideboard drawer for a packet of tin tacks and his mother brought out the box.

Streamers and a few balloons and miracles of coloured paper that opened out into balls or long concertina snakes. On the table his mother spread out some empty cake boxes she'd brought home from work and cut them into shapes like Christmas trees and bells, and he got out his painting box and a saucerful of water and he coloured each one and left it to dry—green for the trees and yellow for the bells, the nearest he could get to gold.

His father had bought something special.

'Jist a wee surprise. It wis only a coupla coppers in Woollies.'

From a cellophane bag he brought out a length of shimmering rustling silver.

'What dis that say daddy?' He pointed at the label.

'It says UNTARNISHABLE TINSEL GARLAND.'

'What dis that mean?'

'Well that's what it is. It's a tinsel garland. Tinsel's the silvery stuff it's made a. An a garland's jist a big long sorta decoration, for hangin up. An untarnishable means . . . well . . . how wid ye explain it hen?'

'Well,' said his mother, 'it jist means it canny get wasted. It always steys nice and shiny.'

'Aw Jesus!' said his father. 'There's only three tacks left!'

'Maybe the paper-shop'll be open.'

'It was open a wee minnit ago!'

'Ah'll go an see,' said his father, putting on his coat and scarf. 'Shouldnae be very long.'

The painted cut-out trees and bells had long since dried and still his father hadn't come back. His mother had blown up the balloons and she'd used the three tacks to put up some streamers. Then she remembered they had a roll of sticky tape. It was more awkward to use than the tacks so the job took a little longer. But gradually the room was transformed, brightened; magical colours strung across the ceiling. A game he liked to play was lying on his back looking up at the ceiling and trying to imagine it was actually the floor and the whole room was upside down. When he did it now it looked like a toy garden full of swaying paper plants.

Round the lampshade in the centre of the room his mother was hanging the tinsel coil, standing on a chair to reach up. When she'd fixed it in place she climbed down and stood back and they watched the swinging lamp come slowly to rest. Then they looked at each other and laughed.

When they heard his father's key in the door his mother shooshed and put out the light. They were going to surprise him. He came in and fumbled for the switch. They were laughing and when he saw the decorations he smiled but he looked bewildered and a bit sad.

He put the box of tacks on the table.

'So ye managed, eh,' he said. He smiled again, his eyes still sad. 'Ah'm sorry ah wis so long. The paper-shop wis shut an ah had tae go down nearly tae Govan Road.'

Then they understood. He was sad because they'd done it all without him. Because they hadn't waited. They said nothing. His mother filled the kettle. His father took off his coat.

'Time you were in bed malad!' he said.

'Aw bit daddy, themorra's Sunday!'

'Bed!'

'Och!'

He could see it was useless to argue so he washed his hands and face and put on the old shirt he slept in.

'Mammy, ah need a pee.'

Rather than make him get dressed again to go out and down the stairs, she said he could use the sink. She turned on the tap and lifted him up to kneel on the ledge.

When he pressed his face up close to the window he could see the back court lit here and there by the light from a window, shining out on to the yellow snow from the dark bulk of the tenements. There were even one or two Christmas trees and, up above, columns of palegrey smoke, rising from chimneys. When he leaned back he could see the reflection of their own kitchen. He imagined it was another room jutting out beyond the window, out into the dark. He could see the furniture, the curtain across the bed, his mother and father, the decorations and through it all, vaguely, the buildings, the night. And hung there, shimmering, in that room he could never enter, the tinsel garland that would never ever tarnish.

ALAN SPENCE

The Rain Dance

❖❖❖❖❖

WITH improvised maraccas—a shake of small stones in a tin can; with tambourine, cymbal and drum—assembly of biscuit-tins and lids; with a bell, a rattle and a party squeaker left over from Christmas; with streamers, with a rose, with a paper hat, Kathleen was paraded through the lamplit streets of the scheme. Her maids and ladies-in-waiting were girls from the same office, Agnes and Jean linking arms with her, the rest of the clattering procession straggled out behind.

Faces appeared briefly at windows as they passed, drawn for a moment from the television before fading back into its blue light, jerking shadows on the ceiling. Curtains were opened on living-room windows, screens that the procession moved across and was gone. Curtains were closed.

Some there were that leaned out and waved, or stood watching from closemouth and pavement, some smiling and glad, others tight-lipped and knowing.

'Tommy Brady's lassie.'

'Gettin merried at Martha Street themorra.'

'Merried oantae a Proddie tae.'

Passing silent judgment on this double heresy. Not only marrying a Protestant, but marrying at Martha Street Registry Office. And for a Catholic girl, that was no wedding at all.

But the girls were untroubled as they sang into the night. The bells are ringin for me and my gal. The clamour and racket of the bridal dance.

> 'Everybody is knowin
> To a weddin they're goin
> An for weeks they've been sewin
> Every Susie and Sal.'

Breaking off into shouts and laughing whenever man or boy should stray across their path. Then they would gather round the victim, willing or not, sometimes lurching across to the opposite pavement, or even stopping cars in the middle of the road. And Kathleen would be jostled towards the captive, offered for the ceremonial kiss, a final flirtation, benediction, farewell.

There was a young boy of about fourteen who blushed and was clumsy and missed her mouth.

There was an old silver-haired man, out for a walk with his dog. He smiled and kissed her forehead and said, 'God bless ye lass.' Then he added, tugging the lead, 'An whit aboot Rab?' So she bent and kissed the dog's wet nose.

There was a boy with the smell of drink on him, who had known Kathleen at school. The girls clapped and stamped and cheered as he gave her a long deep kiss, probing with his tongue.

'Drunken bugger!' said Kathleen, laughing and prising him clear at last.

'It's a bit late fur that, son,' said Agnes.

'That's the wey it goes,' he said.

They moved on, their voices raised again.

> 'And she sang and she sang
> And she sang so sweet
> His name is Brian
> Ah hope ye will agree.'

(A song from their childhood. A memory of long summer evenings. Her friends in a circle moving round her in step, chanting the magic name, the name of the boyfriend, the name that would release her, to take her place again in the circle of linked hands. Songs and games. Just a few summers. Chalkmarks on the pavement.)

They rounded a corner, past a stretch of open ground. The noise and the singing came echoing back from a gable end. Their pace grew slower. It began to rain.

Brian had to get a bus to Hillhead so Tommy saw him to the bus-stop in Hope Street. Tommy had to get a bus to Pollok.

'Ah'll see ye doontae the bus-stoap,' said Brian.

Supporting each other, they made their erratic way down past Central Station towards Midland Street. By the time they got there it had started to rain and they were glad of the shelter of the railway bridge above them.

'Ah'm tell'n ye Brian,' Tommy was saying, 'Canada . . . at's wherr yis should go. See wance yer time's oot at the college . . . land a

opportunity . . . See Peter . . . ye huvnae met Peter . . . Peter's ma
son . . . Kathleen's big brurra . . . ah'll show ye a fotie . . .'

'At's awright Tommy,' said Brian, 'ye showed me it arready. Jist pit
yer wallet back in yer poacket before ye drap it.'

'Aye . . . aw aye. Yirra good boay Brian. Tell'n ye . . . See you an
Kathleen . . .' He broke off as a train rumbled overhead.

'Mon ah'll see ye up tae the bus-stoap,' he went on.

'Naw, look . . .' said Brian, 'wu've arready been up therr; Ah mean,
don't think ah don't appreciate it . . .'

'Sawright,' said Tommy.

'Anywey,' said Brian, 'it's wet. Nae point in the two ae us gettin
soakin. Look . . . here's yer bus comin. Ah kin jist dive roon tae St
Enoch's an get a subway.'

They both got on the bus, Brian guiding Tommy into a seat.

'Ah'll see ye themorra then,' said Brian. 'That's if ye've sobered
up!'

'You don't need tae worry aboot me,' said Tommy, slowly nodding
his head, spreading his fingers like an opening fan. 'Nae bother!'

'Right yar,' said Brian. 'Martha Street themorra.'

'Themorra,' said Tommy, poking the air with an emphatic finger.

Then somehow Brian was outside on the pavement, knocking on
the window. Tommy wiped the steamed-up glass and through the
clear patch saw Brian's face, focused, mouthing words he couldn't
hear. Then he was gone and the window misted over again as the bus
moved out into the main stream of traffic and across Jamaica Bridge.

Kathleen had gone to bed but Mary her mother still sat, leaning on
the windowsill, seeing nothing but the rain streaming down the glass.
The window had clouded a bit from her breath and she drew a face
on it with her finger. Like a child's drawing, the mouth turned down
and doleful. Half past eleven. Tommy shouldn't be long now. She
had made a pot of tea and poured herself a cup. Thinking maybe,
that the smell of the tea would bring him home. Funny how you
half-believed things like that. No sooner would the tea be ready than
somebody's head would be round the door. Tommy or Kathleen or
Peter. Three years now Peter had been gone. And now it was
Kathleen. One more day. The house would be strange without her.
Just herself and Tommy. And Kathleen and Brian would begin it all
again. Mary liked Brian well enough but she was troubled about the
wedding. She remembered the bit in the missal about not marrying
outside the church. And that meant both ways. It meant marrying a

Catholic and it meant a proper church wedding. So she was worried for Kathleen. Father Boyle had put the fear in her about the wedding not being blessed. Not that Kathleen cared, or Tommy either. Little enough he cared about anything, especially the church. Sundays he usually spent recovering from Saturday nights and only rarely could she drag him along to mass.

And now he was somewhere out there, roaming and daft and drunk. Him and Brian both. But he couldn't be much longer now, allowing for the last lingering pint and the chip-shop queue and the time it took him to get a bus . . .

She looked out at the same old street, wet by the same old rain. She saw him turn the corner, unsteadily, and veer across towards the close, and she was relieved and annoyed all at once at the sight of him.

She stood up from the window. The cup of tea she had poured herself was cold and untouched.

Tommy woke, stiff and cold, huddled on the living-room couch. That was where he had slumped, a deep drunk sleep ago, his head drooping forward, his jaw sagging open. The shifting room had closed over him and Mary had taken off his shoes, covered him with his coat and left him be. Now he moved from a dream of creatures like cats or owls surrounding him, waking to a dream of ashes in his mouth, sickness dry in his throat. In the first grey light of the day the room resolved itself into vague familiar shapes, shapes from another dream. There was the table, television, display-cabinet, gas-fire. He gave them names and remembered them as real. He remembered who he was and where. He tried to get up but he was too weak to move. A sick dull throb had replaced his head and the room tilted and threatened to swamp him again. He turned over with difficulty, almost falling off the couch, then pulled his coat tighter about him and went back to sleep.

When he woke again his body was one long ache. He managed to open his eyes long enough to see Mary looming over him, like a mourner at a wake.

'So it's come back tae the land a the livin his it? C'mon, get up!' She clumped into the kitchen.

He screwed up his face and groaned. The light was too bright and harsh. Mary was banging about in the kitchen. He could hear outside the noises of the morning, voices, traffic, children on their way to school. Then he heard Kathleen ask the time and he remembered what day it was and why he was not at work. The wedding. Christ! Still, it wasn't till the afternoon and another half-hour wouldn't . . .

'Oh Jesus, ma guts!' He creaked to his feet and wobbled towards the door. As he fumbled with the doorknob it came away in his hand and the knob on the other side thudded on to the hall floor.

'Oh ya bastard!' He glowered accusation at the crucifix on the wall.

When he had replaced the handle and opened the door, Mary stuck her head out of the kitchen and bawled.

'An ye kin fix that door before we go oot!'

'Ach!'

A little later, purged, he braved the kitchen. Mary was scraping the cinders from bits of charred toast. She shoved them in front of him, banging down the plate, rattled out cups and saucers and poured him some tea.

He sipped at it, fingering the blackened, brittle toast. He pushed the plate aside and started to retreat.

'Ah canny face the burnt offerin hen.'

'Ye need somethin in yer stomach.'

'Aye, maybe efter, Ah'm no feelin too good.'

'Aye, well hell mend ye, that's aw ah kin say.'

'Noo don't start! Ye gave me enough shirrikin last night. Bloody dog's abuse.'

'And no bloody wonder!' she said. 'God forgive me.' (Slipped in like punctuation as she put down a plate so she could cross herself.)

'Ach be reasonable Mary. Ah mean it wis the boay's last night a freedom before e pits is heid 'n the auld noose.' He yanked an imaginary rope above his head and jerked his neck to the side. But that brought back the nausea, so he sat down before going on.

'We hid tae gie um a wee bit send aff, ye know whit ah mean.'

'Ah know whit ye mean awright, an ah know wherr ah'd send the perry yiz! Noo get ootma road. An will ye go an . . . DO somethin ABOUT yerself!'

He went back into the living-room and fumbled in his coat pocket for his cigarettes. His hand met the grisly remains of a fish supper and a copy of the *War Cry*, absolute proof of how he'd spent the night before. He wondered vaguely if the *War Cry* was ever sold anywhere else but in pubs. He remembered the girl that had sold him it, black cape and bonnet and bright moon face. Into battle with her *War Cry* for the Salvation Army. He didn't know anything about what they believed, just that they were another kind of Protestant, but something in him had always warmed to them for the way they went at it, with their brass bands and their banners. Some of them still had the fire and the joy of it, and that was how it should be. He tried to imagine old Father stoneface Boyle rattling a tambourine or beating a drum. He looked again at the *War Cry* and suddenly saw the words for what they were. A war cry was what an Indian would make, or a Dervish, or a Zulu. He had a sudden picture of the whole Sally Army birling and yelling and charging through Pollok. He looked at the main article on the front page. It was a report of a conference in London with a photo of delegates looking serious and purposeful.

'Ach!' he said. He wrapped the paper round the cold soggy chip-bag and threw it in the bin.

He sat down on the couch again and closed his eyes. He was still feeling crumpled and raw. Kathleen poked her head round the door and asked if he'd like another cup of tea.

'Aw thanks hen,' he said, 'ah'd love wan. Ah've git a tongue in me lik a spam fritter.'

She brought through his tea and a cup for herself and sat down beside him.

'Aye, well,' he said. 'The day's the day.'

'Aye,' she said. They smiled at each other, reassuring.

'Did Brian get hame awright last night?' she asked.

'Och e wis fine!' said Tommy. 'As a matter a fact he wis lookin efter me. We didnae really huv that much.'

'Aye, tell me another wan!' said Kathleen.

'Naw ah'm no kiddin,' said Tommy. 'Some a they pals a his wur merr bevvied than the two ae us pit thegether. Ah mean we knew we hud tae keep wursels right.'

'Away ye go!' she said.

'You're as bad as yer mammy,' he said, shaking his head. 'How wis she when ye wur in the kitchen?'

'Och she's still playin the martyr.'

'Aboot me?' said Tommy.

'Jist aboot the whole thing,' said Kathleen, 'because it's no a church weddin an aw that. Ah suppose you jist made ur a wee bit worse, comin in steamin. But ah think it's maistly that auld priest that's been gettin oantae ur again, pittin ideas intae ur heid.'

'Interferin auld bugger,' said Tommy.

'Never mind,' said Kathleen, 'wance she sees the actual weddin she'll be fine.'

'Suppose so,' said Tommy.

'Anywey,' said Kathleen, 'ah'm away tae huv a bath, so ah'll see ye efter. Oh, could ye take the cups intae the kitchen?'

'Okay hen, ah'll see ye in a wee while.'

He took the cups through and rinsed them out. Mary was sweeping the floor.

'Ah think ah'll go oot fur a wee walk an get the paper,' he said. 'Maybe the fresh air'll clear ma heid a bit.'

'Fine,' said Mary. 'It'll get ye oot fae under ma feet as well.'

'Look hen,' he said, 'Ah'm sorry aboot last night. But ye know how it is. It's jist wan a these things.'

'Aye, well . . .' she said. 'Jist . . . away ye go an gie's peace!'

On his way out he called through to her, 'D'ye want anythin when ah'm oot?'

'Naw,' she said. 'Thanks aw the same.'

And he heard the tone of truce in her voice and was glad. He stepped from the close and felt the wind cold in the shadow of the building. He crossed the road into the sunlight, too bright for his eyes still and it made him feel grubby and sticky, but he welcomed its warmth, enough to ease the chill from his bones.

Brian could see most of the park spread out below, the green hillside stretching down to the fountain and the pond, beyond that, a glimmer, the Kelvin, and further, across Kelvin Way, the Art Gallery, the University tower. Further still he could see the shipyards of Partick and Govan, the cranes, giraffe-necks, jutting, grey. Govan was on the other side of the river and somewhere behind that was Pollok. There was nothing to distinguish it, no way he could recognise it from here. But that was where Kathleen was. He wondered what she was doing, what she was thinking. Probably the same as him, the same inconsequential stream of nothing in particular. Tangle of branches. Flight of ducks. Hunger. A bit of an old song. Let us haste to Kelvingrove bonnie lassie o, through the . . . something . . . let us rove bonnie lassie o. He'd learned that at primary school but only recently had he remembered it and connected it with the park. Every day now for almost two years he'd passed through the park on his way to the university. The park was his calendar. Here he could read the traces, the changes, the slow shift of the seasons. The daft dance of it. In a few more hours he would be married. A few more months he would be a father. Tick tock. On it went. A few more steps in the dance.

He looked up at the statue of the horseman, silhouetted at the top of the hill, and remembered the wedding of Richie and Meg. The papers had called it a mockery and gone on about long hair and bright clothes. None of the parents had come because it was at

Martha Street. But somehow none of it had mattered. They'd all come here to the park afterwards for a ceremony of their own, running mad and laughing across the grass. They'd climbed to the top of the hill, about thirty of them, and they'd linked hands and danced in a huge circle, round and round the statue of the horseman. And as they'd danced they'd chanted, and tried to levitate the statue, and with it the park and the rest of Glasgow, and raise it into orbit for ever.

Richie and Meg were in London now. He'd heard they were living apart.

The grass was still wet from last night's rain. Everything felt fresh and new. It was almost spring now. Nothing definite yet, no riot of leaves on the trees, no blaze of daffodils and tulips, just a feeling of everything hesitant, about to be, of opening, unfolding, a slow stirring to life.

A dog went panting and scampering up the hill, stopped and chased its tail, lay down and rolled and wriggled in the grass. Brian laughed.

'Daftie!' he said, out loud. He made his way towards the gate. On his way home he stopped in at the Indian grocer's, to buy some milk and rolls. He liked the shop, and Mr Rhama who owned it. It had a warmth and a brightness about it, open till all hours, an improbable clutter of boxes and bags, of bundles and packets and tins, piled, haphazard, to the ceiling, and always the smell of spices or cooking from the back shop.

Before him in the queue, two tiny Indian boys with broad Glasgow accents dithered over the penny tray—candy balls or bubble-gum, jelly beans or caramels. Brian reached down and helped himself to a pint of milk from the blue plastic crate perched by a wall of tins—hamburgers and mangoes, creamed rice and Scotch broth, corned beef and pineapple and curried beans. Above the crate hung a sacred heart calendar, Jesus gazing up at the legend PL Trading Co—Cash And Carry—Maryhill Road. Next to it was a poster for a showing of Indian films.

'Anything else please?' Mr Rhama grinned across the counter at him, between a basket of tomatoes and a tray of meat pies.

'Jist four rolls,' said Brian. 'That's all.'

The rolls were in a breadboard balanced across an orange-box. Mr Rhama eased his way between bags of coal and a pile of newspapers, put four in a paper bag and passed them over the counter.

'Today's the big day, yes?' he said. Brian had told him about the wedding.

'It is that,' said Brian.

'Ah well,' said Mr Rhama, 'now you have to stop messing about. You have to settle down and bring up family.'

'Suppose so,' said Brian.

'No suppose,' said Mr Rhama, laughing. 'It's really true. No more messing about. But never you mind. I tell you, married is best.'

At the far end of the counter, his wife moved among packing-cases and sacks, the swish of a blue sari, the glint of a gold-embroidered hem, a jewel in her nostril, a glitter of rings.

Brian wondered about their wedding, how long ago it had been, in Glasgow or in India, what the ceremony had been like. He remembered the West Indians he'd seen in London, just a glimpse as he'd passed, a splatter of bright colours, bopping and jigging out of the church into the street. He was about to ask Mr Rhama about Indian weddings, about his own, but a fresh delivery of milk arrived, the vanboy lugging crates in the door, and Mr Rhama had to see to it. No matter. If he remembered he would ask him the next time he was in the shop.

'Good luck!' said Mr Rhama.

'Thanks,' said Brian.

On his way out the door he turned as Mr Rhama called out to him.

'Hey! Next time you come here you be a married man!'

Kathleen lay, soaking in the warmth and comfort of the bath, nothing in her head but just drifting, lazy, not wanting to stir from it, ever. Steam rose and hung in the air, misted over the windows and the mirror, condensed and trickled down the tiles.

Through the wall she could hear her mother in the kitchen, familiar noises, far away, her mother, she supposed, still troubled and thinking about old Father Boyle, filling her head with purgatory and hellfire. She remembered how he'd seemed to her as a child, arms raised, intoning the mass, glorious in his vestments, exalted and terrible like God himself, the voice of judgment in the deep musty dark of the confessional. Father forgive me for I have sinned. I have committed a sin of impurity. Yes my child. I have kissed a boy on the lips. And is that all? Yes Father. Yes Father. She leaned against the sides of the bath, buoyed up so slightly by the water, stretching, bobbing in the warm stream, and she thought of the life that moved deep inside her, the tiny life that was growing, becoming, the child that would be hers and Brian's. And at twelve she'd wanted to be a nun. It had seemed so beautiful. The bride of Christ. Jesus the lover, the bridegroom, gentle Jesus. Father forgive me for I have conceived out of wedlock. How many acts of contrition and hailmarys for that? Impurity and dirt. Wash it all away. She laughed and lathered herself with the soap. Sandalwood. Brian had bought it for her in the Indian shop. Fragrance. Like the incense he burned in his room. Hail Mary full of grace. Mother Mary working in the kitchen, on the other side of the thin wall. And once Kathleen had been no more than a stirring inside her, had been one with her, curled and safe in the warmth of her womb. She slid back down into the water again, lapped in the warmth surrounding. She brought her knees up to her chest then stretched again, looking down at her body, pale through the soapy water, the curve of breast and belly breaking the surface, the black seaweed tangle of hair, flattened out by the water, felt below it the soft depth of hole, open, the dark emptiness her being centred around. Blessed art thou among women. Blessed is the fruit of thy womb.

The taxis were waiting, purring at the close.

'Huv ye seen ma black tie?' said Tommy.

'It's a weddin wur goin tae,' said Mary. 'No a bloomin funeral!'

'Ye coulda fooled me,' said Tommy, turning, stiffnecked because his collar was up in readiness for the missing tie.

'Whit's that supposed tae mean?' she asked.

'Your face, that's whit,' he said. 'Kin ye no gie's a wee smile hen. Ah mean it is YOUR daughter's weddin tae!'

'Aye, well,' she said. She brought out a blue tie from the wardrobe. 'Here,' she said, throwing it to him. 'This'll dae ye.'

In the next room Agnes and Jean, who had led Kathleen the night before with such devoted rattling of cans, were again fussing over her, making sure that no talisman was forgotten.

'Right,' said Agnes. 'That's the flowers an the horseshoe. Noo make sure ye've got the lot. Somethin old, somethin new, somethin borrowed, somethin blue.'

'This cameo's old,' said Kathleen. 'Used tae be ma granny's.'

'An yer shoes are new,' said Jean.

'Ah huvnae anythin borrowed,' said Kathleen. 'Ye'll huv tae len me somethin.'

'Take this hanky,' said Agnes.

'Where'll ah put it?' said Kathleen. 'Ah'm no takin a bag.'

'Therr's a rude answer tae that wan!' said Jean.

'Jist shove it up yer jook,' said Agnes.

Kathleen wrapped the hanky round the stems of her flowers.

'An mind an gie me it back sometime,' said Agnes, 'otherwise it's no borrowed!'

'Yer dress is blue,' said Jean, 'so that's everythin.'

'Expect yer nosy wee neighbours'll huv somethin tae say aboot that,' said Agnes. She looked down her nose, disapproving. 'And not even a white wedding.'

'Ach they'd huv somethin tae say anywey,' said Kathleen.

'C'mon!' shouted Tommy from the hall. 'The taxis ur waitin!'

At the closemouth, a few peering faces, a handful of confetti, a huddle of children waiting, eager, for the scramble of loose change. Bundling into the taxis, Kathleen and Tommy in the first, Mary, Agnes and Jean in the second.

'Huv you got change fur the scramble?'

'Godalmighty, did ah pit oot that gas?'

'Mind yer flowers in the door!'

A cheer. A flurry of waving hands. Tommy bestowing a shower of coins from the window, jolted back into his seat as the taxis moved off. Agnes turned in her seat for a last look at the scramble before they rounded the corner.

'God, wid ye look at them!' she said, laughing. 'Lik flies roon a toly!'

'Ah remember readin,' said Jean, 'that scrambles go right back tae the aulden days, when they didnae keep records an that. An it wis so's the weans an everyb'dy wid remember the weddin. Then if they ever needed witnesses, they'd aw mind a the money gettin scrambled.'

Jimmy and Ann, like most of the other children, had just been passing, on their way back to school. They were triumphant as they fought their way out of the tangled, scrambling pack, jostling and grappling in the roadway.

'Much d'ye get?' asked Jimmy.

'Tanner!' said Ann. 'An you?'

'Eightpence!' said Jimmy, counting it out into his palm.

'Race ye doontae the café!' said Ann, and they both pelted off down the road. By the time they reached the café near their school, and elbowed their way into the semblance of a queue, the taxis were moving along Paisley Road, towards the town.

Tommy smiled across at Kathleen.

'Ur ye still feelin rough?' she asked.

'Ach, no too bad,' he said.

'Never mind,' she said. 'No doubt a coupla wee halfs'll set ye right.'

'Hair a the dog,' he said.

'Ah thought that would set yer wee eyes twinklin!' she said. 'But we've got the small matter ae a weddin tae get over wi first!'

It was over so quickly, embarrassed introductions, Brian's mother Helen to Tommy and Mary, grins and hello to the friends that had come, crowding, awkward, on the pavement, trying to keep out of the wedding-group photos of the couple that had just come out; confusion over which door to go in, then somebody showing them the way; hustle along a corridor, a few minutes' wait, hushed, in the hall; a door opening, another wedding-group bustling past; another door opening and the registrar ushering them in.

In a low, bored drone he intoned the preliminaries, about how the ceremony was no less serious and sanctified though it wasn't in a church, and about general impediments to marriage.

Tommy thought he was going to laugh, then suddenly for no reason, when he saw them standing there, he wanted to cry. He looked at Mary and he saw the confusion in her eyes.

Kathleen too had to stifle a laugh, changing it to a cough and turning her face from the registrar. Brian was staring at the pattern on the carpet, as if he could read there the meaning of it all, the meaning they all knew at that moment. Not the lifeless ceremony, the cardboard stage-set, the dead script, the empty sham. Not that, but something at the heart of it, something real. In spite of it all, they knew, and that was what moved them, to laugh or to cry.

The exchange of vows. Signatures on the line. Out along the corridor, past the next group waiting to go in, out into the street and it was done.

'We've done it now!' said Brian.

'So we huv!' said Kathleen, and he kissed her and they laughed.

Outside, waiting, were the friends that hadn't gone in. Somebody showered more confetti as they gave themselves up to the backslaps and handshakes and hugs. Ian and Kenny had cars. They were two of Brian's friends from university and Ian was the best man. They took as many as they could crowd in. The rest followed in taxis as they headed back to Pollok, to what had been Kathleen's house, for the reception.

In the boys' playground, Jimmy was finishing the sweets he'd bought with the money from the scramble. He screwed up the bright coloured wrapper and kicked it high over the railings.

In the girls' playground, Ann was pushed, giggling, to the centre of the circle. Her friends linked hands and moved round her in step and as they moved they sang.

'And she sang and she sang
And she sang so sweet
His name is Jimmy
Ah hope ye will agree.'

And when she at last agreed, somebody else was pushed into the centre and the dance began again.

Instead of buying a cake, they'd got Mary to bake an enormous dumpling. Tommy carried it carefully into the living-room and solemnly laid it on the table. With exaggerated ceremony Brian took the knife and flourished it in the air.

'Feels lik a Burns Supper!' he said. 'Great chieftain o the puddin race! Or is it Wee sleekit courin tim'rous beastie?'

'C'mon you an stop yer nonsense!' said Kathleen, laughing.

'See that!' said Tommy. 'She's got ye under the thumb already!'

Brian guided Kathleen's hand and everybody cheered as they carved the first slice. Kathleen went on slicing it and Agnes helped her to dish it out. Mary and Jean carried plates from the kitchen, piled with bread and bun, biscuits and cake, while Brian and Tommy brought through the carry-out, bag after bulging bag. When all the glasses were filled, Ian got up to make his speech and read the telegrams.

'Three telegrams,' he said. 'The first one's from Peter in Canada. It says ALL THE BEST TO MY WEE SISTER AND HER LAD.'

'Aw the nice!' said Mrs Robertson from downstairs. 'Luvly boay Peter,' she said to Mary. 'Luvly boay!' She smiled into the distance.

'The next one,' said Ian, 'is from Uncle Danny and Auntie May.'

'Ma brother in Ireland,' explained Mary to Brian's mother.

'Sure it's from the ould country,' said Tommy.

'It says,' said Ian, raising his voice, 'GOOD LUCK GOD BLESS AND MAY ALL YOUR TROUBLES BE LITTLE ONES.'

That one brought a laugh.

'Nudge nudge!' said Jean.

'The last one,' said Ian, 'is from Gerry in London. It says NORMAL IS REALLY NICE.'

Again everybody laughed.

'Whit wis that aboot?' said Tommy to Kathleen.

'Och it's jist Brian's pals up tae thur nonsense again,' she said.

'An whit's the matter wi a wee bit nonsense?' said Brian, tickling her.

'Aye bit whit dis it mean?' said Tommy.

'The whole universe is a wee bit nonsense!' said Brian.

'A wee bit order therr!' said Ian, who wanted to propose a toast.

'Aye, wheesht the perry ye!' said Kathleen.

'Ah've got no intention of wastin time makin a speech,' said Ian.

'Hear hear!' said Brian.

'So ah'll just say good luck and happiness and long life to you both.'

He picked up his glass. 'The bride and groom!'

All the glasses were drained and set down empty on the table.

'C'mon now people,' said Tommy. 'Get wired in therr!'

'Eat up,' said Mary. 'Yer at yer auntie's!'

Several refills later, Brian turned to Kathleen.

'Tommy's peed already,' he said.

'Yer no doin too bad yerself!' she said.

'Ach well,' he said, squeezing her, 'it's no every week ye get married.

'See Kenny an Ian are gettin quite pally wi Agnes an Jean,' he said, nodding to where the four of them sat squashed on the couch.

'Ah'm watchin ye!' he shouted over. He crossed to where his mother was talking to Mary.

'Gettin on okay mammy?' he asked.

'Ah'm jist fine,' she said. 'Me an Mary are havin a right old natter.'

'Don't believe a word she tells ye about me,' he said to Mary. 'Honest, ah'm innocent!'

'Who's gonnae give us a song then?' asked Tommy, raising his arms and calling for order.

Mrs Robertson let herself be coaxed on to the floor and began the singsong with 'You're the Only Good Thing', then she dragged her husband, protesting, to his feet and he sang 'Green Grow the Rashes O', and 'Of A' The airts'.

'It's nice tae hear an auld Scotch song,' said Mary.

'She better be quiet,' whispered Ian, 'or e'll be givin us "Scots Wha Hae".'

Mary was next with 'Honky Tonk Angels', then Tommy with 'Take Me Back to the Black Hills', and the afternoon grew late and the bottles and cans were emptied , and everybody sang the songs they always sang. 'Nobody's Child', 'There Goes My Heart', 'Please

ALAN SPENCE

Release Me', 'The Blue of the Night', 'You're Free to Go', 'Among
My Souvenirs'. They forgot themselves, they wallowed, grew happily
maudlin as they sang. And through it all Tommy kept calling for
order, 'C'mon now there, one singer one song,' and joining in all the
choruses himself.

'How is it,' said Kenny, 'the whole a Glasgow likes Country an
Western?'

'Everyb'dy likes tae get a wee bit sentimental when they get
bevvied,' said Ian. 'It's a wee escape.'

'Aye,' said Kenny, 'but whit ah mean is, whit is it aboot Glasgow?
Ah mean, how come Country an Western?'

Tommy swayed over to where they sat.

'How aboot youse young yins?' he said. 'How aboot givin us some
ae yer modern stuff? The auld rock an twist an aw that jazz!' He
gyrated his hips and snapped his fingers in attempted imitation of the
dance style of ten years ago.

'Naw,' said Ian, 'we'd need a backin group.'

'Ach!' said Tommy, dismissing them, 'yer aw the same. Canny dae
anythin withoot electricity!' He supported himself, leaning heavily on
the back of a chair, and announced that he was going to sing one
more song.

'For ma wee lassie,' he said, and began singing,

> 'I'll take you home again Kathleen
> To where your heart will feel no pain . . .'

When he'd finished she went to him and gave him a hug.

'Wherr's Brian?' he asked. 'Ah wanty talk tae um.'

'E's away doon tae Mrs Robertson's tae phone a taxi,' she said.
'E'll be back in a minute.'

When Brian reappeared, Tommy took him by the arm and looked
at him earnestly.

'Brian . . .' he said. 'Ah jist wanty tell ye yer a great kid!'

'You too Tommy,' said Brian. They shook hands on it.

'See you an Kathleen . . .' said Tommy, 'Canada . . .'

He took out his wallet and once again showed Brian the photo of
Peter and his family.

'Ah told ye aboot wur hoalidays therr in the summer, din't
ah? Peter peyed wur ferrs. Daein well so e is. Terrific it wis, nae
kiddin . . .' He stopped and raised his hand to cover his mouth. The
room was going up and up and up, like a television when the vertical
hold goes. He belched out an explanation and lurched towards the

bathroom, leaving Brian holding the snapshot. A young couple with a baby between them, sitting in front of a Christmas tree. Bright colours, like a photo in a magazine.

'The taxi's here,' said Kathleen, tugging his arm.

'Ah'll jist give this back tae Tommy,' he said, holding up the photo. 'Ah think it's too precious tae leave lyin here.'

They found Tommy in his own room, rummaging in the cupboard.

'Ye feelin better noo?' said Brian.

'Me?' said Tommy. 'Ah'm champion! C'mere an sit doon a minnit. Ah wanty show ye somethin.'

'We canny wait, daddy,' said Kathleen. 'We're jist gawn.'

'Here's yer fotie,' said Brian. 'Mind ye don't lose it.'

Tommy shook Brian's hand. 'Aw the best,' he said.

'Same tae yersel,' said Brian.

'Cheerio daddy,' said Kathleen, hugging him again.

They shouted a quick farewell into the living-room and hurried to the door. Mrs Robertson was in the hall, and before they fled, Kathleen stopped and said 'Could ye gie ma mammy a wee warnin. Tell er ma daddy's lookin fur is souvenirs, an that prob'ly means e'll be givin is party piece any minute.'

'Right yar hen,' said Mrs Robertson, opening the door for them. 'Good luck tae ye.'

Outside on the landing stood Father Boyle, his hand raised to knock the door. Kathleen and Brian almost banged into him as they rushed out. They all stood for a moment, embarrassed, looking at each other.

Then Brian grabbed her hand.

'Cheerio Father!' she called back to the priest as they clattered down the stairs.

'Ur ye comin in Father?' said Mrs Robertson.

'Well, I . . .'

'Mary!' she shouted. The priest stepped into the hall and she closed the door behind him.

Tommy still sat in his room, looking down at the floor. That was it. She was gone. He looked again at the snapshot he was still holding in his hand, then turned his attention to the cupboard and the cardboard box full of souvenirs from Canada, a heap of mementoes he'd brought back from their holiday. A pair of moccasin slippers, a chipped plaster ash-tray shaped like a maple-leaf, a miniature Canadian flag, a doll dressed like a mountie, a stick-on plastic badge and all the other wondrous, useless things he'd gathered.

Digging under a jumble of postcards and guide-books and leaflets, coins and maps and assorted tickets, he unearthed what he was looking for. It was an Indian head-dress, made up of red and white feathers, fitted on to a cardboard headband and bordered at the front with brown fur.

'Yes,' said Father Boyle, 'I wanted a wee word with you and Thomas, but it looks as if I've chosen an awkward moment. Maybe tomorrow . . .'

'Yes Father,' said Mary. 'Well you see . . .'

'Oh Mary,' said Mrs Robertson. 'Ah nearly forgot. Kathleen says tae tell ye Tommy's lookin fur is souvenirs.'

'Aw naw,' said Mary. 'No another performance! If ye'd excuse me a minute Father, ah'll jist . . .'

'Ah ya bastard!' Tommy was struggling with the door and the handle had come away. The door thudded twice under his boot then there was a final crash as it swung open and he came stumbling into the room. 'Wahoo!' he shouted, brandishing the doorknob. The head-dress was perched on his head, tilted forward so that the fur covered his brow.

'I think I'll just be going,' said Father Boyle, but Tommy came over and grabbed him by the arm.

'Hello therr Father Boyle,' he said. 'Wull ye huv a wee half tae drink ma daughter's health?'

'I really must be going,' said the priest.

'Ach c'mon,' said Tommy. 'Melt yer auld stone face fur wance in yer life!'

'Godalmighty!' said Mary, looking in despair at the ceiling.

'Wish ah had a camera,' said Kenny. 'This is jist too much.'

'Auld Father Gilligan widnae uv said naw,' said Tommy. 'He liked is wee dram wi the best ae thum. Fine man e wis tae. Red nose an aw! Jesus, d'ye mind the time e hid the weans up dancin a paddy ba oan the altar, the time the bishop came! Ye shoulda seen aw the frozen faces tut-tuttin away. By Christ they wurnae long in gettin rid ae um efter that.

'But ah'll tell you,' he went on, waving the doorknob at Father Boyle, 'E wis twice the man you'll ever be, God rest um.'

The priest was making his way towards the door, Mary behind him, apologising.

'Perhaps some other time,' he was saying, 'when Tommy's sober.'

'An anyb'dy that says ma wee lassie's no right's a no-user!' shouted Tommy after him. 'An that goes fur yer church an aw!'

THE RAIN DANCE

'C'mon Tommy!' said Ian, laughing. 'Do yer Medicine Man! Give us a Rain Dance!'

Tommy straightened his head-dress and stamped a rhythm with his foot, shaking the doorknob like a rattle above his head, howling and patting his pursed lips with his palm.

'Gawn yersel!' said Kenny, as some of the others shouted encouragement and took up the rhythm, beating it out on the furniture or clapping their hands.

'Ah don't believe it,' said Ian, as Tommy twisted and shook, waving his arms in the air, getting faster and faster till he finally collapsed, exhausted, face down on to the couch, and his head-dress dropped to the floor, a few of the feathers crooked and bashed.

Tommy was still lying there, huddled, dead to it all, long after everyone had gone home. Only Mary still sat, thinking she should tidy up the debris left from the party, but feeling engulfed by it, and unable to move.

'The tea'll be ready in a minute,' said Kathleen. 'Ah'm jist lettin it mask.'

'Great,' said Brian, who was busy filling the paraffin stove.

She took a joss-stick from the packet and lit it, blowing out the flame and watching it smoulder and glow. She placed it in the brass holder on the mantelpiece, watched the smoke curl and rise past the wooden image of Siva that Brian had bought at the Barrows, Siva with his four arms, his fire and his drum, dancing in a circle of flame.

She went to the window and looked out. It had begun to rain again and it was just beginning to get dark. A few people were passing on their way home from work. She could hear, faintly, the stream of traffic from Great Western Road. Through a gap between two gable ends opposite she could see the shapes of trees in the park, branches dark against the sky. The streetlamps went on then. She could see five or six, reaching to the end of the street. She thought of them going on all over Glasgow, a linked network of lights, strung across the city, and everywhere people coming home.

She could smell the incense now, the fragrance of sandalwood permeating the room, and with it the warm smell of paraffin burning. The tea was brewing. The stove was lit.

Looking down below, outside the close, where they'd stepped from the taxi, she could still make out a few tiny specks of colour, bright flakes of confetti, scattered on the pavement, wet by the rain.

GEDDES THOMSON

Pride of Lions

⬥⬥⬥⬥⬥

I WAS twenty-one. I had just left university after completing a degree in English. I knew nothing. I wanted to be a writer. I was working on the Glasgow buses as a conductor, to see life. Later, I intended to work on the night-shift at a power station like William Faulkner and write my first novel. That would take about six weeks.

But at the moment I was sitting on the back seat of a double-decker bus smoking a Sobranie Straight Cut cigarette. Opposite me sat my regular driver, Sardar. He was reading the Manchester *Guardian*. Not for the first time, I thought we were a strange pair to be in charge of a Glasgow bus.

I liked these day-time rests at the terminus. Passengers were few. The city had a peaceful semi-deserted look in the sunlight. The inhabitants seemed to consist of old people, young mothers and infants. Later it would be very different, as successive waves of truculent humanity invaded the bus at their appointed hours.

'Has he died yet, Sardar?' I asked.

The paper shook like a white flag in a breeze and then collapsed to show Sardar looking at me. He was never quite sure how to take my interest and always began by studying my face carefully for signs of mockery.

'He is my man,' he said. 'He fights for freedom.'

'Is he related to you, Sardar?' I knew that he wasn't, but the question would lead to further conversation.

'Sardar Singh. My name and his name. But we are not related. All Sikhs are called Singh. Did you know that?'

'Yes.'

He studied my face. 'Do you know what it means?'

'It means "lion".'

'Ah, but "Sardar"?'

'No.'

'It means "chief". I am "Chief Lion",' he said with emphasis.

' "Sardar" is a common name. There must be a great many "Chief Lions".'

He laughed. 'Yes, a great many. Thousands and thousands.' He flung back his turbaned head and laughed. We both laughed heartily, falling back on our seats, our chests heaving with the humour of those thousands of important kings of the jungle.

'You know something, "Chief Lion"?' I said. 'It's time you were driving this bus.'

I liked him a lot. He didn't support Celtic or Rangers. He read the Manchester *Guardian* and he worried with pride about his namesake who was fasting till death in far-off India.

'Will you come for a drink with me, tonight?' he asked, picking up the hat he never wore. We arranged the place and the time.

'No overtime, tonight, then?' I asked Sardar when I met him in the pub.

He smiled. Once I had asked him how he was able to endure the long hours of queuing for overtime. He had said, 'At home I once queued for two days with my son to see the doctor. This is easy.'

After five rapid drinks Sardar was ready to come to the point.

'I have a favour to ask.'

'Fire away,' I said like a benevolent sport in one of the thrillers I despised but read in dozens.

'Could you go there and ask for the keys?' He handed me a newspaper clipping advertising a house for sale. At the bottom was the estate agent's address. 'Say you are interested in the house and wish to view it.'

I felt a flush warm my face.

'You mean—'

'They won't give me the keys. You know why.' In his eyes I could see shame. Shame for me, for himself. A shame so palpable that it seemed to radiate out to include the people in the pub, the people in the streets beyond. I also saw fear and suppressed rage.

'Of course I'll get them.'

The next day I got the keys and we looked at the house. Sardar was pleased with it and with me. He invited me up to his flat for a meal.

'This is my friend,' he said, standing at the kitchen door.

Faces stared at me. Half-a-dozen faces which broke into smiles. The room seemed full of light. A tangy redolence tantalised my nostrils.

'Now I am in the lions' den,' I said.

Sardar laughed. He explained the joke to the others and we all laughed again.

The meal was good. We ate it with fellowship in the kitchen of that Glasgow tenement. When I left, the streets were grey and wet with rain.

Last run of our shift. A late-night bus-load of drunken and aggressive Glaswegians, who shouted, sang, swore, urinated, vomited, as the mood took them. Collecting fares required devious diplomatic gifts.

At the terminus a group of youths surrounded Sardar's cab. They chanted insults, hammered the windows with clenched fists, challenged him to come out and fight.

A pale youth with jagged blonde hair stood on the platform grinning at me.

'You just stay where you are sonny,' he said. 'You're goin nowhere.'

He couldn't have been more than fourteen. He was thin and undernourished. I was more afraid of him than I have ever been of anyone in my life.

'You like darkies?' he asked.

I couldn't answer.

'Ah asked you a question, cunty.'

I heard my voice hoarse and choked: 'They're all right. In their own country. Not over here.'

He gestured. 'C'mon.'

We walked round to the front of the bus. I could see Sardar sitting in the cab, his turban white in the gloom. He stared ahead, impassive as Buddha, as if waiting for overtime or the doctor.

'See, who ah've goat,' the youth said to his mates. 'Says he doesny like darkies in this country.'

'He'll have tae prove it,' a low voice said.

They crowded round and suddenly my money-bag was knocked up. A shower of coins flashed in the air.

'Better than a weddin,' one shouted as he scrambled for his share.

I heard the low voice again—'He'll have tae prove it.'

'He'll have tae dae somethin,' the blonde youth said.

'Spit at him,' a voice suggested.

'Aye, that's it. Spit at the darkie.'

'C'mon, ya mug. Spit at him!'

My throat was parched with fear. I tried to swallow but couldn't. My tongue desperately searched my mouth for moisture.

'C'mon, spit. Spit at the darkie.'

My mouth opened. I tried to gather some saliva. My lips moved, but nothing came.

'Christ, he's no spittin. He's blowin him kisses, the pouf!'

I was knocked over. My body shook as the kicks thudded in. Then the sound of running feet. And silence.

Gentle hands uncurled me. Sardar's face above me. I saw with shame his concern and his pride.

'You are truly a lion,' he said. 'You wouldn't spit.'

VALERIE THORNTON

Another Sunday Morning

❖❖❖❖❖

CAMERA, film, light meter, keys . . . she muttered to herself as she opened the door.

Instead of the blue peeling walls and garish orange carpet, she saw a large black and white animal on the stairs and let out a cry of fright before she realised that it must be the dog from the next flat. Almost at once she noticed that their door was wide open. She hoped no one had heard her, and hurried on down the stairs.

Uncertain, the dog preceded her down, until it stopped halfway down the last flight and barked timidly.

'It's all right, beast,' she said, 'I'm a friend.'

They each seemed equally unsure of the other.

She felt foolish for over-reacting. Must have been something to do with her dream of two nights before, when she had found herself being bitten painfully on the left toe, by a small foxy animal. People around her were smiling indulgently with 'it's all right—he's only playing' expressions, but she had been in real pain and wondered how she could prise the rows of sharp white teeth from her foot.

Eventually she had hit the animal on its back, fairly gently, with some object akin to a jam-jar, whereupon it had stopped biting her toe and had lain on the floor unmoving. She had then felt the cold, silent disapproval of those around her, whoever they might be.

This flashed back into her head as she paused, equally uncertain, on the stair. The dog was between her and the door, and she was between it and its master.

A whistle from upstairs solved the problem. The dog shot past her, tail and ears down, and she breathed a sigh of relief.

Outside, it was cool, clear and mild—ten to ten on a Sunday morning.

She climbed into the old Morris Minor, adjusted the cushion and checked the amount of water that had leaked in during the night.

It started first time, thank goodness. She was glad not to have to use the starting handle, because it hurt her back.

She drove quickly through the quiet streets, down to the docks, watching the speedometer needle creep towards forty and hoping there were no cops watching. Just my luck if they get me now, she thought—the one time I'm in a hurry.

They hadn't been much help last night, the police. She'd phoned them up, the ones on the north side of the river first, because someone had said that they'd known about it last week.

'Cranstonhill Police Station.'

She had waited for the pips, then shoved her 5p in.

'I wonder if you can help me. They blew up a crane at the docks last week and they're supposed to be blowing up two more soon—can you tell me if they're doing one tomorrow?'

She'd been lying in bed, last Sunday morning, when an enormous double explosion had shattered the silence. There had been no explanation on the local radio news, and it wasn't until she saw the paper the next day that she discovered they had blown up one of three cranes and were going to be blowing up the remaining two 'over the next few weeks'.

'Sorry, dear,' the policeman had said. Why did people always call her 'dear' on the phone? Did she sound so much younger than her twenty-seven years? 'No one here knows anything about it. Try the other side of the river—it's on their side and if anyone knows, they should.'

They didn't, but they did add that the cranes were owned by British Steel.

So she'd tried the paper where she'd seen the picture. Their news desk knew nothing either and suggested trying Clyde Port Authority.

Clyde Port Authority wasn't in the phone book, and Clyde Port Stevedores weren't answering on a Saturday night.

So she'd decided to go along, for ten o'clock, on the offchance that they would be demolishing the second crane.

She loved watching things like that. Once when she'd been very young, her father had taken her and her younger sister for a winter's walk in the country. There had been sheets of white ice over the ruts in the track and they had splintered them noisily with their heels. All the time they could hear the whine of a circular saw on the cold still air. They traced it to its source and found a few men about to pull down a tall tree, at the edge of a wood.

They were told to stand back, and protectively, her father had led them a very safe distance from the tree. There was a red tractor in the field next to it, with a long steel cable running from the back of it to the tree. It was attached around the trunk about twenty feet up.

Things happened quickly. The saw stopped, the tractor revved and then a loud creaking and groaning filled the air, and the topmost branches of the tree shuddered. The tractor began to move, the steel cable went taut, the tree whined deeply and started to topple. It was so tall that its fall was like slow motion, but the tearing, shrieking sounds filled the air with harsh reality.

It tilted through the air, gracefully, then hit the ground with a vast crashing and cracking of branches, almost bounced, then settled, rustling, as the booming echoed through the forest and hills.

She'd never forgotten that morning, long ago. There had been tremendous excitement at the noise, yet also she had felt pity for the tree which seemed to be crying in anguish as it fell.

Much more recently, she had watched a big hotel in the city burn to a shell. She had followed the screaming sirens there soon after the fire had started, and had seen the six cooks, in white with pale faces, sitting on the wall of the church across the road, describing how the drums of cooking oil kept beside the grill had exploded.

The traffic had been diverted and the streets were running with water. There were loud cracking noises and sparks flying up into the dark evening air.

She had returned, several hours later, near midnight, to find every window ablaze with orange, as if there were a wild party. Only the tongues of flame licking through the glassless windows and darting from the roof, confirmed that destruction rather than celebration was in progress.

The firemen were on strike at the time, and the only fire fighters were soldiers, using Green Goddesses—ancient inefficient monsters which could only just spit water to the level of the second floor. It had been both tragic and exhilarating. There was the threat of the fire spreading along the length of the whole terrace, and a few brave soldiers were on the roof where the hotel half of the terrace ended, hosing through the roof to try and save the rest of the block. All the occupants had been evacuated, one with his five pedigree cairn terriers, another with her two priceless Ming vases.

She would have watched, enthralled, all night, but those who were with her dragged her home when they got bored.

Next morning, she had returned to marvel at the roofless black-ened shell, still smouldering, with blue sky showing through the windows and a handful of smudged and exhausted soldiers, hosing out the last smoking remains. The rest of the terrace had been saved, but the hotel was no more than a shell with a few steel supports stretching across its gaping interior.

She felt privileged to have been witness to its demise.

She parked on the north bank of the river, and looked across its still, flat, brown surface to the huge cranes known as the three sisters. They loomed side by side on General Terminus Quay, the farthest sister crippled and broken from last Sunday's blast.

Once these docks had been among the greatest in the world. Now the miles of docks, quays and warehouses were abandoned, overgrown and decaying. The docks were being ignominiously filled in with tons of rubble; the roofless buildings, patterned with red and cream bricks, gradually crumbling.

There was no sign of movement. She took some pictures of the cranes, juxtaposing them ironically with a gay red and white life-belt, and wondered which of the remaining two would go that morning. One of them had a large sign on it with the name of the demolition company. Surely not that one—they wouldn't waste their sign. She half hoped to see a squad of demolition men with bright yellow safety helmets, climb up the rusty girders of the crane and disentangle their sign from it, prior to blowing it up.

But no one stirred.

The tiny figure of a man in grey walked along the pathway behind the cranes and disappeared.

She took some more pictures of the ailing docks. The warehouses were half destroyed, with their gable ends open to the elements; an overhead tunnel of corrugated iron had collapsed in the middle and its broken ends hung absurdly from the two warehouses it had once joined.

Everything was rust-coloured and disordered, except for the crisscross girders of the two remaining cranes which formed an ordered pattern against the grey sky. Pigeons wheeled round the dark orange counterweights, the size of large barns, high on the massive jibs. Hanging down motionless in the centre of each of the airy constructions, were the jaws of the crane, bigger than a caravan, closed, and in the shape of a droplet of rusty liquid. As she watched, a pigeon flew through a gap in one of them.

She walked along the river side to get a better silhouette of the jagged ruin of the first sister. The river was quiet enough to give a near perfect reflection. She looked through the viewfinder at the angled edges of the crane and its reflection. I'll turn this one on its side and call it butterfly, she thought to herself as the image of a huge, ragged brownish butterfly presented itself to her eye.

Half an hour passed. Still nothing had stirred on the opposite bank. She hoped her film wouldn't run out just when the action started. She took another picture hoping it might finish the spool. It didn't.

A boy in denim walked past her.

Then it started to drizzle. She moved back from the river's edge to shelter under the lee of a warehouse. There was a smell of liquid plastic and under her feet the khaki slush of pigeon shit.

Gradually she realised that more and more people were turning up, with umbrellas and cameras and children. They must know, she thought, although she shied away from going along to them and asking if they did know. Then they too drifted off, leaving only three young boys and herself.

Her fingers and toes were freezing. The two pairs of gloves she wore scarcely warmed her, and almost prevented her from holding the camera properly. Everything was ready to shoot whichever of the cranes went up. She checked the light reading and adjusted the camera to compensate for the gloom of the rainclouds.

The reflections were blurred by the rain. She watched as a square of green frame floated past, very slowly and revolving slightly, in an oily slick on the murky water.

The drizzle stopped and it became lighter and the silhouettes of the cranes became sharp again.

On the far bank, a man in dark clothes walked quickly past with a bright orange bag in his hand. He walked purposefully into the distance and disappeared from sight.

Then she noticed a police car had drawn up on the far quayside. The engine was still running—she could see the exhaust fumes.

Great! It must be going to happen soon. It was now after eleven, she discovered, as she looked unwillingly at her watch. Last week's explosion had been long before now. I'm not waiting after half past, she said to herself, as she tried to convince herself that it might happen very soon now.

The police drove off. Sometimes they came down to the docks just to sit for a while and keep a professional eye on things, but today she was sure they had come to monitor the demolition.

She was alone on a strip of river path in front of the long curved row of warehouses; the three boys were beyond the edge of them, on a more open piece of grass. She felt a little vulnerable and hoped no weird men would come along. Several isolated figures had passed along the broad path between the warehouses and the river. She hadn't looked at them and they hadn't paused. But she was wary.

She glanced up and down the river and noticed a little man stepping briskly along the far edge of the path, coming towards her. He had on a shabby colourless suit, and a matching cap. She caught a glimpse of his silhouette and realised with a shock that he had no chin. His face tapered back from his nose into his neck. She looked away, hoping he might not notice her.

She saw from the corner of her eye that he had slowed down and was beginning to curve towards her. He was quite close now—only a few yards away. She turned round to look at him and began to move out from her corner and head away from him.

He made an inarticulate sound and she noticed his left eye socket hung low in his skull and was a watery red colour. He didn't look evil, just pathetic and mis-shapen. He seemed to want to attract her attention. She paused, half ashamed of being poised to flee, half expecting to have to run at any moment. He was waving his arms and trying to show her a piece of paper he had in his hand. He stopped far enough away for her not to feel threatened, indicated the paper and made a sound.

She moved a little towards him and looked.

On a tiny scrap of rough-edged paper was scrawled in shaky big capitals, the word 'BOMB'. Another end-of-the-world freak, she began to dismiss him in her mind.

He turned the paper over and it read, equally shakily, but clearly—'NEXT WEEK'.

'You mean the cranes are going up next week?' she asked.

In reply he turned to them and jabbed his arm first at one, then at the other, and made a noise of confirmation in his throat.

'Thanks for letting me know! How do you know?' she said clearly. 'Are they both coming down next week?'

But already he was backing away from her, to continue his walk along the river edge. He saw she had understood and that was enough, or perhaps all that he could do. He turned away from her as she again called thank you, and walked quickly along the path, away from her.

She felt ashamed of her fears. She almost wanted to go after him and talk to him and show him the respect he had shown her.

She remembered the deferential distance he had maintained and hoped he hadn't noticed the annoyance and fear on her face as he approached. There were so many questions in her head—how did he know? Why did he tell her? What was wrong with him? What did he do? Where did he come from? Did he write it? And why 'bomb'? . . .

Slowly she retraced her steps. It was near enough to half eleven anyway. A breeze disturbed the river's surface lightly—the stillness had left the day.

Nothing happened.

She drove off still awaiting the thunderous blast at her back.

All remained quiet.

She would come back next week and every week, until the two bereaved sisters were also 'bombed'; until she had photographs to tame the images in her mind.

BILL TURNER

The Shoes

❖❖❖❖

THE midden-raker was looking for a shoe. He was doing his seventh back court, and his sack was nearly full, but a shoe would have merited an early finish to his day. With his elbow he supported a pile of cans while his fingers expertly explored the surface ashes. He uprooted two bottles and twirled them across his sleeve, whisking away the dust. One was a vinegar bottle which he slid into the sack between his knees. The other was quite unfamiliar, like a sauce bottle but of fancy glass. It had a blue label with words, but no picture or clue. Old Mick could not read.

As he hesitated, a woman came down the stairs in the next back, carrying a rolled carpet. Her slippers flapped as she walked over and heaved the carpet across the railings. Old Mick knew the signs. He stooped and picked up his sack. The woman muttered something as he limped away, but he did not acknowledge her abuse. She could vent her spleen on the carpet: may it fall to bits. Children ran past him giggling as he went out of the close. The fierce 'Whup!' of the carpet being beaten sounded behind him, and above it rose the tuneless unison of the children yelling:

'Mick, Mick, the midden-man, combs his hair with a fryin' pan!'

When he came out of the close the bin-men were across the street. They greeted his appearance with shouts and friendly gestures: he was a familiar figure to them. One little red-haired man turned from emptying his basket into the long dusty van, and beckoned him over.

'What'll it be, Mr Mick?' he enquired, with a grin. 'Would you care to inspect our stock, or was you after anything special like?'

'It's a boot I'm needing. I really do need it, son, if you've anything that would serve a turn.'

The bin-man glanced down at the old man's feet.

'In the Name!' he cried out. 'What on earth's that you've got on?'

Mick's left foot was like a cartoonist's idea of gout, wrapped round and round with sacking tied by string. He shrugged.

'It's just bits of things tied together. I'll surely come across an old boot soon.'

The wee bin-man was concerned.

'Look, you'll get us doing opposite the Park the morrow. You see me, and I'll have either a boot or shoe for you. Let's see, about size eight. Right? You watch for us.'

He slapped Mick's arm and went off, following his mates. Mick looked after him, and waved doubtfully. Then he gathered up the sack, and set off towards his den.

As he crossed the muddy stretch of waste ground, he heard Pal barking. He quickened his step, though it meant a fresh twinge in his sore foot. Pal was a good watch-dog, and only barked when a stranger ventured too near. The bark was not repeated, a warning heeded, perhaps. Approaching the bushes, he heard hurried footsteps. Then a man burst past him, hugging a roughly wrapped parcel to himself. Mick had a quick impression of black jeans and a drape jacket, before the fellow passed with chin down on chest: a bad lot, that one. For a moment he feared some harm may have come to his hut, but the alarm faded when he saw Pal relaxed on his haunches before it.

Old Mick's dwelling was a triumphant testimony to his opportunism. An abandoned watchman's hut had been the start of it. To this was added a length of corrugated iron that may have come from an Anderson shelter. It was not clear how this was supported and fixed to the hut, for the joins were covered with strips of yellow oilskin, and all the gaps stuffed with newspaper, but little clumps of tangled wire stuck out oddly here and there. There was no door. A black tarpaulin draped the entrance, giving a kind of dignity to the absurd shape of the place.

Mick drew back the flap, and heaved his sack to the rear. Pal, with his ears up, watched expectantly as he fished in his coat pocket. He made a little ceremony of producing the poke of paper and unwrapping the contents, such scraps of edibles as he had been able to salvage. These he laid at the entrance with a grand gesture, and the dog inclined its head in a graceful motion of acceptance and dismissal. They got on fine together.

Mick seated himself on a heap of sacks, and took off his boot. It took him a minute or two to undo the string round the sacking on his sore foot. Then he carefully eased away the handkerchief which had stuck to the skin as the blood dried. In spite of his caution, the sore began to bleed freely again, and he muttered crossly at it. Reaching over for the day's haul, he emptied the sack out in front of him.

The vinegar bottles were his immediate concern. There was a factory which paid ninepence a dozen for sound bottles. He had six on hand, and today had collected four more. With luck there would be a bag of chips for supper tomorrow. Mick's idea of sheer luxury was to walk into Frank's chip shop and put down a sixpence for a fourpenny bag, so as to get twopence back. He always waited till the shop was empty, for the shining cleanliness of the place made him uncomfortable about his own appearance. But Frank always had a cheerful word of greeting for him, and sometimes would slip a fish into the bag without saying anything. There weren't many about like Frank. Glasgow was more or less a city of Sunday Christians, no doubt of it. Most people seemed to think that anybody in rags was necessarily a beggar.

He put the vinegar bottles in the sack containing the others, and pushed the assorted items he had salvaged to the back of the hut. Time enough later. He turned to face outside. For a while he sat appreciating the cool air about his bare feet, and looked out of his den at the distant roofs, debating where he should take his last few bundles of firewood for sale. After some time his gaze returned to the bushes in the foreground, and he frowned with concentration. There was something white lying just where the leaves were thickest. He put on his socks, and his boot, and hobbled carefully across the bare ground to the bushes. Nothing could be seen from a standing position, but when he stooped a white box was clearly visible. After a bit of effort he managed to get a grip of it, and tugged it out. It was a new clean shoe-box.

Remembering his suspicions of the stranger at whom Pal had barked, he surmised that the man had been visiting a 'plank' of stolen goods. This had been left. Mick carried the box back to his den before he dared open it. He smelled the leather even before he lifted the top layer of tissue paper. Inside, the glossy shoes shone like the sleek limousines in showroom windows.

Staring at them, he was afraid. These were the fruits of commerce, polished to dazzle and tempt. Vanity of vanities, a forgotten sermon shouted out of the grey flux of memories. Yet it would be a shame not to try them on, at least.

'Oh, you beauties!' he said, as if in astonishment.

They fitted perfectly, with room enough to wiggle his toes. He stood up and looked down at the new shoes, the wicked shine on them. He took a few steps round in a half-circle. His feet felt peculiarly light, and somehow more confident. He raised one foot and pointed its gleaming toe-cap at the dog.

'Oh Pal, Pal!' he cried, in his old man's voice, and capered about a little. He clicked the heels together, and took a few exaggerated mincing steps. The shoes were leading him into forgotten manoeuvres.

'Oh it's the jiggin' the night, for sure! The jiggin', the jiggin' for me the night.'

It was almost a song and it was quite a dance. The dog watched gravely, without any sign of approval, as he jumped and kicked away in fierce concentration. He stopped and mimicked it, putting his head to one side and allowing his tongue to hang freely as he recovered breath.

'Ach well, maybe you're right.'

He sat down gingerly, and tugged the tongues loose. Then he took the shoes off quickly, with a long sigh. and held them up, looking at them. They were never meant for feet the likes of his, that was certain sure. He picked the mud from the heels, and wiped them with his elbow. Now he would just have to hunt for a policeman to give them up. There might—no use looking for it, mind you—but there just might be a wee reward, you never know.

Back in the white box went the shining shoes, and the soft tissue paper was smoothed over them, and the lid replaced. Then Old Mick started to wrap the sacking round his sore foot again. He would have to get some sort of boot for that foot before it got any worse, he could see that. Various people had said they would see about finding an old shoe for him, but people sometimes forgot their promises. Mick was convinced that his friend, the little red-haired bin-man, was a sincere little fellow. He had the same kind of relaxed expression as the man in the chip shop. You can tell about people like that. The bin-man wouldn't forget the plight of Mr Mick. Tomorrow, surely, some kind of old shoe for his blistered bleeding foot would turn up. He lifted the box and tucked it firmly under his arm.

'Now you,' he said roughly, addressing his dog, 'you mind them sacks now. There's a bob's worth of good bottles in there.'

He set off through the bushes, without looking back at the dog. He walked jauntily, not really limping.

JOAN URE

Kelvingrove Park

◇◇◇◇◇

SHE was sure she could sit where she was for only a short time. Why she had come even into the park she could not explain to herself. The scummy Kelvin in front of her moved slowly towards its fall, brown-coated as if clots of sand were sliding along its surface.

The sun reached the surface of her face and her hands. It was the beginning of spring and birds practised their newly discovered vocabularies, finding their songs at the same instant as the sounds revealed themselves. This was the heart of her city, the centre of quietness and trees.

The University clock chimed as the sand clots on the river's surface were blown backwards upstream.

Three young men, hands in pockets, threw their voices ahead of them along the path, taking their morning walk between one lecture and the next. She turned her head away. Her habit of escaping dictated the movement.

From the turbulence that waiting in the Clinic created in her, sucked by her spirit from her disgust at the sickness round and within her, she grew peaceful there as she sat. This morning the ageing woman on the bench beside her had laughed at her childish shape. The woman's hair stuck out dry and straw-coloured around her head, as if she were part of a Renaissance painting. 'Only old men and kinks fall for those, don't they, hen?' The girl had not answered. These open-eyes women did not speak with the same words as she did, it seemed, and yet they all had to share the same vocabulary. She shuddered at a touch from the other patients. They had only their sickness to share. And now even her sickness was gone—almost certainly gone. A new nurse, with shoulders like a man and narrow hips, gave her the last injection. The pressure against her skin stopped for a second, as if the nurse drew a breath of surprise at the trembling of the girl. Then the needle plunged, almost more pain-fully than usual and, as it did, the girl felt on her skin a whisper that

175

could have come out of a nightmare. 'You took their money and now some man has left his receipt. That's fair enough.' The girl had lain for the required minute or two on the couch, her tears salt-tasting on her fingers. Some resistance was growing in her and when she was dressed she raised her eyes to the nurse who gave her the Clinic's card. She separated herself from the judging certainties of that nurse and gave her a deliberate, insolent look, like the look she had seen in the eyes of the other women. Walking away, she was glad that she had been unable to explain why she was here at all, glad at last, instead of ashamed. This might be madness, but she did not care.

Sitting in the park now, she felt the slight breeze ruffling her hair and pushing against the skin on the right side of her face. The first of this year's hot suns beat at the sleeve of her coat and caressed the left side of her face, drawing the skin where tears dried against her nose.

It was a long time since she had been in this park across that river there, a long time, many months, many, many months. Yes, it was surely madness to be there, even in the full day.

A cough across the water was the warning that a man walked along the path. She watched him walk, one foot ahead and then the next, careful of his corpulence. His brow was shining. He carried in his hand his smooth business hat, giving it at each third or fourth step a little twitch. He walked and paused; looked momentarily at the river. The Kelvin just where he walked, just there where he had stopped at the railinged edge, where the trees had made deep shadows across the path, the Kelvin had been given to her once in the darkest of the evenings by a man whom she had never seen anywhere afterwards. The river had been forced upon her by a man whose name she did not know, whose voice she could not remember. Somehow she had expected to see that strange, strong face again. Opening a newspaper perhaps, she would see that face surrounded by the newsprint of sensation, but she had not. He had given her, along with the imposition of himself, the grass verge beyond the railings, the river itself and the sharp pinpoints of the stars, each individually. With a cloth that tasted of paraffin tied around her mouth, he had, within that infinitesimal infinity, thrust against her memory the impress of a moon of different sizes, from the thin scimitar that it was as her startled eyes caught sight of it beyond his awful head, to the certainty of the completion of it as a sphere on some other night, some future night, some far, far, future night.

Now in the daylight, two years later, the river looked dirty, small and scarcely moving. It was almost impossible for her to believe, sitting there opposite, alone, that she had ever possessed the river at all. It was tender now, pathetic, puny, a travesty of the river that had held life's whole brutality and had forced it on her body and into her mind. It was today a human river, tentative, scummy, smelling, hardly purposeful, and yet moving towards the sea. She looked across at the railinged edge of the pathway and saw her own tortured drama as if she was outside of it, as if she wept sentimental tears for it, like the child-adult woman at the pictures. She was really unmoved.

Middle-aged women walked singly past, or men of the same age wearing caps, alone. She would move away from the smell of the river. The scum on its surface was blowing more quickly now but it was only the surface that moved.

She spiralled and spiralled along the pathways of the park, from the scum-encrusted river to where the possibilities of that scum lay gently like white thread-vines on the brown silk water. The trees were sprouting their vigorous yellow greens; other trees were dark still, with tiny pink buds caught in the light as a promise of later good, strong colour.

She spiralled from the river's edge upwards, from the city's green centre and its peace and loneliness. She spiralled upwards. She passed old men pushing their grandchildren in prams to spend the open air of time till lunch. They all stopped, children and old men, to take crusts from a paper bag and to throw the broken bread to the ducks swimming their patterns out upon the water. More water separated into traps for light and shot upwards from the fountain upwards and outwards, caught by and catching the daylight, the spray drifting out in the breeze so that the concrete was wet on one side of the fountain, like its shadow.

As she zig-zagged on the pathways uphill, more and more fitted into the growing canvas of her vision. The oriental Art Galleries added the University to itself in solid red stone and beyond the University a new pale building and steel girders supporting its rough edge. Dark tenements drew up alongside the carnival skyline of the Galleries and piled back and back. A high factory chimney stretched its sucker into the blue air. Beyond the etched beauties of the shipyard cranes, at last the hills. The city surrounded its natural centre and was encircled by it. The noise of buses rose upwards, punctuated comically by the high-pitched hiccuping of a motor scooter engine hurrying like an ant.

Closer, birds tried out their songs hidden in pale trees. She heard them carolling, knew why they sang and yet could marvel at the sound they made. The possibility of summer was there almost to be touched.

Her clinical condition now was, almost certainly, clear. 'But keep in touch,' the doctor had said, keeping expression carefully from his face. 'If you had consulted us when you suspected at first, we could have been swifter, and of course, surer.' He was signing a paper and did not look at her as he spoke. He might, she realised now, sitting there, in spite of his precise, mathematical movements, even have understood what had kept her back. She watched the far hills, bare of the city, empty hills able to touch the sky. You cannot get close enough to anyone to ask an explanation or to begin to expect the possibility of an answer. There is no vocabulary at all when life is all new and strange.

She offered her return to life to the city's quickening heart and looked up to where a veil of cloud moved slowly across the sun. She felt her neck turn, following with her eyes, as a young man chased a girl across the park. She did not need to turn her eyes away to hide herself from the meaning of the chase. Their laughter rose to her and she was not afraid. Summer was close enough to touch. She felt with her thin fingers the regular purpose of the surviving beat upon beat of her heart.

FURTHER READING

More Glasgow short stories by these and other authors will be found in:

Scottish Short Stories, Faber and Faber, 1932; 2nd edition 1947; 3rd edition revised 1957.

LINDSAY, Maurice and URQUHART, Fred, eds., *No Scottish Twilight*, Maclellan, 1947.

HENDRY, J. F., ed., *The Penguin Book of Scottish Short Stories*, Penguin Books, 1970.
   Scottish Short Stories, Collins, 1973–
   Annual volumes, produced in conjunction with the Scottish Arts Council.

GORDON, Giles and URQUHART, Fred, eds., *Modern Scottish Short Stories*, Hamish Hamilton, 1978. (Paperback edition, Faber and Faber, 1982.)

MURRAY, Ian, ed., *The New Penguin Book of Scottish Short Stories*, Penguin Books, 1983.
   Includes some stories from the 1970 edition above.

CAMPBELL, James, ed., *The Panther Book of Scottish Short Stories*, Panther Books, 1984.
   Selected from the Collins/SAC volumes above.

NOTES AND ACKNOWLEDGMENTS

GEORGE FRIEL (1910–1975, b. Glasgow) wrote five distinguished novels set in Glasgow, the finest probably being *Mr Alfred M.A.* (Calder, 1972). 'Onlookers' is from *Outlook*, August 1936.

EDWARD GAITENS (1897–1966, b. Glasgow) has a secure place in Glasgow literature for his short stories, collected in *Growing Up* (Cape, 1942), and the novel partly based on them, *Dance of the Apprentices* (Maclellan, 1948). 'Growing Up' first appeared in the *London Mercury*, September 1938 and 'The Sailing Ship' in the *Scots Magazine*, May 1939.

ALEX GILKISON (b. 1955) lives in Inverness. 'Atthis' is published here for the first time.

ALASDAIR GRAY (b. 1934 Glasgow) is a painter and writer whose books combine literary and artistic elements. He has published two novels, *Lanark* (Canongate, 1981) and *1982 Janine* (Cape, 1984), and a collection of short stories, *Unlikely Stories, Mostly* (Canongate, 1983) from which the two stories here reprinted come. Further stories will appear this year in *Lean Tales* (Cape), a collection by Gray, James Kelman and Agnes Owens, as well as another novel, *The Fall of Kelvin Walker* (Canongate).

ALEX HAMILTON (b. 1949 Glasgow) reproduces Glasgow speech patterns in his stories, collected in *Gallus, Did You Say?* (Ferret Press, 1982; also available as audio cassette). Earlier versions of 'Moonlighting' appeared in *GEM* magazine, 1980 and in *Gallus*.

MARGARET HAMILTON (1915–1972, b. Glasgow) is perhaps best known as the author of the Glasgow poem 'Lament for a Lost Dinner Ticket'. She wrote many short stories and a novel, *Bull's Penny* (MacGibbon and Kee, 1950). 'Jenny Stairy's Hat' appeared in *No Scottish Twilight*, 1947.

J. F. HENDRY (b. 1912 Glasgow) is a poet and critic, and author of the fine Glasgow novel *Fernie Brae* (Maclellan, 1947). He edited the 1970 edition of *The Penguin Book of Scottish Short Stories*. His latest book is *The Sacred Threshold: a life of Rilke* (Carcanet, 1983). 'The Disinherited' appeared in *Scottish Short Stories*, 1957.

JAMES KELMAN (b. 1946 Glasgow) has collected many of his stories in *Not Not While the Giro* (Polygon, 1983), from which 'Remember Young Cecil' is taken. His first novel *The Busconductor Hines* (Polygon) appeared in 1984. His second novel, *A Chancer* (Polygon), is due this year. 'The Hon' is taken from *Short Tales from the Night Shift* (Glasgow Print Studio Press, 1978).

JOHN J. LAVIN (b. Lesmahagow) is known for one powerful Glasgow novel, *Compass of Youth* (Museum Press, 1953). 'By Any Other Name' appeared in *Scots Writing* 2 (c. 1950).

NOTES AND ACKNOWLEDGMENTS

TOM LEONARD (b. 1944 Glasgow) is best known as a poet, particularly for his Glasgow dialect poems. A volume of selected writing, *Intimate Voices* (Galloping Dog Press) came out in 1984.

'Honest' was included in *Three Glasgow Writers* (Molendinar Press, 1976) and 'Mr Endrews Speaks' is from *Words* 3, Summer 1977.

FREDERIC LINDSAY (b. Glasgow) has published poetry in *Akros* and written for radio and television. A play has been produced by the Scottish Youth Theatre and his first novel, *Brond*, was published in 1984 by Macdonald (Edinburgh).

'People of the Book' is published here for the first time.

HUGH MCBAIN (b. 1920 Glasgow) has written radio features, plays, stories and the novel *The Undiscovered Country* (World Distributors, 1964).

'Supper on the Wall' first appeared in *Scottish International*, December 1971.

CARL MACDOUGALL (b. 1941 Glasgow) has had two collections of stories published by the Molendinar Press, *The Cuckoo's Nest* (1974) and *A Scent of Water* (1975). He founded and edited *Words* magazine and was Creative Writing Fellow, Dundee University, 1977–79.

'A Small Hotel' first appeared in *The Glasgow Magazine* 4, Spring 1984.

FARQUHAR MCLAY (b. 1936 Glasgow) has published widely, mainly in magazines. A collection of poems, *Cry Anarchy*, was published by Autonomy Press in 1984.

'Headlines for Whitey' appeared in *Words* 7 (1979).

J. FULLERTON MILLER. The editors have been unable to trace this writer or any work by him or her apart from the story 'A Lover of Nature' which appeared in *Saltire Review*, Winter 1955. Information would be welcomed.

WILLIAM MONTGOMERIE (b. 1904 Glasgow) has compiled with his wife Norah several collections of Scottish rhymes and tales. He edited *Lines Review* 1977–82. His latest collection of poems is due this year from Canongate.

'Daft Jenny' appeared in *Life and Letters Today*, October 1944.

STEPHEN MULRINE (b. 1937 Glasgow), poet and short-story writer, has also written plays and documentaries for radio and television.

'A Cold Coming' first appeared in *GUM*, Martinmas 1967 and was reprinted in *Scottish International* 9, February 1970.

ALAN SPENCE (b. 1947 Glasgow) charts boyhood, adolescence and other facets of Glasgow life in his short-story sequence *Its Colours They are Fine* (Collins, 1977, reprinted by the Salamander Press, 1983), from which the stories here reprinted come. He is also a playwright (*Sailmaker, Space Invaders*, both published by Salamander) and is currently working on a novel, *The Magic Flute*.

GEDDES THOMSON (b. Ayrshire) is a poet and short-story writer. He edited *Identities* (Heinemann, 1981), an anthology of modern West of Scotland writing.

'Pride of Lions' is taken from *Chapman* 33, Autumn 1982.

NOTES AND ACKNOWLEDGMENTS

VALERIE THORNTON (b. 1954 Glasgow) has written poetry and feature articles. Her short stories have appeared in *New Writing Scotland* (ASLS, 1983 and 1984).

'Another Sunday Morning' is published here for the first time.

BILL TURNER (b. 1927 York) is a poet, playwright and novelist. He edited the Glasgow poetry magazine *The Poet*, 1951–56.

'The Shoes' first appeared in *Saltire Review*, Winter 1957 and was reprinted in *A Scottish Sampler* (Blackie, 1960).

JOAN URE (1919–1978, born Elizabeth Carswell, near Newcastle) wrote many poems and stories but was best known as a playwright. *Five Short Plays* (Scottish Society of Playwrights, 1979) is the only collection of her work so far.

'Kelvingrove Park' is taken from *GUM*, January 1962.